"KA NAMA KAA LAJERAMA!" BREDON SHOUTED TO THE MACHINE

"Get into the war room as fast as you can! Cut your way in if you have to!" It occurred to him that even if the machine couldn't open the door, maybe a human could, and he yelled, "Emergency override! Human in danger!"

Then he dove off his perch and landed rolling. The door slid open. Moving swiftly and silently, Bredon got into a tense crouch, ready to spring or flee. Then he leaned forward and peered around.

The war room was huge, and every inch of it was filled with monstrous implements of death!

D0695855

DENNER'S WRECK

LAWRENCE WATT-EVANS

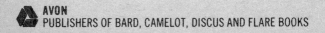

AVON
PUBLISHERS OF BARD, CAMELOT, DISCUS AND FLARE BOOKS

AVON BOOKS
A division of
The Hearst Corporation
105 Madison Avenue
New York, New York 10016

Copyright © 1988 by Lawrence Watt Evans
Front cover illustration by Ron Walotsky
Published by arrangement with the author
Library of Congress Catalog Card Number: 87-91689
ISBN: 0-380-75250-6

First Avon Books Printing: April 1988

AVON TRADEMARK REG. U.S. PAT. OFF. AND IN OTHER COUNTRIES, MARCA REGISTRADA, HECHO EN U.S.A.

Printed in the U.S.A.

K–R 10 9 8 7 6 5 4 3 2 1

Dedicated to my agent
Russell Galen

Clarke's Law: Any sufficiently advanced technology is indistinguishable from magic.

Arthur C. Clarke

Some of the physical characteristics of the planet Denner's Wreck were determined using "World Builder," a computer program designed by Stephen Kimmel with the assistance of Dean R. Lambe. The author extends his sincere appreciation.

Chapter One

"Lord Grey the Horseman rules a vast domain far to the south and west of our village, a broad expanse of open grassland where his horses roam free, and no mortal is permitted to set foot without first proving his worth to the land's master. Here Lord Grey's horses run unhindered—and what horses they are! Faster, stronger, smarter than mere animals, these creatures are a match for any man. They run like the wind itself, their hooves like thunder and their manes waving like the grass before the storm, and woe betide any hunter fool enough to venture near. The horses of Lord Grey can dodge any trap, tear any rope, outrun any pursuit. And if a man should somehow capture one despite these obstacles, then he must face the Power himself, for Lord Grey knows instantly when one of his proud children is touched by a mortal's hand . . ."

—FROM THE TALES OF ATHERON THE STORYTELLER

The sun was high in the heavens at mid-secondlight, shining fiercely down on the shadeless plain. Bredon could feel its light clearly, bright and warm on his back, pouring over him like honey as he crouched in the tall grass.

He blinked away sweat, then cautiously raised himself up to peer over the waving blades.

The plain lay palely green before him, flat and even to the mountain-rimmed western horizon. Warm wind hissed and muttered around him, through grass already half-bleached by summer and well on its way to becoming golden hay.

His gray hunter's vest lay crumpled on the ground at his heel, dropped there when he had stopped to crouch. The thin leather garment had been designed for comfort and convenience and had served him well in the year he had worn it, but in the long wakes of pursuit it had begun to chafe him, to feel unbearably hot and confining by light, and heavily clammy in the cool darks. He had removed it a couple of hours ago, just after the wake's second sunrise. He now wore only short bleached cotton breeches, but he had carefully dragged the vest along rather than risk losing it.

His companion crawled up, eerily silent in the tall grass, and lay beside him. The newcomer followed the first youth's gaze to where a magnificent gray mare stood quietly grazing, then whispered, "Give it up, Bredon. The horse is bewitched, probably a creature of one of the Powers—no ordinary mare could have eluded us this long. You'll never catch her."

"Oh yes I will," Bredon hissed back. "I don't care if I have to chase her all summer, I'll keep after her until I catch her. Look at her! With a horse like that I'll have my pick of any girl in the village. Riding her, I could be the greatest hunter in the grasslands. I'll be rich enough to be an Elder inside a year."

The other stifled a sigh. "Bredon," he said, "She's chewed through our ropes, dodged our traps, outrun us and outwitted us for six lights and five darks. What's left to try? How do you plan to catch her?"

"I'm not sure yet, but I'll do it somehow. If you want to give up you can go home without me."

The answer was quick and definite: "Walk back a hundred kilometers alone and unarmed? No thank you!"

Bredon rolled over and looked at his comrade with mingled affection and annoyance. "Mardon, has anyone ever told you that you're a coward?" he asked politely.

Mardon shrugged. "No more often than you've been called a stubborn fool," he replied, plainly unoffended.

Bredon smiled. "That's probably true," he admitted. "Well, if I'm a fool, O Wise One, then why don't *you* devise some means for trapping that mare?"

Considering the challenge, Mardon peered dubiously about at the empty grassland and asked, "Have you ever been here before?"

Bredon glanced back over his shoulder at the mare. "I think so," he said. "I believe my father and I came near here hunting rabbits once. It's hard to be sure, out here, but I think this was the place."

"Rabbits?" Mardon was puzzled. "Why did you come so far?"

Bredon shrugged. "Why not?"

Mardon had no answer to that. He knew, but did not understand, that Bredon and other members of his family often acted on whim. He ignored the question and asked, "Did you get as far as those mountains?" He waved vaguely in the direction of the peaks that adorned the western horizon.

"No," Bredon answered, "I'm not really sure we even got this far, but I *think* we did. It looks familiar. And those mountains are farther away than they look. My uncle said he rode for five full weeks once, lights and midwake darks both, and only got to the foothills."

Mardon wiped sweat from his cheek and waved a hand to dismiss any thought of traveling so far. "It's probably just as

well," he said, "I don't think I'd care to meet the Powers of the mountains, Gold and Brenner and the rest. It's said they're an unfriendly lot."

Bredon snorted. "The mountain people probably say that the Powers of the plains are a nasty bunch."

"Well, it doesn't matter, anyway," Mardon said. "The mountains are too far away to do us any good."

It was Bredon's turn to look puzzled. "What use could mountains be?"

"In the mountains we could trap the horse in a canyon or a cave," Mardon explained patiently.

"I guess that's true," Bredon said. "We *could* trap it somewhere, couldn't we?" His expression turned thoughtful as he considered for a moment.

"That gives me an idea," he said. "If I remember correctly, if this is the place I think it is, there's a water hole back that way a bit, with deep, sticky mud under about five centimeters of water. I got my hand stuck in it when I tried washing off the blood after I gutted a rabbit. If it's still there and we can find it, maybe we can herd her into the mud. It won't stop her completely, but it should slow her down enough for us to get a rope on her that she can't chew off."

Mardon mulled that over for a moment, then admitted, "It *sounds* good."

"Good. It's northeast of here, I think. You circle around and we'll start the chase."

"Right." Mardon slithered back through the grass and vanished.

Bredon waited patiently for Mardon to reappear. Finally, just as he was beginning to grow uneasy, Mardon suddenly jumped up from the grass on the mare's far side, yelling and waving his arms wildly.

The mare shied and started toward Bredon. He, in his turn, jumped up and shouted.

The horse started, then turned and galloped northeast, in exactly the direction Bredon wanted her to take.

Grinning and yelling, he set out after her. Mardon followed less enthusiastically. By staying well apart and varying their noise they controlled the mare's direction fairly well; if she attempted to turn to either side, the man on that flank would shout more loudly and pursue more closely.

Whenever she was actually galloping she would quickly gain on her tormentors, who would fall silent and lower their arms. Each time this happened she would slow and stop, thinking she was safe, only to be forced into a new burst of speed when the humans drew near again and resumed their noise.

There was little danger that the mare would flee farther than her hunters could pursue. Bredon and Mardon both knew that men are far more persistent than horses.

During one slow amble toward the tiring mare Bredon paused, his vest hanging from one finger, and sniffed the air. "I smell water," he said. "We're getting close."

Mardon sniffed, and nodded agreement.

A few moments later, as Bredon scanned the plain, he noticed a break in the even green of the grass. "There," he said, pointing.

Again, Mardon nodded without comment, and circled out a little farther, correcting the mare's intended course.

A moment later, at Bredon's signal, he began whooping. The mare shied and ran straight toward the pool. She plunged heedlessly through the grass and into the water. The youths heard her hooves beat on the hard ground, and then a moment of tremendous splashing, which ended abruptly when, tripped by the mud, the horse fell and vanished from their sight behind the waves of green.

Ignoring everything but their prey, the two charged headlong across the plain and reached the water hole within seconds of each other.

The mare had struggled to her feet, but was up to her fetlocks in muck, her whole hide soaked and dripping. She turned her head, staring at them with eyes wide with terror.

Bredon readied his only remaining rope, determined to keep it where she could not chew it this time. He was scarcely four meters away when the mare abruptly stopped her thrashing. Her great brown eyes went calm as she said, very distinctly, "I wouldn't do that if I were you."

Bredon's mouth literally dropped open, a reaction he had always before considered to be artistic license on the part of the village storytellers, rather than something that really happened. Mardon, in turn, was so shocked that he tripped over his own feet and fell flat on his face in the mire at the edge of the pool.

The air was suddenly full of roaring laughter. Following the sound, Bredon and Mardon both looked up at what should have been empty sky.

A glittering platform that looked one instant like crystal and the next like metal hung unsupported in midair, about three meters off the ground. Bredon estimated it at perhaps a meter wide and twice that in length. Upon it stood a small, brown-haired, spade-bearded man clad in gleaming violet plush, laughing uncontrollably. His laugh seemed far too big for his stature.

Mardon cowered, trying to compose a good final prayer, cer-

tain he was doomed. There could be no question that he was facing a Power. The stories he had heard since childhood rarely made the Powers out to be unthinkingly hostile, but always emphasized incredible supernatural abilities, short tempers, and a ferocious disregard for the sanctity of human life. Mardon could not imagine surviving an encounter with a Power. He was certain he would make some little error in protocol, or trip over his own feet again, or otherwise bungle, and that this Power would take offense and destroy him.

Bredon simply stared, unable to cope with what was happening. He had never entirely believed in the Powers. Despite the assurances of the tellers, he had secretly assumed the stories to be myths, or at least exaggerations. His view of the world was a pragmatic and logical one, and there was no place in it for whimsical demigods.

The man on the platform laughed heartily for several seconds, reveling in the youths' confusion, before allowing his mirth to trail off into a smile and the relative silence of the wind in the grass.

"My apologies, gentlemen," the little man said when he had finished his laugh. "I'm afraid I've been having my fun at your expense."

Bredon stared up at him; then, as some of his scattered wits returned and his priorities reasserted themselves, he threw a quick look at the mare. She was standing calmly motionless in the mud.

"You made the mare talk?" Bredon asked.

"Yes, I'm afraid I did," the violet-garbed stranger replied, grinning.

"Is she yours?" Bredon demanded.

"No," the stranger said, his smile growing broader in response to Bredon's single-mindedness, "but I brought her here, and I'm afraid you can't have her. She belongs to a friend of mine by the name of Grey; I merely borrowed her."

"Oh." Bredon's disappointment was so obvious that the man on the platform laughed again, somewhat more quietly this time.

Mardon, still lying in the mud, cringed at the mention of Lord Grey the Horseman. The stories about him were few, but they all described him as one of the least tolerant Powers. He favored his horses over all else, especially mortal men—and they had trapped one of his mares!

Bredon was still confused. He had been so intent on the mare, had her so firmly fixed as the most important fact of his existence, that his mind was still refusing to function properly regarding anything else. He realized that he was facing a stranger, however, and as childhood training leaked to the surface, he remembered his manners. "I'm Bredon the Hunter, son of Aredon the Hunter," he said. A glance showed him that Mardon was still speechless, and he added, "That's Mardon the Cornfarmer, son of Maldor the Cornfarmer."

The man on the platform burlesqued a bow. "Honor to both your families, Bredon the Hunter. I am known as Geste."

A dozen childhood tales came back, even to Bredon, at the mention of that famous—or infamous—name. Mardon's terror abated slightly—or at any rate changed its form. Geste the Trickster was not reputed to kill on a whim, but he was dangerous in other ways.

Still, Mardon did not dare speak aloud to a Power.

Bredon was less reticent. "Geste the Trickster?" he asked. "The one who tamed the giants, and tricked Arn of the Ice into melting his own house?"

Geste smiled. "I see you've heard of me, but the tales seem to have grown in the telling. I don't recall that I've ever tamed any giants. And Arn only melted a part of the Ice House."

"And now you've tricked *us?*" Bredon was recovering himself finally, and found himself filling with rage.

"Yes, I believe I have." The little man grinned infuriatingly.

"You led us on for three wakes for a stupid joke? And *we can't even keep the horse?*"

Geste stared for a moment, then burst out laughing again. Bredon stared back at him coldly, and when the hilarity showed signs of subsiding, he said with intense dignity, "I had always heard that you were one of the more compassionate Powers, that you weren't vicious or petty or vindictive, but I think that this trick of yours was . . . was . . ." Words failed him, and he simply stared accusingly.

"Oh, calm down, Bredon," Geste said, still smiling down from his platform. "Don't take it so seriously. I like you; you say what you think, don't you? There aren't many mortals who would dare talk to me like that anymore. But really, Bredon, what's three wakes? Besides, you enjoyed every minute of the hunt. Don't claim you didn't!"

"But that was because I knew I'd catch her!" Bredon insisted.

Geste's smile faded. Struck by the young man's persistence and sincerity, he sobered. "Maybe you're right," he said, looking at Bredon thoughtfully. The smile was gone, or at least buried, as he said, "Listen, Bredon, I'm sorry. I didn't realize it would upset you so greatly. We sometimes forget how important these things can be to you mortals. Let me give you a gift to make it up to you. I can't give you this horse because, quite sincerely, she isn't mine to give, and we Powers don't break our promises, to mortals or to each other. I gave my word that I would return her unharmed, and so I must return her unharmed. I'm sure you understand that. However, instead, I will do you any other favor within my power—which is considerable, as I'm sure you know." He waved a hand and drew a glowing rainbow through the air, which burst into a thousand golden sparkles and then vanished. "Ask, and it's yours." His smile returned, bright as ever.

"I want the mare," Bredon said.

"You can't have her," Geste replied immediately.

"I don't want anything else," Bredon insisted.

"I could fetch another horse, perhaps," Geste suggested.

"No." Bredon's answer was prompt and definite, his mouth set in a scowl.

Geste repressed a smile at Bredon's petulance. "All right, Bredon, have it your way. You can't have the horse, and if you won't take anything else, you won't. I won't argue about it. I like you, and I'll respect your decision. That's for now, though, and you may reconsider eventually. I owe you something, and if you won't take it now, maybe you will later. Take this." He plucked something from the air and tossed it to Bredon, who caught it automatically. "Break that when you've decided what you'll take instead of the horse."

Bredon looked down at what he held. It was a shiny, bright red disk perhaps five centimeters across, made of some completely unfamiliar material that seemed as hard as metal, but with an odd slick texture like nothing he had ever felt before. "What is it?" Bredon asked, turning it over in his hands.

Mardon, who had been huddled silently throughout the conversation, suddenly sat up in the mud at the sight of this gift and demanded, "What about me?"

No one answered either question. Bredon looked up and discovered that Geste and his platform had vanished as suddenly as they had appeared.

What's more, the horse was gone, leaving only a gentle rippling on the surface of the muddy pool.

Chapter Two

". . . the stranger said, 'What? You haven't found it? Well, that's no surprise, for the truth is that I had it all the time, in my back pocket, and had only forgotten it.' Then he looked about at the ruins, at the broken cupboards and tumbled walls, and he burst out laughing.

"The farmer and his wife were shocked that the traveler could laugh so at another's misfortune, and the wife began to berate him soundly, whereupon he laughed all the more, until he was gasping for breath, his hands clutching at his belly.

"This enraged the wife so that she forgot herself and snatched up a spoon and went to beat upon the stranger, but she found that the spoon itself refused to strike him, no matter how hard she tried. This is hardly in the nature of a spoon, of course, and that was when her husband realized that this stranger was no mortal man at all. But he could not stop his wife, for so great was her fury that she would neither listen to reason nor consider the spoon's actions for herself, but only tried the harder to bring it down upon the stranger's head.

"The stranger lifted a hand, and caught his breath enough to say, 'Halt, enough!' Then he waved a hand, and behold, the walls rose up from the ground and rebuilt themselves, as sound and whole as ever. The cupboards jumped back into their accustomed places, and the furniture flew back together and arranged itself as it had been before the traveler ever set foot within the door.

"The wife dropped the spoon in astonishment and watched as the miracle took place, allowing the stranger to recover himself. He stooped and picked up the spoon, and handed it to her, saying, 'Here, my good woman, you may find this of use.'

"She took it, and saw that the ordinary wood had been transformed into solid gold.

" 'My apologies,' the stranger said, 'I'm sorry for any inconvenience. I must go now, but you have the thanks of Geste the Trickster for your most enjoyable hospitality.' And then he was gone, vanished as if he had never been.

"And the farmer and his wife looked around at their home and saw all that they had, that they had not appreciated—four sound walls and a warm roof, well-stocked cupboards and a comfortable home, and they saw how foolish they had been. And they did not sell the golden spoon, or melt it down, but hung it above the fireplace as a reminder of their encounter with the Trickster."

—FROM THE TALES OF ATHERON THE STORYTELLER

"It's not fair," Mardon insisted, as he sat poking at the dying cook fire with a broken turnspit.

Bredon sighed. He had heard this a good many times in the forty-odd wakes since he and his companion had arrived safely back in their home village. "Life is rarely fair," he pointed out, without moving from where he lay sprawled on his blankets. "You could have spoken up, just as I did, instead of hiding your face in the mud."

"I thought he was going to kill you!" Mardon said, giving the coals a particularly vicious jab. Sparks sailed upward.

"According to the stories," Bredon repeated wearily, "the Trickster never kills anyone." He rolled over and looked at his comrade, toward whom he was feeling distinctly less comradely of late. "Look, Mardon, you wouldn't have gotten to keep the horse if we'd caught it, we agreed on that, so why do you care about this stupid trinket we got instead?" He sat up and pulled the disk from his pocket. "It's not worth anything. I don't think it will really work, if I ever decide to use it. That was *the Trickster,* remember? If the stories are true, he lies all the time! He just gave me this to shut me up. If I break it I'll probably just get a faceful of stinkweed or something." He flipped the disk into the air with his right hand and caught it neatly with his left.

Mardon was not to be talked out of his sulkiness as easily as that. Abandoning the fire, he turned, still seated cross-legged, to face Bredon and asked, "Why do you keep it, then? Why not give it to me?"

"Mardon, he gave it to me, not you! Why should I give it to you? You're my friend, but that doesn't mean I need to give you everything I have. Look, you met Geste the Trickster, saw a Power face-to-face. You've got something to brag about to every girl in the village, a tale for your grandchildren, if you ever have any you care to acknowledge. You can pretty up the story all you like and no matter what you say I won't contradict you, you know that. I haven't told anyone that you didn't dare talk to him, and I'm not going to, so no one knows what you did or didn't do. The trinket proves we met him, so no one can doubt that we did. Atheron said so, and everybody accepts that. It doesn't matter which of us has it, for that, and Geste gave it to *me.* He might not like it if I gave it away. You don't need it, and you wouldn't dare use it if you had it, so why do you care about this thing so much? Isn't the tale enough?"

"No. Maybe. Oh, I don't know. It's just not fair." Mardon picked up the turnspit again.

Abruptly, Bredon felt he had had enough. His strained good

humor fled completely. He rose suddenly, almost jumping to his feet, and shouted down at Mardon, "Then go call Rawl the Adjuster about it, but stop whining to me! *I* didn't make you a coward, and I'll be damned and my soul eaten by demons before I'll give you the stupid thing!" He strode out of the tent, leaving the flap hanging open and Mardon staring after him in dumb astonishment.

The sun was on the eastern horizon and the midwake darkness was fading rapidly; full daylight would arrive in minutes, and the population of the village was already out and about, abandoning the quiet conversation and indoor work of the midwake dark for the outdoor work that could only be done while the sun was up. The long lights of midsummer were past, and sunlight was not to be wasted.

Several of his fellow villagers saw Bredon emerge from his bachelor's tent. His brother Kredon smiled and waved from the steps of their parents' house, and Bredon waved back perfunctorily. Kittisha the Weaver, on her way home from the village well, also waved, and changed direction, heading across the street toward him.

He growled quietly to himself. He liked Kittisha well enough, and had thoroughly enjoyed her company in his tent just two sleeps before, but in his present mood he did not care to talk to her. She tended to prattle on endlessly. When he was in the right frame of mind it was funny and endearing, but just now he knew it would only irritate him more. He pretended not to see her—just enough darkness remained that he could do that without risk of insulting her—and instead veered off to the right, around the side of his own tent and those of the other unmarried young men, and headed out of the village by the shortest available route.

He marched on past the tidy herb gardens, past the cornfields—which, he recalled with annoyance, were the domain of Mardon's father, cultivated by the entire family—and well out into the surrounding grassland before he calmed sufficiently to think at all. His pace gradually slowed, and on a whim he turned his steps eastward.

He walked on, and he thought.

His life was not going right. He felt that, but he could not really explain it. It all seemed to hinge somehow on his encounter with Geste the Trickster, the most playful of all the Powers. Before that, he had seen nothing wrong with his life, but now he could see little that was right.

Had Geste played some subtle trick on him, perhaps? Something that altered his feelings, something far more devious than the rather silly and simpleminded stunt with Lord Grey's mare?

He shook his head at the thought. He did not really believe that was it.

Fifty wakes earlier he had been a normal young man, happily pursuing wealth, glory, and young women. He was a fine hunter, one of the best in the village—that was no boast, but simple fact. He was tall, strong, and if not staggeringly handsome, certainly not ugly. His family was respected and respectable, his brother and three sisters all well enough behaved, both parents alive and healthy, his various aunts, uncles and cousins causing no problems. He had had no bitter quarrels or disagreements, nothing beyond the ordinary household squabbles that every family had, and even those had been few and mild of late.

He had almost no money, of course, but that was nothing. An unmarried man needed little enough. All he really owned was his bachelor's tent and a few personal items, but he had never lacked for the essentials, and his future was bright. Hunting was steady work, and prestigious, and a good hunter could make plenty of money once he had paid off his debt to his parents. Bredon's debt was down to a matter of a dozen meals or so, and his parents were not pressing him. If anything, pleased and proud as they were at how quickly he was paying, they seemed to be encouraging him to take his time.

As for women, for the past few seasons, since he had reached man-height and his complexion had begun clearing, he had had little trouble in finding willing females to share his bedding—though not always those he might have preferred. He had taken the occasional romantic setback in stride. He had had friends of both sexes, and was rarely lonely.

He had been happy, he knew he had.

Then he had glimpsed the mare when she wandered near the village, and he had set out in pursuit. A fine horse was wealth he could appreciate. He had spent three wakes chasing her, almost six full lights and five darks, with his childhood friend and inseparable companion beside him, and they had trapped her.

And that was where everything had gone wrong. By rights, they should have struggled with her, tied her, dragged her back home, and spent weeks breaking and training her. They would have worked hard with her, certainly, but their efforts would have been rewarded with the respect of the village, and with the knowledge of their own skills proven, as well as with a superb mount.

Instead, they had left the horse out on the plain and had come back with nothing but the strange red disk. A legend had come to life, appearing out of nowhere and snatching their quarry from them.

Even coming back empty-handed because the mare had escaped or died would have been more satisfying, he thought. They would have been honorably defeated, but learned from their mistakes and been better prepared the next time.

Instead, they had come back and told their story, which Atheron the Storyteller had declared fully authentic and consistent with the known characteristics of the Powers. They had shown the disk. The villagers had smiled, applauded them, honored them, feasted them—but it was all somehow unsatisfying and empty.

Bredon realized, with a start, what was really lacking. The villagers treated him with awe and wonder, they honored him—but the respect that he had sought was not there.

And why should it be? he asked himself silently. He had done nothing worthy of respect. He had not proven his worth as a hunter, as he had set out to do. He had, instead, been the butt of a demigod's stupid joke. People might stare at him in awe, they might honor him outwardly for his contact with divinity, but inwardly they thought no better of him than before. His encounter had been sheer luck, after all. Geste might have picked on anyone, anyone at all. He had not cared in the least that Bredon was the best young hunter in the village. What did a Power care about hunting?

And had Bredon come out of the encounter with honor? No, not really. He had done nothing.

The respect that was truly lacking, he saw, was his own self-respect.

He should have defied Geste, he thought. The little man was a Power, certainly, but that was no reason for Bredon to have stared at him so stupidly, gaped so awkwardly, spoken so foolishly. He should have at least *tried* to take the mare, despite what Geste said.

Of course, Geste was a Power, a demigod.

But then, the tales said that most of the Powers, including Geste, respected those who stood up to them despite the incredible danger of doing so. Some stories said that the Powers were only men and women come from another, higher world, a world where fortune had gifted everyone with immortality and magic. If that was so, if Geste was just a man, then Bredon had disgraced himself, given up his own dignity as an adult, in not standing up to his tormentor. He had forsaken his own commonsense view of the world and been overawed by Geste's supposed supernatural power.

He had done better than Mardon, though. Mardon had cowered and cringed, and that had been eating away at both of them since they had returned to the village. Their friendship was breaking up, Bredon knew. Mardon did not want the red disk so much as he wanted not to have behaved so badly, but there was nothing either of them could do about it. It was all in the past. Neither of them could change the past. The disk was just a symbol of the parts they had played, and if he gave it to Mardon he knew it would do no good. In fact, he suspected it would make things worse, as Mardon could then accuse Bredon of patronizing him.

Mardon was a coward, and had acted like a coward, and was ashamed of it. He was redirecting that shame into envy of Bredon, and it was destroying a friendship that had endured since the days when both wore diapers.

Bredon sighed.

Geste had done more harm than he knew. Bredon wondered whether the little man would laugh at the unhappiness he had caused.

He stopped walking, pulled the disk from his pocket, and studied it. It gleamed like a ruby in the light of the fast-rising sun.

If he broke it, would the Trickster really come?

And if he did, could he put right the wrong he had done? Could he cure Mardon's memory of his own cowardice, give Bredon back his self-respect?

Surely, such things were beyond even the Powers. They could move mountains, but could they repair a damaged soul?

Even if Geste could cast a spell of some sort, and make Bredon and Mardon once again happy and content, would either of them want a magical cure of that kind?

He put the disk back in his pocket.

He turned and faced westward for a moment, considering. The sun was well up; he had been walking toward it for an hour or more. If he hurried a little he could get back to the village before the sun reached its mid-secondlight zenith.

Did he want to?

What would he find in the village? Mardon might still be in his tent, which would mean chasing him out. That would be unpleasant. He did not want to see Mardon again for a while.

There was no one else he wanted to see, either. None of his relationships with the village girls had progressed beyond casual entertainment, really. His siblings were busy with their own affairs, and were still amused by the story of his meeting with the Trickster. His parents steadfastly refused to intervene in his life now that he had reached manhood and pitched his tent, and for the most part, despite their pride in him, they acted as little more than polite strangers—strangers he owed money. And most of his old friends had fallen away, somehow, in the last forty wakes.

He would be alone in the village.

That was a depressing thought. He hated being alone.

If he was going to be alone, he decided, he might as well be alone out in the open. Having other people around him would only make it worse. He turned eastward again and marched on.

Only hours later, when the last light had died and he had trampled himself a bed in the tall grass for the sleeping dark, did he suddenly decide where he was going.

Not far to the east stood the so-called Forbidden Grove. He knew the place was reputed to be the territory of one of the Powers, a female Power, called Lady Sunlight of the Meadows. She was by far the closest of the Powers—excluding the wanderers like Rawl and Geste, of course, who could be anywhere. She was more or less the patron deity of the area, as much as there was one. He could not remember any tales about her, or at least none of the details—he had never taken any interest in the stories Atheron and Kithen told—but she was said to be an important Power all the same. Somewhere in the grove, or just beyond it, she was supposed to have her personal demesne, her place of power, a place called, naturally, the Meadows, where she had a great glittering palace.

Bredon's uncle Taredon had pointed the grove out to him once, when a hunt brought them this way, so he knew where it was. He should, he thought, be able to reach it by the next wake's second sunrise.

He would go there, he told himself, go right into the grove, taboo or not. He had survived an encounter with one Power already, but had lost his self-respect in doing it. Maybe if he trespassed fearlessly on the lands of another he could regain a little of his pride, show himself that it had been surprise, more than fear, that had let the Trickster get the better of him.

Of course, that assumed he would survive trespassing in the grove. He could not be sure of that.

Before meeting Geste, he had never paid any attention to the Powers. No one else in the village had ever met one—at least, no one still alive, though tales were told about various ancestors. The Powers had been nothing to him but stories for children, and he had not considered them relevant to the real, everyday world around him.

He now saw that he had been wrong. The Powers were real and relevant, and if he wanted to understand the world he needed to know how to deal with them, whether to ignore them as he always had, or to actively avoid them, or to seek them out. This mysterious Lady Sunlight was close at hand—if she actually existed—and as good a subject for investigation as any.

He would not embarrass himself again.

With that thought circling through his mind he fell asleep.

Chapter Three

" . . . Lady Sunlight of the Meadows is among the most shy and retiring of all the Powers, at least as far as mortals are concerned. She takes no interest in worldly matters, and in fact barely lives in our world at all—her glittering palace is almost impossible to find, for the paths in the Forbidden Grove twist and turn beneath mortal feet, always leading away from the Meadows. When one perseveres and finally, by charm or luck, does reach the place where her palace stands, one might not even see it, for it is not always there. And no one can enter it, for there are no doors. Lady Sunlight wants no guests. Her interests lie in the sparkle of sunlight on a dewdrop, or the shape of a flower's petals, not in the mundane affairs of everyday people. She has no desire to speak with mortals—if, in fact, she can speak at all, for no mortal has ever heard her voice. Those who wander near the Forbidden Grove sometimes glimpse her, as a flash of movement in the corner of the eye, or a reflection in a stream, or a shadow in the sun, but none has ever heard her speak. Those who dare venture into the Grove, perhaps to the boundaries of the Meadows, can sometimes catch sight of her briefly, as she runs laughing through the fields, or tenderly cares for her flowers, or combs the golden hair that reaches to her ankles. Of these who glimpse her, those who return to their villages—and not all of them do, for some pine away for love of her, spending their lives watching for another glimpse or waiting in hope of hearing her speak—but those who do return to them are never quite the same. They speak often of her beauty, though they can never describe any details, and they spend much of their time staring off into space, in the general direction of the Meadows . . ."

—FROM THE TALES OF ATHERON THE STORYTELLER

The grove made him uneasy. He moved forward cautiously, the rich, earthy smell filling his nostrils with every step.

Bredon had rarely seen trees except at a distance. Few trees grew on the grasslands around the village, and he, like all his people, almost never ventured away from the open plain. The plain was big enough for anyone. Besides, other lands belonged to other tribes, or to the Powers, and one did not intrude uninvited.

At least, not without a good reason. Bredon was very aware that he was intruding uninvited.

The presence of not one, or two, but four or five hundred trees

in a single place was almost overwhelmingly alien. He had seen
the forests cloaking the distant mountainsides, but to be *among*
the trees, close enough to touch them, to smell them, to see the
individual leaves, was very different. Despite his bold intentions,
Bredon had entered the Forbidden Grove very slowly and cautiously, moving as silently as he could and staring up uneasily at
the strange, towering plants on every side.

Something felt wrong almost immediately; he paused to try
and identify it.

When he had stopped moving, when his feet no longer rasped
against the underbrush and his clothes no longer rustled as they
slid across his body, he realized what it was. The woods sounded
wrong.

Every hour of his life, every wake, every sleep, every light
and dark, ever since his birth, whenever he had been outside
solid walls, he had heard the wind in the grass. In the spring the
wind hissed through the green young shoots. In summer the grass
was tall and whispered in the wind. In autumn the brown stalks
rubbed and chattered, until at last came the winter, coating the
grass in ice, knocking the blades to the ground and sometimes
burying them in snow, but not quieting them as they tinkled
together or crunched underfoot. The sound had been faint when
the wind was gentle, a harsh howling when the winter winds
ripped down from the mountains, but always present. The air on
the plain was never still, and the grass was never still. When a
man walked anywhere beyond the village, he walked through
rustling grass.

Here in the Forbidden Grove the grass did not grow and the
wind could not reach. Overhead leaves rustled, but that was a
different sound, an alien sound, a *wrong* sound. His feet moved
silently, moving aside nothing but air, and the air around him
was calm—not dead, because it still stirred faintly, but calm and
quiet.

A bird chirped, loud in the closed-in stillness.

He was hungry, he decided. After all, he had not intended to
make so long a journey, and had come away with nothing but a
pocket full of corn chips. He had reached the grove, he had
entered it; now it was time to go home and get something solid to
eat.

He was actually starting to turn when he caught himself.

He was not Mardon, he thought scornfully, to be terrified by
anything that was at all out of the ordinary. There was nothing
unnatural in the grove's stillness. He had experienced similar
quiet in his parents' house, he told himself.

That was not strictly true, he immediately corrected himself. Houses did not have leaves that rustled overhead. Houses were built, not grown. Houses had distinct walls and small rooms, not great ill-defined spaces that seemed to wind on forever. Houses were lit by lamps or straight-edged windows, not by dapples of sunlight that spilled randomly through a myriad of leaves, all shifting in the breeze.

Still, he was no child to be frightened by something simply because it was strange. He forced himself to march on into the grove.

It occurred to him that, here among the trees, he was walking between the stems of plants as an insect walked between blades of grass, similarly sheltered, and that he was in no more danger from the trees than an ant was from grass. However, the analogy did not really comfort him, but instead made him feel insignificant.

As he moved on in the still air beneath the rustling leaves, he quickly noticed something else about the grove: it was cool. The sun was almost straight overhead, yet he was not at all uncomfortable. Out in the open he knew that he would have been sweating heavily. Summer was dying, but not yet dead, and the autumn cooling would not arrive for another few tensleeps.

With that, with the realization that he was not sweating and hot, his opinion of the grove began to change. He began to see the beauty, as well as the strangeness, in the scattered light, the soaring trunks and reaching branches, the open ground. Looking up, he began to distinguish between the different varieties of tree.

His pace had shifted from a tentative creep when he first passed under the shade of the trees to a confident stride when he conquered his fear. Now it shifted again, from a stride to an amble, as he began to take in the details of his surroundings, not as potential dangers but as potential delights.

Best of all was when he rounded a huge old oak and found himself on the bank of a stream. The water gurgled around tree roots and polished stones, and the sunlight shattered into dancing glitter on its surface. He almost thought he heard a distant music, as of children singing or someone playing lightly on a fidlin.

The streams he was familiar with out in the grasslands were little more than meandering ditches. They did not sing and sparkle.

It was no wonder, he told himself, that people thought a place as weird and wonderful as this must be linked to the Powers. He saw no sign of any Lady Sunlight, but only the sunlight on the leaves and water.

He looked out across the stream and saw an open meadow, a

few hectares of wild flowers and short grass surrounded by trees. That, he told himself, was surely the Meadows, but he saw no Lady Sunlight, and certainly no great palace. For an instant he thought he saw something tall and glittering in the center of the meadow, but when he could not find it again he dismissed it as a trick of the light, something caused by emerging from the dimness of the trees into the meadow's brightness.

Weird and wonderful, he told himself as he sat down to rest by the stream, but nothing of the Powers about it.

He did not see the glittering column flicker again. He did not know enough to realize that, even when planted with trees, the plain would not naturally have babbling brooks full of water-rounded stones. As the life of the grove went on around him, he could not distinguish the artificial insects and flowers from the natural ones. He was unaware of the hidden machines that scanned him, analyzed him, and decided he was harmless.

He sat quietly by the stream until the wake's second sunset and dozed off there, convinced that he sat among wonders of nature, and only of nature.

The sun was well up the sky, and firstlight well advanced, when he awoke again. He was in the habit of waking at dawn, but he was not accustomed to the cool shade of the grove.

He rose and stretched, then knelt and splashed a little water on his face. The stream was clear and clean and cool. He bent down and drank.

His stomach growled, ruining the mood. Something chittered overhead, and he looked up in time to see leaves closing behind some small scampering creature. A dislodged vine slithered across a branch.

He had not brought any weapons, and besides, he had no idea how to hunt among trees. He reached in his pocket for the last of the corn chips, and stuffed all but the smallest fragments into his mouth.

When he had taken the edge off his hunger by chewing the corn chips to liquid, he sat down at the base of a great tree and looked around, admiring the scenery. In the rising light it took on a different aspect from what it had had when he first arrived. The meadow across the stream was somehow more colorful, he thought; the air itself seemed to glisten, and the impression of distant singing in the sound of the brook was stronger than ever.

This, he thought, would be a wonderful place to bring a woman. There was a serenity to the place that he judged would appeal to most of the girls or women he knew. He was sure

Kittisha would like it. The mossy bank of the stream would be a very pleasant place to lie together.

He let himself imagine that for a moment as he gazed across at the meadow.

Then he saw that the air really *was* glittering. He stared, realizing that it was no illusion, or at least none he had ever encountered before.

He asked himself if it could be some peculiar sort of diurnal firefly, and was on the verge of convincing himself that that was exactly what he was seeing when a woman stepped out of the glittering air onto the meadow grass, accompanied by strange music that was definitely neither singing nor the sound of water.

She was tall and slender, her long, flowing hair the golden yellow of sunlight on wild flowers. She wore a filmy pale something that seemed to shift both color and shape every time she moved, and which hung drifting in the air despite a complete lack of any breeze to account for such motion. Small fluttering things, like tiny glowing butterflies, flashed a thousand colors in a halo about her, and furry things moved through the grass at her feet.

Bredon stared, and felt something stir within him.

The woman paid no attention to him. She gave no sign that she had noticed his presence at all. She stood in the meadow and took a deep breath, filling her lungs with the morning air. The flutterers swirled away for a moment, then returned, and the sourceless music rose into a brief crescendo.

Bredon watched hungrily. This woman was, beyond any doubt, Lady Sunlight of the Meadows.

She was also the most beautiful thing Bredon had ever seen.

He was, he realized, looking at another Power. This was what he had come here for, to see another Power and see if he could recover some of what he had lost in his meeting with Geste. Looking at Lady Sunlight as she stretched lazily, he knew exactly what he wanted, what would more than make up for the lost mare and his lost self-esteem.

He wanted Lady Sunlight. He wanted her with a raw and simple lust stronger than any he had felt in years.

His breeches had grown uncomfortably tight as his body reacted to the sight of that sleek and inhumanly beautiful female form; he shifted his legs, trying to accommodate himself, then got awkwardly to his feet.

"Hello!" he called.

Startled, the woman dropped her arms from above her head to cover her breasts, and whirled to face him. The flutterers abruptly vanished, the music stopped, and the animals at her feet disappeared into the grass. She whispered something; he could see her lips moving, but even without the music Bredon heard nothing over the rustle of leaves and the splashing of the brook.

There was no one else in sight save she and himself. Bredon wondered who she was talking to—the invisible musicians, perhaps?

Then there was someone else in sight, or at least some*thing* else. It was shaped more or less like a man, but was obviously not a man, not even a man in a costume. It was eight fell tall, covered in gleaming silver metal, its face a dark nothingness. It stepped across the brook in a single stride and stood towering over him.

"Sir," it said in a polite and completely human masculine voice, "you are trespassing on private property. I must ask you to leave at once."

The thing was blocking his view; he tried to peer around it, to see what Lady Sunlight was doing. "I just—" he began.

"Sir, I must ask you to leave *at once*. There can be no discussion."

"But—"

He felt himself being picked up, but the thing's arms still hung motionless at its sides, a meter or two away. Before he could figure this out he was being whisked back through the grove at an incredible speed, though he had not felt anything throw him. Trees flashed by on either side, and for an instant he was terrified by the thought of striking one; at the speed he was traveling he knew such an impact would break his skull or his spine.

Then he slowed, and tumbled to the ground on the open grassland at a speed no greater than if he had stumbled over his own feet.

Driven by lust and his native stubbornness, he immediately untangled himself, jumped up, and started back into the grove.

His face smacked into something invisible, and he fell back, his hand flying immediately to his nose.

He felt the damaged area carefully. It was not broken, not even bleeding, but he thought it would develop a nice purple bruise in another few hours.

He advanced again, more cautiously this time, his left hand held out before him.

His hand pressed up against something he could not see. The invisible barrier was still there. He shoved at it.

It did not yield. It felt like a solid wall, yet he could see nothing, not even the odd glitter that he had seen above the meadow.

He stepped back and considered, then circled around a dozen paces to the left. There he advanced into the grove again.

Once again, he encountered the invisible barrier just past the first ring of trees.

This, obviously, was magic. This was power. This was what made the Powers respected and feared throughout the world.

He leaned on the barrier with both hands, digging his heels into the soft earth, but could make no impression. He pushed until he could feel the muscles in his thighs and upper arms knotting with the strain.

The dirt beneath his heels gave way; his feet went out from under him and he fell ignominiously face-first onto a patch of moss.

Fuming, he pushed himself up onto his knees and spat out moss and dirt. He glared at the grove, serene and beautiful behind the barrier, looking just as it had when he first awoke. The only difference was that now he was outside and could not get back in.

He had given in to Geste, but by all the gods and demons, he promised himself, he was not going to lose to Lady Sunlight without putting up a fight.

He backed out onto the grassland for a running start.

He bruised his shoulder on the unyielding barrier.

He glared at the grove, rubbing absently at his injured joint. He had bruised his shoulder, but he did not give up. He would never give up.

He did not give up, and at last, considerably later, he stood, somewhat battered, in the center of the meadow, trying to decide what to do.

He had struggled against the invisible wall for hours, as the sun passed its zenith and hurried down the western sky. He had rested briefly at the wake's first sunset, but when full dark had arrived he had renewed his efforts. When the secondlight sunrise came he had rested again, finishing off the last crumbs of corn and washing them down with water taken from the stream where it emerged from the southeast corner of the grove. There, he noticed, the stream became an ordinary ditch, with no rocks and rills, and he began to suspect that the entire grove was an artificial creation, devised by Lady Sunlight for her own enjoyment.

He tried sneaking upstream to slip under the barrier beneath the shallow water, but succeeded only in covering himself with mud; water did indeed pass under the barrier, but the opening was too small for him.

He climbed out and dried himself off, and after sitting for a moment, thinking, he decided to try digging his way under. He felt his way forward, looking for the barrier in order to know where to start digging, and did not find it.

The barrier had vanished. He walked into the grove unobstructed, and found his way to the meadow.

There was no sign of Lady Sunlight there. He could see glitter in the air sometimes, and once or twice he bumped into invisible somethings, but he could not locate anything out of the ordinary more than once. He found no supernatural doorways, no hidden caves, no messages, nothing but an empty meadow where, every so often, he would brush against a wall that wasn't there when he turned to investigate further. The bright little fluttering things were gone without a trace, as were the small furry creatures that he had glimpsed at her feet, and there was no music, but only the whisper of the wind in the leaves, the gurgle of the stream, and an occasional call from a lonely bird.

He stood there, baffled.

He wanted Lady Sunlight more than he had ever wanted anything. He knew that was irrational, but he could not help it. He thought it was not really for her own sake—she was staggeringly beautiful, but he knew nothing more about her than that, and beauty meant little. It was for what she represented. She was a Power. That meant she was unobtainable. It also meant that she was a part of the group that he felt had wronged him. The combination was irresistible.

This was not love, in any form. It was lust. He knew that.

He understood his motives, and he was not proud of them, but he was unable to change his feelings. He wanted her, very much indeed. Quite aside from the sexual element—and powerful as it was, he thought he could resist that—he wanted to talk to her, to voice his complaints and challenge her to answer them.

She was not there. All he saw was the empty meadow.

Defeated, he thrust his hands in his pockets, hunching forward and glaring balefully at the unmindful wild flowers.

His finger touched something hard and slick, and he stopped, startled, as he realized what he was touching. A smile spread slowly across his face, then faded again.

It might, as he had told Mardon, produce nothing but a faceful of stink. If Geste had told the truth, though, Bredon had his answer. He had a demand to make that would surely be a challenge even for Geste. If Geste gave him what he asked for, then he would have Lady Sunlight and a victory over the Powers; if Geste failed, then he would have shamed Geste as Geste had shamed him. He pulled out the red disk.

"If this doesn't work, you bastard, I'll do my best to kill you," he said. Then he grabbed the disk in both hands and pushed against it with his thumbs.

It cracked easily, then crumbled, and suddenly he held nothing but red powder.

Bredon brushed the powder from his hands and looked about expectantly.

Nothing happened. Leaves rustled, and somewhere a bird whistled plaintively.

He waited, quickly growing angry.

"May demons suck the marrow from your bones for lying to me, Geste the Trickster!" he shouted at the rustling leaves overhead, after a moment passed without incident. Disgusted, he started toward the stream, intending to cross it and head home. He was very hungry now, and he had found nothing to eat anywhere in the grove.

Chapter Four

"... neither woman would relinquish her claim to the child.

"Rawl the Adjuster looked at them carefully, and said, 'Long ago, an ancient king revered for his wisdom faced a case exactly like this, and proposed that the baby be cut in half, that each mother might have half. What would you think of that solution?'

"Both mothers gasped in horror at the idea, and each quickly offered to give up her claim to forestall such a catastrophe.

" 'I thought as much,' said the Adjuster. 'That story never sounded right to me. Let us see if we can't do better. Give me your hands.' And he reached out to the two women.

"Well, naturally, both were hesitant to touch the actual flesh of a Power, but first one reached out, and then the other, not wanting to be bested, did the same. They held hands with the Adjuster for a moment, and then he released them and stepped back. He picked up the baby, then returned it to the cradle.

"A moment later he announced, 'This woman is the child's true and rightful mother, the woman who bore him,' and he pointed to the woman on the left. 'The sheens prove it.'

"No one knew why Rawl spoke of sheens, but it's sworn by all who were there that that was his word, or one very like it.

"When he had made his announcement, the other woman flung herself at his feet, confessing that it was true, that her child had died and she had taken the other in its stead, and the Adjuster bade her rise and stop weeping.

" 'I cannot give you back your dead child,' he said, 'but I can give you another just like it. Bring me the remains of the dead child.'

"And the woman ran behind her house and began scraping at the dirt where she had buried her babe.

"The Adjuster followed, and the dirt flung itself aside at his gaze. He reached out and pinched the dead child's arm, then returned it to its grave.

" 'In three days,' he said, 'I will bring you your child.' And he vanished.

"The people wondered mightily at this, and for three days they spoke of little else. Most of them doubted that even a Power could create a new child without a mother's womb, and certainly not in three days; some ventured to guess that Rawl had gone to search the world for an orphan to take the place of the lost infant.

"But lo, when the three days had passed, the Adjuster returned with a baby in his arms, and the child was newborn, and in fine health, *and was in every way the exact image of the poor dead boy that lay behind the house, with hair and eyes and features just the same.*

" 'A clown,' the Adjuster said. 'This is a clown of the one that died.' He handed the baby to the dead boy's mother, and then he vanished again.

"But the odd thing is that the Power's prophecy was wrong, and when the boy grew up he became a fine blacksmith, and not a clown at all."

—FROM THE TALES OF ATHERON THE STORYTELLER

Crystal shimmered white in the air above the terrace, and Lady Sunlight stepped down onto the pavement. A polychrome torrent of flying sparkles poured after her, glittering in the sun, and a golden-furred creature the size of her hand leapt out beside her, nose up and alert.

"Hello!" she called. "I'm here!"

"Hello, Sunlight," a hoarse voice replied.

She turned, startled, and found a short man dressed in black standing at one corner of the terrace, where he had been admiring the view to the west. A thick black disk perhaps a dozen centimeters in diameter hovered above one of his shoulders, and a black-furred and bat-winged creature glared at her from the other. A small feelie vine was wrapped around his wrist.

"Oh, hello, Rawl," she said. "I didn't know you were here."

"I'm here," he replied.

"I can *see* that," she said, annoyed. She shifted her shoulders, drawing her flowing polychrome gown more closely about her and sending her insectile aerial circus into an uproar. "Is Sheila here yet?"

"She's inside," Rawl said, jerking his head toward the gleaming windows.

As he spoke one of the transparent panels vanished, and a tall, handsome woman in a brown bodysuit leaned out, brown hair stirring in the breeze. Music spilled out around her, the mellow droning of an ancient Fomalhautian mood piece, and the accompanying images swirled behind her.

"Hello, Sunlight!" she called. "I'm glad you could come!"

"Hello, Sheila!" Sunlight answered, waving gaily, "I wouldn't miss it! I brought some flutterbugs to brighten up the place!"

"Well then, don't just stand there, come on in, and bring them with you! You too, Rawl; Autumn House is now officially open."

"It isn't autumn yet," Rawl said, as he turned away from the panoramic view of the western foothills and the desert beyond. The floating disk spun slowly, and faded from sight; his creature blinked slowly and curled itself up to his neck. The feelie vine stroked his wrist soothingly.

"Oh, I know that," Sheila said. "But I felt like coming up here a little early this year. It's just another hundred hours or so, anyway; that's close enough. Come on in!"

When his inhuman passenger was secure on his shoulder, Rawl strode across the terrace with calm assurance. Lady Sunlight hesitated.

"Sheila, who else is here?" she asked, reaching down to scoop up her golden-furred companion.

"No one, yet," Sheila replied, momentarily puzzled. Then her expression cleared. "Oh, you mean Geste. I haven't gotten hold of him yet; they tell me he's out bothering the natives again. I don't think he knows I came early, so you should have a couple of days—local days, at the very least—before he gets here."

"Good!" Lady Sunlight said.

Rawl passed her on his way to the house. "They aren't natives," he said, almost to himself.

"Oh, certainly they are," Sheila retorted. "They were born here, weren't they? They've been here for thousands of years, so they're natives *now*, and it doesn't matter where their ancestors came from."

"Yes, it matters," Rawl insisted, as he stepped into the lounge.

"Well, yes, it *matters*," Sheila admitted, annoyed, "because they're human and not extraterrestrials or artificials, but damn it, Rawl, they're natives now, and we need *some* term to distinguish them from our own little expedition."

Rawl just shrugged at that, and gestured for a drink. A silver dish—actually a small, self-aware machine, akin to his own disk-shaped device—that floated in midair appeared, a ball of crystalline fluid held in a field above it.

Sheila helped Lady Sunlight into the house—not that she needed it, but simply as a gesture of welcome. The glittering flutterbugs scattered across the lounge, transforming the seething Fomalhautian imagery to something much quicker, more cheerful and more scattered. The music changed to match, improvised by the household machines, and an odor of cinnamon and new grass wafted through the room. "I wish you and Geste got along better," Sheila said.

"Oh, sometimes I wish we did, too," Lady Sunlight replied, sighing as she settled into a floating red chair. A feelie vine offered itself to her ankle, but with a gentle twitch she sent it away. "We did once, you know—we were lovers for about a decade once. But he's just *so* childish and immature with his stupid pranks! Do you know what he did? He—''

Sheila, sinking into her own seat, cut her off. "Yes, I *do* know, dear, because he came and told me about it himself, and you shouldn't hash it over again.''

"I suppose he was bragging about it.''

"No, he was apologizing, explaining why he wouldn't be able to visit at the same time you did for a while.''

Rawl sipped his drink through a pseudopod of force, and asked, "What *did* he do? I hadn't heard.''

"Oh, this isn't anything new," Sheila said before Lady Sunlight could speak. "I told you about it. It was almost three years ago, now.''

"Oh, that," Rawl said, shrugging. "Nothing.''

"Nothing!" Lady Sunlight exclaimed.

"Nothing *important*," Rawl amended.

"Maybe not to you, Rawl, with your damned high ideals, but it's important to *me* when some young idiot ruins a party for some stupid joke that he should have outgrown before they ever let him leave Terra!" She settled back, stroking her tiny pet. The creature chirrupped softly.

"Is Geste Terran?" Rawl asked with mild curiosity.

Lady Sunlight hesitated. "Is he?" she asked Sheila.

Sheila shrugged. "I don't know," she said. "I never worried about it.''

"Housekeeper, is Geste Terran?" Lady Sunlight demanded of the ceiling.

"I'm sorry, my lady, but that information is not in any of the household records. Shall I ask the mother ship?''

"No, don't bother, it doesn't matter," she said.

Rawl, his curiosity piqued and disappointed in his companion's disinterest, closed his eyes and put through his own call internally. He learned that Geste had been born in Three Rivers, on Achernar IV, which seemed very appropriate for a prankster; that said, he declined the automatic tell-me-more before it went any further. He was not particularly interested in any of the details of Geste's past just now. He opened his eyes again without having missed a word of the conversation.

"The housekeeper should have asked Mother without waiting for orders," Sheila was saying. "I think the programming must have deteriorated pretty badly. I've been putting off redoing it for sixty or seventy years now, but I think it's about due.''

"Sometimes I hate roughing it here, with these inadequate machines Aulden brought along—I mean, they *work*, but they aren't exactly state-of-the-art, are they?'' She waved at the flutterbugs, the light show, the stone-floored, wooden-beamed room. ''But then I remember what it was like back home and decide that it's worth a little inconvenience to have the elbow room,'' Sunlight said. She sighed. ''Sometimes I wonder what the poor machine does with itself when you're not here, don't you?'' she asked. ''Do you leave it awake?''

''I let it decide for itself, of course, and I honestly don't know what it did this year.''

Rawl already knew that the housekeeper had remained awake, fussily removing every fleck of dust or trace of wear, shooing away every form of wildlife from the larger bacteria up to fair-sized goats, always without harming them. He knew because he had stopped by to visit with the machine once or twice. He suspected that Sheila knew as much, but neither of them mentioned it. Sunlight, he knew, already considered the wanderers, especially Geste and himself, to be crazy, and would be even more firmly convinced of it if she knew he took pleasure in visiting a mere machine. She thought it was quite bad enough that he spent so much time with the first-wave colonists—the natives, as Sheila insisted on calling them, a name that was at least preferable to *primitives* or *savages*, terms some of the other recent arrivals used.

Not, he admitted to himself, that their arrival was all that recent anymore. They had been on this planet, listed in the ancient records under the curious name Denner's Wreck, for roughly four centuries by local time, four and a half by Terran standards.

He finished his drink and sat down, trusting the housekeeper to make sure that a good chair, customized to his particular proportions, was waiting beneath him.

The housekeeper did not fail him. It was not *that* badly deteriorated.

''Who else are you expecting?'' Lady Sunlight asked.

''Oh, I'm not really sure,'' Sheila replied. ''I've told Mother that I'm having my annual autumn housewarming, and I expect Grey to put in his usual appearance and spend the entire time talking about horses and pseudoequines and so forth, and Brenner will probably show up and argue the whole time, and the Skyler may come if I can convince her it won't be too crowded—the usual people. I haven't bothered with actual invitations in almost a century, you know, I just wait to see who turns up. I'm sure that Geste will come by eventually, when he stops teasing the natives long enough to notice what time of year it is.''

"Is that what he's doing?" Rawl asked.

"Probably," Sheila replied. "You know what he's like."

Rawl nodded agreement, disturbing the creature on his shoulder so that it flapped awkwardly upward and set out to find a better perch. "At least he has the grace to try and make amends when he's through abusing them. He doesn't treat them like just more machines or creatures."

Lady Sunlight sniffed derisively.

"You think I'm overprotective of them?" Rawl asked. He knew perfectly well what Lady Sunlight thought, and for that matter what each of the others in their group thought, but he asked in the interests of provoking discussion, in hopes of deepening his insight.

"I think you're too *concerned* with them," Lady Sunlight said. "I won't say they don't need protection from themselves, but it isn't any of our business, is it? There's no need for us to involve ourselves with them at all."

"That's what you said when we landed," Rawl remarked mildly. "You haven't changed your mind?"

"No; why should I?"

"You've had four hundred years to observe them now."

Lady Sunlight looked at him in genuine surprise. "*Observe* them? Why in the universe would I do that? I've done all I can to *avoid* them! Just today, before I left to come here, I had one of those stupid robots chase one of the natives away, because he was spying on me. They're just a nuisance, Rawl; I leave them alone, and all I ask in exchange is that they leave me alone."

"They're people," he reminded her.

"Oh, yes, well, I suppose so, but they aren't anyone I care about. I don't even know why we all insist on speaking their language all the time!"

"Well, we have to, now," Sheila pointed out, "because a lot of the machines and creatures don't understand anything else."

"And whose idea was *that?*" Lady Sunlight said, glaring at Rawl.

"Aulden's," he replied mildly. "He was all for sharing our technology, even more than Imp and Geste and I were."

"Giving them anything isn't our business," Lady Sunlight insisted. "That's the job of a cultural analysis team. We're just tourists. I said then, and I still say now, that they're none of our business, and that's the way the vote has always gone."

"The majority is not necessarily right," Rawl muttered. Lady Sunlight did not hear him.

"It's not as if we expected to find them," she was saying.

"When we came here looking for a lost colony we never expected to actually *find* it! I thought we might find some interesting ruins or antiques, an abandoned settlement, or maybe even a little civilization out of the mainstream, but I *never* thought we'd find short-lived primitives!"

There was that word again, and Rawl shut up, rather than risk a messy argument over it. He reminded himself that he had picked the quarrel himself, in the interests of livening up the conversation.

He resolved to keep his mouth shut henceforth—at least for a few days. Maybe only the fourteen-hour local days, but a few days.

"I mean, really," Lady Sunlight was continuing. "How can they go on like that, century after century, living their pointless little lives, farming their crops and killing animals to eat and never getting anywhere? I know they had to start practically from nothing, but they've been here for thousands of years now, and there isn't a city on the planet, and they don't know the first thing about building any kind of machine, let alone engineering themselves useful plants or animals or even bacteria. How can they have lived like this for so long without dying out? It's a mystery to me, I'll tell you that!"

How, Rawl wondered, could anyone live as long as Lady Sunlight had, and remain so ignorant? History held hundreds of examples of stable agrarian societies, on dozens of planets.

He had resolved on silence, however, and silent he remained as he gestured to the floater for another drink. He noticed that his companion creature had found itself a place atop a wooden beam overhead, and he amused himself for a moment by looking at the room through its eyes. The entertainment system had given up on any attempt to coordinate its images with the independently minded flutterbugs, so the low music was now only sound, and the view unimpeded.

"Excuse me, my lady," the housekeeper said, slipping into a break in the conversation and fading the music still further, "but you have a call from Brenner of the Mountains."

"Brenner? Put him through," Sheila said, brightening. Rawl guessed that she too found Lady Sunlight's attitudes somewhat irritating, and welcomed the distraction.

Immediately, Brenner's image appeared before them, black-bearded and frowning; he had not bothered with full-figure transmission, so his head and leather-clad shoulders floated in the air unsupported.

"Hello, Sheila," he said. "I'm calling to let you know that I may not be able to come to your open house this season."

"No? But why *not?*"

"Oh, well, it seems that Thaddeus is upset about something; I don't have the faintest idea what the hell he thinks I did this time, and the idiot won't tell me, so I couldn't apologize even if I wanted to. Whatever it is, he's shooting at me, and using some fairly serious stuff, too. I don't think it would be a good idea to leave home right now. He might slip something in somewhere, or try to pick me off while I'm traveling." He shrugged. "I'm sorry, but it's really not my fault."

Intrigued, Rawl shifted his vision back where it belonged and brushed away his new drink.

"He's shooting at you?" Sheila asked.

"Well, yes, but—"

"He can't do that!" Lady Sunlight exclaimed.

Rawl rose and stepped into Brenner's field of vision. "Brenner, I know you don't think much of me," he said, "but I've made a hobby of settling disputes, if you'd like my help in this one."

"Rawl? Well, I'll be damned, I haven't seen you lately!"

"I've been around."

"I'm sure you have. No, I don't need any help, thanks."

"Brenner, wait," Sheila said. "Thaddeus hasn't got any business shooting at you, no matter what you did. The party hasn't started yet; we're coming down to give you a hand, all three of us. All right?"

Brenner's mouth twisted slightly, as if he were not sure whether or not to permit himself a smile. "Well, I won't stop you," he said. "But Thaddeus might."

Rawl thought he heard relief in Brenner's tone. He ran the recorded words through an emotional analysis in his internal computers, and concluded that yes, Brenner was relieved. He was far too proud to ask for help, or to admit even to himself that he might need it, but he was worried.

Thaddeus, Rawl thought, must be making a serious attack indeed, to worry Brenner, master of the impregnable High Castle.

"We'll be there in an hour," Sheila said.

Lady Sunlight started to protest, but Sheila waved her to silence, out of Brenner's sight.

"I'll see you then," Brenner said. His image flicked out.

"But, Sheila—" Sunlight began, obviously distressed.

"We *have* to go, Sunlight," Sheila said. "If Thaddeus is causing trouble—well, you know what he's like. He's dangerous.

He might really hurt someone. Besides, I told Brenner we'd come, and I won't go back on my word."

Sunlight hesitated, mouth set, and then yielded abruptly. "Oh, all right," she said. "But I don't like that castle of his, and I don't like Thaddeus much, either."

"I don't think *anybody* likes Thaddeus," Rawl remarked.

"I have the airskiff I used to bring my things from Summer House up on the next level," Sheila said. "We'll take that." She rose smoothly and led the way to the lifter.

Rawl followed calmly, his creature fluttering back down to his shoulder and his floater returning to visibility, while Lady Sunlight came more reluctantly, her creature in her hand.

The music faded gracefully into silence.

"Good-bye," the housekeeper said behind them, as brightly colored flutterbugs danced wild airborne dances in the empty lounge. "I'll keep the place warm for you."

Chapter Five

". . . when they returned to their village they told their friends and families what had befallen them, and poured forth glowing praise of Isabelle's hearth and hospitality. They spoke at length of her kindness and generosity, how she had taken them in from the storm and met their every need, even before they could ask. They described the fine foods they had eaten, and the exotic beverages they had drunk. They showed the magical cloaks she had given them that were so thin that they could easily be folded up and put in one's pocket, but which would keep out even the coldest wind.

"And most of the people of the village marveled, and remarked on how fortunate the travelers had been, and then thought no more about it.

"But a handful of greedy villagers, upon hearing these stories, resolved to see these wonders for themselves, and bring back some of these heavenly foods, and magic capes, and other prizes, that they might sell them and become rich. 'Why should these fools have such good fortune,' they said, 'when clever and worthy men such as ourselves do not?'

"So they set out into the northern hills, following the tales they had heard, and at length they came to the gates of Isabelle's demesne.

"There they did not wait for an invitation, but pounded loudly upon the delicate carvings, demanding entrance. And a voice called out, 'What do you want?'

"Their spokesman replied, 'We have come for dinner and a night's lodging!'

"'This is not an inn,' the voice replied. 'But you may come in and warm yourselves at my hearth.' And the gates swung open, and a great wind pulled them forward and deposited them at the door of the house.

"They wasted no time, but hurried inside, boots still caked with snow and mud, coats dripping, pulling sacks from their shirts to carry off whatever they were given. They did not look at the statues, or at the paintings, or at the fountains. They did not pause to warm themselves before the fire. They ran straight to the great table.

"When all had seated themselves, golden dishes and silver platters came sailing out of the kitchens, bearing strange and wondrous foods—square fruits and golden meats and other things we mortals can't even imagine. Crystal goblets sprang up out of the table itself, brimming full of liquor as red as blood, and soft music played—but still they had not seen their hostess, nor could they see any musicians.

34

"The journey had made them hungry, so they fell to, and ate heartily, but however much they ate, more would appear, so that the table was always full. And they drank the red liquor, thinking it nothing but some concoction of fruit juice. But, of course, it was more than that, and none of them were accustomed to a brew fit for the Powers, so they quickly became tipsy, and grew careless.

"And one man picked up his crystal goblet, and held it up to the light, and said, 'This will bring its weight in gold, I should imagine!' Then he popped it into a sack.

"Suddenly the lights all went out, and the shutters slammed tightly closed on every window, and the room was plunged into darkness except for a single ray of light that seemed to come from nowhere, but which shone directly onto the man who had taken the goblet.

" 'What did you say?' the voice demanded. 'Did you say you plan to sell my tableware? Is this the way you treat your hostess? Is this the way you accept my hospitality?'

"The man shuddered and dared not reply, and then, lo and behold, with a boom and a bang and a flash that blinded all the others, a bolt of lightning struck down from the ceiling and burned the thief to black ash.

"The others all fell from their chairs and groped toward the door as their vision slowly returned, and they all fled screaming into the night.

"When they had gone a few kilometers, they slowed, thinking themselves safe, and some even spoke of perhaps returning again to the house—but then one of them screamed, and turned black and fell dead at their feet, though they had seen nothing touch him and could find no mark on him save the blackening. They saw that they were not safe yet, but still they did not realize that none of them could ever escape, that the last would live only long enough to tell the tale— But I get ahead of my story.

"After their comrade had fallen dead so mysteriously, the others took counsel among themselves . . ."

—FROM THE TALES OF ATHERON THE STORYTELLER

"Excuse me, sir, but there's a message I think might interest you."

Startled, Geste looked up from where he lay on his belly, seemingly adrift in midair. "What?" he said. "What message?"

The floater above him blinked an apologetic blue, then said, "A termination signal has been received from a gift disk, coded as Bredon the Hunter, second-priority response."

"Bredon?" He glanced down through his platform at the three young women bathing in the river below. He had intended to do something to startle them, though he had not yet decided exactly what. He hadn't sent a bunch of teenagers squealing in ages.

Well, he could always find more naked women to embarrass,

and he had promised Bredon a favor. "All right," he said. "Where is he? His village?"

"No, sir. The disk was broken in the immediate vicinity of the Meadows."

"Which meadows?"

"*The* Meadows, sir. The normal-space location of the home of Lady Sunlight of the Meadows."

"Really?" This was suddenly very interesting; the nubile creatures below him were instantly forgotten. "He's been bothering Lady Sunlight?"

"I couldn't say, sir. The openly available information from Lady Sunlight's household intelligences indicates that a trespasser was recently expelled from the Meadows, but no indentification was made, and no information is available on what the trespasser was doing or why he was expelled."

Geste got to his feet, grinning. The platform turned opaque, first black, then silver. "Oh, this sounds as if it should be interesting. I wonder what Bredon thinks he's doing?"

"I have no idea, sir," the floater said.

"I didn't suppose you did. Put up a field, then, and let's get over there and see what he wants."

"Yes, sir."

The air around him was suddenly dead, motionless and silent, as the force field snapped into place. Geste felt a very slight tug of acceleration, and when he glanced down, the ground below the platform was moving past in a blur.

He should not have felt the start at all, though; he frowned, and promised to remind himself to have the airskiff overhauled at the first opportunity.

Soft music played. He ignored it.

Within minutes he was over the Forbidden Grove, the trees thick and green below him. The platform came to a gentle stop over the center of the Meadows and obligingly turned transparent before he could give the order. The music faded away.

At least, he thought, the basic programming still seemed sound, even if the transition-smoothing systems were weak.

The floater hovered anxiously at his shoulder as he peered down at the clearing.

"I don't see him," Geste said after a moment.

"Neither do I," the floater said.

"Did he get into the house somehow?" He made a gesture to the platform, which promptly extruded a small, spherical image-field. It floated up to Geste's eye level like a bubble rising in a glass of sparkling wine, and transformed itself into a flawless three-dimensional representation of the main entrance to the Meadows.

To the unaided human eye, of course, the entire palace was usually quite invisible, save where sparkles of light refracted from its turrets and trim.

The image scanned across the extradimensional facade of Lady Sunlight's residence, stepping the available radiation up or down into the visible spectrum for him, refracting it from bent-space to normal-space where necessary. Walkways, gardens, terraces, and blank walls slid across the screen, all bereft of inhabitants.

"The door guards say no one has gotten past them," the floater said, "and the internal systems that will talk to me all agree. Incidentally, I've spotted the remnants of the signal-disk. It was definitely here when it was broken."

"Well, I don't see him. Is Sunlight here? Maybe she knows what happened to him."

"Lady Sunlight is not presently at home, either figuratively or literally. Her messages are being forwarded, but their destination is shielded."

"That's no surprise," Geste muttered. He and Lady Sunlight had not gotten along well for the past century or two; she had never forgiven him for intercepting and altering some of her transmissions, including party invitations. He had thought the results were funny and harmless, but she had taken affront, and had, in his opinon, been acting stuffy and humorless ever since. Among other things, she was avoiding him, refusing even his most innocuous calls. He rather hoped that Bredon's request would be something that would annoy Sunlight and that was within his power.

The floater had not finished speaking; it ignored his interruption and continued, "However, the extended defense systems report that the trespasser who was expelled several hours ago returned to the Meadows after the fields were dropped, and has only very recently departed. He is currently nearing the western edge of the grove. Recordings of your previous conversation with the native of Denner's Wreck who called himself Bredon the Hunter indicate that you neglected to mention that it would be advisable to wait in one place after breaking the disk. In keeping with the local perception of you and the other off-worlders as supernatural beings, he probably expected you to materialize out of thin air immediately after the disk was broken, and has now departed in anger."

"Ha! Of course! So that must be him to the west, then!" Geste chortled. "Let's go find him!"

"Yes, sir." The platform turned and skimmed westward, and the floater, in accordance with Geste's standing orders regarding contact with the natives, faded from sight.

Bredon neither saw nor heard Geste's approach. He had just left the edge of the grove behind and was marching out into the grass when someone called loudly from behind him, "Hello, Bredon the Hunter, son of Aredon the Hunter!"

He whirled, startled, half expecting to see the faceless metal thing pursuing him.

There was nobody there. He saw only the trees of the grove, the mossy stones, the scattered wild flowers, and a shadow that did not belong.

He looked up, and there was Geste, standing on his platform. This time his clothes were green and shimmering, instead of violet plush, but otherwise he was unchanged. He was smiling broadly.

Geste, looking down, noticed that Bredon looked rather battered. A large bruise was spread across his nose, and a wide variety of cuts and scrapes adorned his limbs.

He hoped that the native hadn't summoned him just for a little medical service.

"Oh, it's you," Bredon said. "Hello."

"Hello. I believe you called me," Geste replied.

"Oh," Bredon said again. There was something about Geste that was curiously unnerving. Perhaps, Bredon thought, it was the way the little man seemed to accept everything with a smile, as if he spent every day standing on a platform in midair, mysteriously appearing and disappearing.

Of course, for all Bredon knew, that was exactly how he *did* spend every day.

No, the unnerving part, Bredon decided, was that this harmless, rather foolish-looking little person was a Power. Geste simply did not look the part of a demigod.

"Uh . . . I broke the disk," Bredon said.

"Yes, I know. You want to collect, I presume. I said I would grant you any favor within my power. What would you like?"

Now that the moment of truth had arrived, Bredon found himself horribly nervous. Looking up at Geste in his glistening clothing, standing blithely unsupported a good four meters off the ground, Bredon could not help remembering all the childhood tales of people who had dared too much, and of wishes gone wrong. One man who had been granted wishes by Brenner of the Mountains, and had used them for cruel revenge against all who had ever slighted him, had had everything he owned, including his home and family, taken by Rawl the Adjuster to balance the scales. A woman who had demanded unlimited wealth of Hsin of the River had almost starved to death surrounded by the mountains of gold she had asked for, piles of coins that had blocked every exit from her house. A young couple who had intruded on the demesne of Gold the Delver with some harmless request had never been heard from again; Bredon's own maternal grandmother, as a girl, had known that pair personally.

And that did not even touch any of the stories about people who offended the Powers directly, as his request might well offend Lady Sunlight. There were the guests who had insulted Isabelle, and the girl who matched her beauty against the Nymph, and all the people who ever had any contact at all with Thaddeus the Black. A large percentage, perhaps a majority, of the tales about the Powers were cautionary in nature.

But this was exactly the sort of cowardice he had castigated himself for, and despite his location and attire Geste looked harmless enough. "Lady Sunlight," he said, forcing the answer out without preamble.

Geste stared at him for a moment, his grin broadening. This was better than he had really expected. He had guessed that Bredon would simply want to see the inside of Sunlight's house, or some other such harmless whim; he had not dared hope for anything so audacious as asking for Sunlight herself. "Just how do you mean that?" he said at last.

Flustered, Bredon could only stammer.

"You say you want Lady Sunlight," Geste said in his most pompous manner. "Do you mean you want to own her, as if she were a beast of burden? Or that you want to take her as your wife? Or that you just want to lie with her once? Or do you merely want to speak with her?"

Again, Bredon could not answer coherently.

"I'm afraid that I can't give her to you outright," Geste said. "That's beyond my power. She's as free as you or I. And for that same reason, I can't compel her to marry you. As for bedding her, all I can do is to do my best to assist you; I can make no promises." He was rejoicing inwardly at the entire situation. Finding some way to coax Sunlight into this poor native's bed would tax his ingenuity to its fullest. Sunlight wanted nothing to do with *any* native.

I . . . I don't want that," Bredon said, losing his nerve. "I just want to speak to her." That was a lie; he wanted very much

to bed Lady Sunlight, but he did *not* want to become the subject
of some new cautionary tale that would be told to future generations of children. Geste, after all, was the Trickster; he had a
reputation for doing anything for a laugh, regardless of the
consequences. Looking at Geste's expression, Bredon could readily see the comic possibilities in tricking a Power into bed with a
mortal, and could also guess at just how Lady Sunlight might
react. She would probably not see the humor, and might well
take it out on him. She would be unable to harm Geste, but any
number of mortals had been casually killed or maimed by Powers
before this, and with far less cause.

Disappointment was plain on Geste's face, and Bredon was
suddenly much more certain of his decision.

"All right," Geste said. "You want to speak with her. Is that
all?"

"Yes," Bredon said, relieved. "That's all."

"You're sure?"

"Well, I . . ." Bredon began, amid a swarm of second
thoughts—and urges that, while they did not qualify as thoughts,
still had a strong influence. He drove them away with the memory of how Lady Sunlight guarded her home. If she could call on
such defenses against a simple trespasser, what might she do to
her seducer?

No, he dared not ask for more in regard to Lady Sunlight, but
a twinge in his belly reminded him of another concern.

"Well," he said, "if you have anything to eat, I'm awfully
hungry."

Geste smiled. Oh, he thought to himself, he did love these
poor people they had found on Denner's Wreck! They were so
full of surprises. He supposed it had something to do with the
brevity and simplicity of their lives; they didn't have the time to
fall into firmly fixed patterns, or the need to close out most of
their environment in order to be able to handle its complexities.
They could come up with the most astonishing non sequiturs.
And their lack of material resources kept the basic survival urges
always near the surface.

"Of course," he said. "I'm sure that I can give you something
that will help." He made the sign for acquiescence to another's
wishes with one hand, and the sign for descent with the other.

His command floater, still invisible, produced a foil-wrapped
packet of concentrate from somewhere. It fell into Geste's waiting palm as the platform sank gently to a few centimeters above
the ground.

Bredon stepped back warily as the platform brought Geste

down nearly to his own level, but forced himself to stop after that single step.

"Here," Geste said, offering a gleaming blue-silver packet.

Bredon accepted it gingerly, then stared at it, puzzled.

"It's food. You peel the wrapper off," Geste explained. "It tears easily and comes off, like the skin of an orange."

"A what?" Bredon looked up.

"A fruit. Here, climb up on the platform and I'll show you."

"On the platform?" Bredon eyed the floating surface doubtfully.

"Yes, on the platform." Geste tapped it with the toe of one slipper. "Lady Sunlight isn't home just now, and if I know her, if I call ahead she'll arrange not to be anywhere I call. It's much harder to not be there if we go in person, however, so we'll have to go find her, and the easiest way to do that is for you to climb up on the platform and save me the trouble of finding you any more elaborate transportation. Besides, I don't want to stoop, or step down and get my shoes all dirty, so if you want me to show you how to eat that thing, you'll have to get up on the platform."

Still reluctant, but unwilling to admit it, Bredon stepped forward. The platform's top hung at roughly the height of his knees. He hesitated, then put one foot up, expecting it to give beneath his weight.

It did not yield at all. It was as solid as a stone ledge, firmer than the floor of his parents' house.

Startled, he picked up his other foot and nearly lost his balance when the platform still remained absolutely motionless. He *knew* it was floating unsupported on air, despite what his first step had told him, and he had unconsciously adjusted for a sinking, like that of a small boat or a well-sprung wagon, that never came.

He recovered quickly, and found himself standing on the platform beside the Trickster. His breath caught as he found himself looking *down* at a Power, mere centimeters away. The top of Geste's head was even with his own jaw.

From this angle it was easier than ever to think of Geste as a man, not an invulnerable supernatural being.

But that was wrong, he reminded himself. Geste was *not* a mortal man, but one of the Powers that ruled the world. He could be anything he chose; that he chose to look harmless simply meant he was not to be trusted.

"Here, let me show you," Geste said, reaching for something.

Startled, Bredon looked down and discovered that the mysterious packet was still clutched tightly in his right hand. He had completely forgotten it, absorbed as he was in boarding the flying platform and seeing Geste close up.

He held it out. Geste took it and neatly tore open one end.

Steam swirled out, though the packet had felt cool in his hand, and a rich, savory odor filled Bredon's nostrils. Geste handed the packet back to him; he stared at it in wonder, then cautiously lifted it to his face.

The smell was irresistible. He took a bite of the brown gel inside the foil.

He had never tasted anything even remotely like it. He had no words to describe the taste, nothing he could compare it to. It was warm, spicy, meaty, with an oily texture that seemed to vanish into dry crumbliness in his mouth.

It was absolutely delicious, and only after he had devoured every last trace did he pause to ask, "What did I just eat?"

Geste glanced at the empty wrapper before tossing it up into the air, where it vanished with a brief flicker of white light.

"Michaud's Delectation #3, Burgundy style," he said.

"What's Mish . . . Misho's Delegation #3?"

"What you just ate."

Bredon was not satisfied by this answer, but before he could ask anything more, Geste said, "I'll take care of those injuries, if you like."

"Injuries?" Bredon was sincerely startled; he had already forgotten the various scrapes and bruises, which were far less serious than he could expect to receive anytime he went after big game.

"Yes, the bruises on your nose, and those cuts; and that shoulder looks stiff, the way you're holding it. Here, take my hand."

Cautiously, Bredon reached out and took Geste's right hand in his own.

A strange tingling sensation brushed lightly across his palm, and then vanished.

"There," Geste said, smiling. "That should take care of it; I've put a whole microscopic repair crew in your bloodstream."

Bredon had no idea what he was talking about, but thought better of inquiring.

For one thing, he had just noticed that the platform had not remained still while he ate, and while Geste did whatever it was he had done to Bredon's hand.

He had felt no motion, no acceleration, but when Bredon looked down he saw that they were flying over the grasslands, a dozen meters above the ground, so fast that the land beneath was a blur.

They were streaking westward, toward the mountains, and

moving so swiftly that the mountains were growing perceptibly larger with each passing instant.

Not only that, but the soreness in his shoulder was dissolving, and his nose had suddenly stopped hurting; he had no longer been consciously aware of any pain, but its abrupt cessation certainly registered. A tentative touch found no tenderness at all, in either his nose or his shoulder. He glanced at his left arm where he had scraped it on a root and saw the red marks fading away, as were all his other injuries, major or minor.

He blinked, blinked again, and then turned away and simply watched the scenery flying by; he was too frightened to ask any more questions.

Besides, he knew that if he did ask, his voice would tremble, and he refused to give Geste the satisfaction of knowing how frightened he was.

Chapter Six

"The Lady of the Seasons spends every year in search of her lover—though who that lover might be differs depending on who tells the tale, I fear, for the facts are not known to those of us condemned to someday die. Some say that it's Geste the Trickster, whose wandering soul cannot be held even by the love of a Power greater than himself. Others maintain that it's Rawl the Adjuster, and that his sense of justice drives him forth for three seasons each year, to correct the wrongs of mankind and to return only during those bright wakes of spring when all's right with the world. Still others say that it's not one lover she wants, but many, and mortal—that each year she picks anew, but that those she chooses cannot survive her attentions for long.

"Whatever the truth is, in the summer she dwells in the North, holding back the cold and wind, waiting patiently for her love to return. When he comes not, and she grows angry at his dawdling, she moves to her western home, and her rage blasts the leaves from the trees, withers the crops, and drives the sun away, bringing autumn upon us.

"When her fury can no longer be sustained she yields to despair and flees to the south, where she can weep unseen, and the whole world lies cold and dead beneath unchecked winter.

"And there, at last, her love finds her again, and takes her to their bower in the east, where their love brings springtime back to the land . . ."

—FROM THE TALES OF KITHEN THE STORYTELLER

"Where are we?" Bredon asked shakily as the platform finally slowed and began its descent. They had soared up across the mountains, across peaks wrapped in snow despite the lingering summer, across heights Bredon had never imagined and drops—into canyons, over cliffs, down rubble-strewn slopes—that he had only considered in his worst nightmares. He had lived his entire life on the plains; to be able to look down at treetops, without so much as a railing between himself and kilometers of empty space, was terrifying—but oddly exhilarating, as well.

Most strange and wonderful of all, he had felt not the slightest gust of wind or change in temperature the entire time. This dealing with Powers was an awesome thing.

44

"That's Autumn House ahead," Geste said, pointing. "It's just about the time of year when Sheila opens it for the season, and I thought Sunlight might have come to help. She often does. And if she hasn't, Sheila still might know where Sunlight is. If Sheila's here, that is."

Bredon followed the pointing finger and saw a rambling structure that straggled down from a hilltop in a succession of wings and terraces. Autumn House was larger than his entire village. Even if Lady Sunlight were somewhere in it, he thought, it might take hours to find her.

The prospect of seeing Lady Sunlight again, of perhaps speaking to her, was, like the ride through the air, both frightening and exhilarating. His memory of her beauty stirred his lust for her anew, and he forced himself to stay calm and think of other things. "Who is Sheila?" he asked, his voice a little steadier this time.

"I believe you call her the Lady of the Seasons," Geste replied.

"Ah." Even Bredon had, of course, heard of her. She was a major Power, who lived in the east in the spring, the north in summer, the west in autumn, and the south in winter. She was said to control the weather, among other things; the spring rains did not come until she had moved from south to east, the grass did not turn brown until she had gone from north to west, and so forth.

Bredon had always considered this to be unlikely, but he had never argued the matter or come up with a better explanation for the turning seasons. He had accepted the Lady of the Seasons as a metaphor or a symbol, and had left the question of her existence open.

It had never occurred to him that she might not only exist, but would have a name, as well as a title, and he would certainly never have guessed she might bear so simple a name as Sheila.

Of course, that name might just be a nickname Geste used.

It had also never occurred to Bredon that he might someday meet her.

He was reminded again that he was here, in midair, dealing with the Powers directly and familiarly—not just people with mysterious powers, but *the* Powers. This was not *just* an immense mansion, it was the supposed home of autumn itself. He stared at Autumn House for a moment longer, then stole a glance at Geste.

Geste was whispering, though there was no one on the platform save the two of them. Bredon thought for an instant that

Geste was talking to him, then that Geste was talking to himself, and finally decided that he was talking to someone or something that mere mortals could not see or hear, a familiar or spirit of some sort.

"We could call ahead now and tell Sheila we're coming," Geste said aloud. "And if Sunlight is here she wouldn't be able to slip away without our seeing her—at least, not easily—but I think it should be fun to surprise them. I've arranged for our approach to be silent and unheralded, no courtesy announcements or alarms or anything. I haven't done anything very fancy, so I suppose the guards will spot us, but they know me, and we shouldn't have any trouble in just walking in."

Bredon nodded. It was all the same to him, however they approached. He had no idea what the proper protocol might be, or what might best win Lady Sunlight's favor; he was simply following Geste's lead. He was trusting the Trickster with his life—but then, could the Lady of the Seasons's guards be more dangerous than flying through the air on an open platform? He had already trusted himself to that.

Well, yes, he supposed they *could* be more dangerous, but he was resolved to trust Geste.

The platform passed smoothly over the roof of Autumn House and settled gently onto a broad stone-paved terrace, a few meters away from a wide-open doorway. Bredon saw no guards, nor any sign of life whatsoever. On two sides, the north and south, he saw forested mountains in the distance and nothing else. To the west he had a magnificent view of foothills tumbling downward, row after row, and sinking at last into a vast, desolate plain—not a grass-covered prairie like his home to the east, but a golden expanse of wasteland. He was too far up to make out any details.

On the fourth side, the east, stood the stone and timber walls of Autumn House, broken by several large openings into the dim interior.

The air around them, which had been utterly still, was suddenly moving across them in a cool breeze.

"Come on," Geste said, stepping off the platform and beckoning.

Bredon, breathing deeply of the fresh mountain air, followed the Trickster across the terrace and through an open doorway into the largest, most luxurious room he had ever seen.

The houses in his native village were walled with various kinds of brick or woven grasses and roofed with thatch over timber. Timber was scarce and expensive in the grasslands. A room more than four meters across was a rare extravagance; his parents' home had none over three.

This room was easily ten meters across and twenty meters long. Wide windows took up most of three walls, using as much glass as half his village—the openings he had seen from the terrace, save for the single doorway they had entered through, were all such windows, and Bredon marveled that they could be made so large and yet not have the glass collapse of its own weight.

The floor was stone, matching the terrace, but much of it was hidden beneath fur rugs. Looking at the rugs, Bredon could not identify what creature had provided the fur for any of them. A faint scent of cinnamon and woodsmoke reached him.

The sweeping emptiness of the room was broken up by half a dozen scattered couches and an assortment of small tables. The wall that held no windows consisted in large part of an immense alcove that Bredon realized was a fireplace only after he had spotted both the ash in the bottom and the flue at the back.

Tiny spots of color flitted about the room, and Bredon recognized them as the same creatures that had surrounded Lady Sunlight. She *had* come here. He felt the muscles of his throat and chest tightening in anticipation.

"Hello!" Geste called as they stepped inside.

"Hello, Mr. Geste," a smooth, masculine voice replied from the empty air. Bredon looked for its source, but saw nothing. "I regret to say that Lady Sheila is not at home just now, but we expect her back shortly. Is there anything I can do for you? Would you like to wait?"

"Is Lady Sunlight here? I see some of her flutterbugs."

"I'm sorry, sir, but she went with Lady Sheila. The flutterbugs were a housewarming gift."

Bredon felt harsh disappointment welling within him.

"Damn," Geste muttered under his breath. "Missed her!" Aloud, he asked, "But she *was* here?"

"Yes, sir, Lady Sunlight arrived a few hours ago. I understand she will be staying for several sleeps."

"You expect her back?"

"Oh yes, sir."

"When?"

"I don't know, sir."

"Where did they go? Did they say?"

"Yes, sir. Lady Sheila, Lady Sunlight, and Rawl the Adjuster have gone to the High Castle. I believe they felt called upon to

settle a disagreement between Brenner of the Mountains and
Thaddeus the Black.''

Bredon had observed this exchange without comment. He had
determined to his own satisfaction that the voice was not coming
from any of the walls, nor the floor, nor the ceiling. It was coming
from empty air, in the center of the room, which was impossible.
He also did not really know what a castle was, though he had
heard the word in childhood stories. More specifically, he did not
know what the High Castle was, or why so many of the Powers
should be gathering there. The mention of Rawl the Adjuster, the
legendary incarnation of justice and mercy, impressed him, even
here in the home of the Lady of the Seasons, with the notorious
Trickster at his side. He told himself that he should be becoming
accustomed to these casual references to the figures of legend,
particularly since he had yet to actually meet any but the Trickster, but the name still carried an impact, and it added further to
his mounting burden of curiosity, so that he could hold back no
longer. ''Who are you talking to?'' he demanded. ''What's going
on?''

''I'm talking to Sheila's housekeeper,'' Geste replied, a trifle
impatiently.

''Why can't I see him?''

''Because it's invisible.''

Bredon started to protest that that was impossible, but thought
better of it. Among the Powers he had no way of knowing what,
if anything, might be impossible. Instead he asked, ''What's the
High Castle?''

''That's the stronghold of Brenner of the Mountains, about a
hundred kilometers southwest of here. And I think that's where
we're headed.'' He spun on his heel and marched back out onto
the terrace.

Bredon hurriedly followed; behind them the housekeeper's
voice called, ''Safe journey, sir; I'll tell Lady Sheila you were
here.''

Bredon heard no command, saw no gesture, but the platform
glided smoothly over to meet them.

Chapter Seven

" '. . . a strong head indeed, for a mortal,' said Brenner, as he calmly stood up.

"Mighty Konnel looked up at him in shock, still just barely sober enough to realize that although the whole world seemed to be spinning, Brenner was standing straight and steady. Yet he had seen the Power down two drinks to each of his own, and all poured from the same bottles!

" 'I don't understand it,' he said, the liquor loosening his tongue, 'I just don't understand it. I've drunk men twice your size under the table, and now I can't move, while you aren't even staggered!'

" 'Ah,' Brenner said, 'but you can never drink one of us under the table, for we are never drunker than we choose to be. Listen, man, they call you the mighty Konnel, and you're as mighty a mortal as I've ever met, but when you match yourself against an immortal you have no chance. When we matched arms, I drew on the strength of steel as well as bone; when we tested our eyes I saw the target with more than mortal sight, and threw with the aid of demons; when we drank, a spirit in my body took the alcohol when I had had enough. Here, take my hand, and the spirit will draw the drunkenness from you, as well.'

"Konnel managed to bring a hand up where Brenner could grasp it, and suddenly the fog vanished from his head and the strength returned to his limbs, so that he felt better than he ever had before, as if the strength of the mountains themselves was pouring into him. He stood and laughed in amazement and joy.

" 'There!' Brenner said. 'Now go back to your village and tell them that you did as you swore to do, and that I had to cheat to best you, and you caught me at it—that's close enough to the truth, and I've no need to shame you. You're a good man, mighty Konnel, and I'd be glad of your company should you ever care to return. In your honor I swear that I shall never again send the lightning to burn your village, so long as you live there—but that your people, all save yourself, must still stay away from my mountain. And take this as proof.' And he handed Konnel a crystal cup that shone with a light of its own and spoke when questioned.

"And the mighty Konnel thanked him loudly, and they shook hands and parted as friends . . ."

—FROM THE TALES OF ATHERON THE STORYTELLER

Bredon glanced up at the western sky as they flew, and realized with a shock that the sun was still high overhead. Geste had found him early that same light; they had crossed the prairie and the mountains in less than half a light!

As he lowered his gaze to the ground again, something glittered in the distance. He stared, but could not make out any details.

The Trickster appeared to be casually watching the scenery flicker past beneath their feet, not particularly involved with anything, and Bredon found the courage to ask, "What's that?"

Geste looked up and followed Bredon's pointing finger. He squinted, then said, "Give me some magnification."

The air in front of him wavered, like the air above a blacksmith's forge, for an instant. From Bredon's point of view, when the waver vanished it left a discontinuity, as if a little bit of reality had been tucked away out of sight.

It hurt his eyes to look at it; he turned away, looking back at the glitter.

Whatever it was, it was approaching them quickly. He still could not tell what it was, but he could see a shining silver shape growing steadily larger.

"What in hell . . ." Geste began.

"Warning," a voice said from somewhere just above Bredon's left ear. He spun around, almost losing his balance, and found a gleaming *something* hanging in midair, centimeters away.

"Warning," it repeated. "Approaching drone is equipped for heavy assault, and does not respond to attempts at communication."

"We've got the fields up full, don't we?" Geste demanded, glancing up at his floater.

"The standard ones, yes, sir, of course we do. However, the approaching drone is of unknown origin and capabilities."

"It is?"

"Yes, sir."

"What the hell is it doing here?"

"I don't know, sir."

"Can it really hurt us?"

"I don't know, sir."

"Damn!"

Then the glittering thing was on top of them, and for a moment Bredon's world vanished in a blazing fury of light and noise. The platform beneath his feet trembled slightly as impossibly bright colors blinded him and a deafening roar shook his bones.

"Whoa," Geste said as the light and sound died away. "That's serious, isn't it?"

Bredon blinked, clearing spots from his eyes, and turned to see the glittering thing—it was shaped something like a fish, he noticed—to the east, its path curving back around to make another pass at the platform.

"Have we got any weapons with us, any way to shoot back?" Geste asked.

"No, sir," the floater replied. "I wasn't aware that any might be called for."

"Neither was I," the Trickster said ruefully, watching the drone complete its turn and head back toward him. "Drop us down out of its line of attack, would you?"

"Yes, sir," the floater said. Immediately, the mountains rose up around them, though Bredon could not feel any sensation of sinking or falling. They were still speeding forward, as well, so that the sunlit trees and rocks were now flashing past on all sides, rather than merely below them.

The drone swept overhead, but already it was turning to follow and starting to descend.

"Who sent that thing?" Geste demanded.

"I don't know, sir. I'm restricted to on-board systems while maintaining full defensive fields, and I have no data at all on it."

"Whoever it is, he must be crazy, shooting at me like that!"

"I would have to agree with that assessment, sir. Unfortunately, as you know, insanity is common among immortals."

"It is?" Bredon squeaked, startled. The idea of an insane Power was new and frightening, somehow more frightening than the thing that had just attacked them.

Geste and the floater ignored him. "How is it tracking us?" Geste asked.

"I can't be sure, sir," the floater said, "but it appears to be using wide-spectrum scanning."

"Can you hide from it? Take us out of the visible and damp down our emissions?"

"I can try, sir." The air wavered, this time not merely in a small area in front of the Trickster, but all around the platform. Bredon watched with terrified interest.

Then the light faded, though the sun was still high in the sky; the entire world dimmed as if layers of smoked glass were being dropped around them in quick succession, until they were hanging, seemingly motionless, in near-total darkness. Bredon could see Geste as a faint outline in the gloom, black on black, so he knew that the darkness was not absolute, but the floater and the platform beneath his feet were completely invisible, and blackness surrounded him.

"Take us down to treetop level—lower, if possible," Geste

ordered. "Then take evasive action and head for the High Castle as fast as you can."

"Yes, sir."

To Bredon it seemed as if nothing changed. He and Geste stood silent in the darkness for a long moment, tension sharp in the air between them. Bredon could smell his own sweat—but not, he noticed, Geste's. He supposed that Powers did not do anything as ordinary as perspire.

"I believe we have successfully eluded the drone," the floater's voice said at last.

"Where are we, relative to the Castle?"

"Approaching rapidly from the northeast, down a narrow canyon; current distance, twenty-five kilometers."

"Good—but take us up and loop around. I want to approach the Castle from the southeast, directly uphill, where we can get a good view."

"Yes, sir," the floater acknowledged.

"When we get within a direct line-of-sight, if there still isn't any sign of that attack drone, open a window."

"Yes, sir."

The utter darkness made Bredon uneasy, particularly since he knew that the sun was still in the sky; some part of him refused to accept the absence of light. Since the immediate crisis seemed to be past, he ventured a question, hoping to reestablish some sort of contact with reality. "What's going on? What was that thing?"

"I wish I knew!" Geste answered. "Somebody was shooting at us, but I don't know who it was, or why."

"Was it another Power?"

"I suppose it must be; we'd have been notified if anyone came in from off-planet." He paused, struck by a sudden thought. "At least, we'd have been notified if they didn't take out our ship first," he said. Addressing the floater, he ordered, "Put a call through to Mother."

Bredon was startled; surely, Geste had no mother! He was a Power, eternal and ageless.

"I'll have to put a narrow-band hole through the field," the floater cautioned.

"Do it," Geste said. "If anything shoots at us, close it again, but for now I want to talk to Mother."

"Mother ship acknowledges," the floater replied, almost immediately.

Mother *ship?* Bredon asked himself. What did *that* mean? And where was the hole? He saw no light; near-total darkness still surrounded them.

"Is there anything out there?" Geste asked. "I mean, anything artificial in the system that we didn't put there?"

"No, sir, the mother ship has detected no activity indicative of sentience anywhere in the system other than the planetary surface for over a century."

This baffled Bredon completely; he had no idea what system Geste was referring to, and did not recognize the words *sentience* and *planetary*.

"Then it has to be one of us." Geste's words were neither statement or question, but somewhere between. Bredon accepted it as a statement. He could not imagine how there could be any doubt; what but a Power could openly attack a Power thus? Demons, perhaps?

"Yes, sir," the floater acknowledged.

"Did Mother see that drone that came after us?"

"Yes, sir."

"Where did it come from?"

"The drone was launched from an unregistered outpost in the immediate vicinity of Fortress Holding."

"Thaddeus? He sent it?"

Bredon recognized the name with an unpleasant start. The invisible housekeeper had mentioned it, but somehow, perhaps because these spirits pronounced the name a bit differently from the way old Atheron did, it had not really registered. Thaddeus the Black was, according to legend, one of the most inhospitable of all the Powers, prone to destructive rages and possessed of a vicious streak of sadism. The stories about him were not the moral fables or amusing tales that were told about the other Powers; they were horror stories, to be whispered around the fire after the children were asleep.

Fortunately, Thaddeus's domain was located entirely in the western deserts, where few mortals had any contact with him.

"Apparently," the floater agreed. There was an instant's hesitation, and then the machine continued, "Sir, we are approaching the High Castle, and I can detect no trace of the drone that assaulted us previously. However, a great deal of violent activity is taking place."

"What? What kind of activity?"

"Weapons activity, sir."

"Weapons? Damn it, open that window!"

"Yes, sir."

Light poured in from ahead, banishing the darkness; Bredon blinked, half-blinded, then squinted until his eyes could adjust.

Most of their protective bubble was still in place, blacker than the midwake sky, but ahead of them an oval of light had appeared, allowing them to see where the platform was carrying them.

They were rushing down a steep mountain slope, down into a narrow valley. On the far side of the valley another mountain rose to a sharp peak.

Atop the peak stood what could only be the High Castle, built as if growing out of the stone of the mountain itself, spired and turreted, banners whipping from its rooftops; its towers soared upward as if trying to pierce the sky. Between foundation and towers were three great tiers of massive walls and battlements.

Bredon stared at it openmouthed wonder, wonder that mounted steadily as they swept ever nearer and he was forced to repeatedly adjust upward his estimate of the structure's size. He had never seen nor imagined anything like it.

It was only when they were across the valley and starting up the opposite slope that he noticed the glittering specks that flickered on every side of the castle, zipping about it, fluttering back and forth among the towers. Before he had consciously recognized them as being similar to the "drone" that had attacked Geste's platform, something flashed a vivid red from one of the specks, splashing against the stone wall, leaving a black mark—it appeared tiny from his present location, but Bredon realized it was easily three meters across.

Something equally red flashed back from one of the castle towers, and the speck erupted into a golden fireball.

The roar swept over them a second or two later, and glancing to the side, at either end of the "window" in the protective darkness, Bredon could see the trees on either side being whipped violently backward by the accompanying shock wave. The air around him, atop the platform, did not so much as ripple; in fact, despite their great speed, the air felt stagnant and dead, and did not smell very pleasant.

"What the *hell* does Thaddeus think he's doing?" Geste muttered. "These are all his, aren't they?"

The floater took almost a second to reply. "Yes, sir, the mother ship confirms that all attacking equipment originated within a two-kilometer radius of Fortress Holding. Fortress Holding has refused to reply to inquiries."

Another exchange of crimson fire took place; this time the drone escaped unscathed.

"Maybe we shouldn't get too close," Geste said.

The platform immediately slowed to a crawl. As always,

Bredon felt no deceleration; the outside world simply stopped rushing by as quickly.

The stillness of the air in the bubble made the distant battle seem unreal, as if it were no more than an illusion, like the ones Bredon had seen created by traveling conjurors. It was infinitely more elaborate and detailed, of course, but Geste was a Power, not a mere conjuror. Bredon began to wonder whether what he saw was real, or whether Geste was playing some elaborate prank.

Another burst of red fire blossomed, followed by another, and then a full-blown barrage from a dozen or more of the attacking machines. The weapons in the castle towers replied.

"Better stop here," Geste suggested as they drew near the paths of the outermost drones.

The platform halted, hovering a meter or so above the bare rock of the slope. The blackness of the heavy protective fields remained to either side, behind, and below. Above and before them lines and flashes of red and yellow fire spattered fitfully across the castle towers.

"Put a call through to Brenner," Geste ordered.

The floater did not reply immediately, and the Trickster glanced up at it, startled.

"I'm sorry, sir," it said at last, "I can't get through. All communications with the High Castle are being jammed."

"Damn!"

"What's going on?" Bredon asked.

"I don't know," Geste answered. "I don't know, but I don't like it." He stared up at the battle for a long moment.

"Is Lady Sunlight in there?"

"I don't know, but I suspect that she is."

"Is she in danger?"

"I don't know that either," Geste replied, "but I'm afraid she might be."

Bredon looked up at the flashing of incomprehensible weapons. "Is there anything we can do to help?"

Geste did not reply for a long moment. "I don't know," he said at last. "But I don't think we're going to get in there, are we?"

"No, sir," the floater replied. "I cannot take you much closer than this while the castle is under fire, and I certainly can't deliver you to any of the registered entrances."

"If I know Brenner, that castle is even stronger than it looks," Geste said, reflecting. "Unless Thaddeus has one hell of an arsenal built up, he's not going to get through the defenses anytime soon.''

Neither Bredon nor the floater said anything. Bredon knew nothing about either Brenner or Thaddeus save various unpleasant legends, and the floater had no comment to make.

"Maybe Thaddeus has a good reason for this," Geste said at length. "Call Fortress Holding again—tell them that I want to talk to Thaddeus."

A moment later, the floater said, "I'm sorry, sir, but the intelligences at Fortress Holding do not acknowledge. I am certain that several of them are receiving my transmission, but none have responded."

"I think we better call around, see if anyone knows what's going on," Geste said thoughtfully. "Thaddeus may have a legitimate gripe against Brenner—though I can't imagine any that would justify *this*—but he has no business endangering Sheila and Sunlight."

"That assumes that Lady Sheila and Lady Sunlight are, in fact, in the High Castle," the floater pointed out.

"Well, that's another reason to call around," Geste said. "To see if they're anywhere else."

The floater acknowledged the point with a bluish flicker, but then said, "Sir, I believe that the mother ship constantly monitors all members of your expedition, through their internal systems, in order to provide information in the event of an emergency. Would you say this constitutes an emergency? If so, I can inquire as to the exact whereabouts and state of health of Lady Sheila and Lady Sunlight."

Geste nodded. "Do it," he said.

"Yes, sir. The signals from Lady Sheila and Lady Sunlight have been lost due to interference, but at last contact both were in their usual excellent health and had just entered the High Castle in the company of Rawl the Adjuster and Brenner of the Mountains."

Bredon marveled; how could the mysterious invisible talking thing possibly have learned that so quickly? He had heard nothing, seen nothing; the thing—spirit, familiar, whatever it was— had simply pulled its answer out of nowhere.

He would have guessed that the spirit was just making up its answers, had not Geste put so much faith in them.

If it was right, then Lady Sunlight was in danger, and he felt a coldness in his veins at the thought.

"So they *are* in there," Geste said.

"Yes, sir."

"Thaddeus *is* endangering them. This is serious." He paused to think. "Khalid lives closest to Thaddeus; put me through to him," he ordered after a moment's consideration.

The floater paused before replying, "The intelligences at the Tents of Gold report that Khalid departed seventy hours ago, in response to a shielded call, bound for Fortress Holding. He has not returned and his present whereabouts are unknown."

Bredon saw, in the light from the "window," that the Trickster was shaken by this news; no trace of his customary smile remained.

"What does Mother say?"

"No signal is being received from Khalid. At last contact he was entering Fortress Holding, which is heavily shielded against all signals, including the mother ship's telemetry."

"Try Madame O," Geste said.

"The intelligences at the House of Delights have been told not to converse with me," the floater said, "but they will acknowledge that Madame O is not at home. The mother ship reports loss of contact upon entrance to Fortress Holding, sixty-one hours ago."

"Damn! That's everyone west of the mountains!" Geste exclaimed. "What's Thaddeus *doing?*"

"I don't know, sir. I would point out that the Ice House lies west of the mountains."

Geste waved that away. "I suppose it does, but it's so far north it doesn't matter. Ah . . . get me Lord Grey."

Bredon marveled at how ready Geste was to call upon so many of the Powers—but then, why shouldn't he? He was a Power himself!

Bredon shivered slightly. He had very little idea of what was happening, but he knew that he had somehow gotten himself involved, at least peripherally, in affairs far beyond his understanding. He had simply asked to talk to Lady Sunlight, and now he was tangled up in some sort of widespread dispute involving at least half a dozen of the Powers! Worst of all, Lady Sunlight herself was in some sort of danger. The image of her standing in the meadow as he had seen her, her multicolored dress drifting in a wind that he had not felt, filled his thoughts. He shivered again at the thought of any harm befalling anything so beautiful.

Geste was thinking aloud. "Khalid, O, Brenner, Sheila, Rawl. . ."

A face appeared in the air before them, a dark weather-beaten face, half-hidden behind a bristling black beard and shoulder-length gray-streaked hair. It seemed to glow fiercely in contrast with the darkness of the protective field. Bredon started, but realized quickly that this was not an actual head floating unsupported, but an apparition or illusion of some sort.

"What do you want, Geste?" the face demanded.

Geste's relief at the sight of this forbidding visage was ludicrously obvious.

"My apologies for disturbing you, Grey, but I am inordinately glad to see you there. It appears that we may have a problem developing."

Lord Grey's disembodied head eyed the Trickster suspiciously. "What sort of a problem?"

"I don't really know—at least, I don't know what started it. Thaddeus appears to be attacking Brenner—*seriously* attacking him. Take a look for yourself."

Lord Grey seemed to glance away, then looked back at Geste and Bredon. "Is this one of your stunts, Geste? Where would Thaddeus get all those drones? You've been playing with images again, I suppose. Well, I'm not interested."

"No, Grey, I haven't—"

Geste was speaking to empty air.

"Damn!" he said. "Get me Leila."

"The intelligences at the Mountain of Fire tell me that Leila does not wish to hear anything you have to say," the floater replied.

Bredon wondered who Leila might be. Another Power, presumably, but one he did not recall ever having heard of. This was all proving very educational; when he got home—*if* he got home— he would have stories to tell for the rest of his life. He might well become a storyteller without even trying.

He listened with interest as Geste continued calling.

Chapter Eight

"... still he refused to give up. He chased her ever deeper into the forest, never gaining a centimeter, but never quite losing sight of her, either.

"At last he collapsed, exhausted, beside a river. He lay there gasping for breath, dipping his hands in the water and cooling his face with them. And the mysterious woman appeared among the trees on the far side, calmly watching him.

" 'Hello,' she called to him. 'Were you looking for me?'

"He just stared, too tired to call out to her, and nodded weakly.

" 'Well,' she said, 'here I am. Come and get me.'

" 'Witch,' he called, drawing strength from his anger, 'you know I haven't the strength to swim the river!'

" 'Then I suppose I must come to you,' she said, and she rose up into the air and transformed herself into a bird. And in that form, she flew across the stream to him, and then transformed herself back into a woman.

"When he saw this magical shape-shifting, Harlen knew that this was no mere witch-woman. Even the most powerful witches in legend needed spells and chants and potions for the very simplest of transformations, and surely, to take the form of a bird cannot be simple. Harlen knew that he faced either a Power or a demon. And when she knelt down over him, her long red hair brushing his chest, he was afraid, and called out, 'Get away, demon!'

" 'Demon!' she said, as she stepped back in surprise. 'You think I'm a demon?'

" 'What else could you be?' Harlen asked.

"She laughed, and said, 'Oh, I can be anything I please, anything at all. Shall I be a demon for you? Do you want a demon lover?' And she was suddenly a demon, three meters tall and scaly black, her eyes pits of fire and her fingers curving talons. 'Or something more comely?' And she was a woman again, but a different woman, tall and slender, no longer naked, but wearing a gown of spun silver embroidered in gold. 'Or would you prefer a simple companion, and not a lover at all?' And suddenly a man much like himself stood there, clad in buckskin, smiling down at him.

" 'Who are you?' he asked, terrified.

"She did not answer immediately, but returned to her own shape, naked once more, and looked down at him. 'You know,' she said, 'if you're too tired to swim the river, then I can't hope for much from you as a lover, can I? And if you think me a demon, you probably don't *want me at all. I suppose I should just go and leave you alone, shouldn't I?'*

"Before he could answer, she vanished, disappeared into the empty air.

"Her voice lingered, though, and said, 'As for who I am, I'm called Imp, but I'm not a demon at all.' And then she laughed, and her laughter gradually faded away until there was nothing left at all.

"And although he was tired he got to his feet and ran after her, first one way, then another, looking for some trace of her. But he found nothing, and he never saw her again, though he looked for her many a time, spending many, many wakes and even whole seasons wandering through the forest in search of her . . ."

—FROM THE TALES OF ATHERON THE STORYTELLER

Geste's calls were not going well. Bredon watched and listened closely, but said nothing.

Gold the Delver said that Brenner deserved anything he got and it was all one of Geste's pranks, anyway. This said, he broke contact.

Lady Tsien giggled and flirted and refused to take Geste seriously, until at last Geste broke the connection himself. Bredon was fascinated by her appearance; although she looked human, she had small folds at the corners of her eyes, and an odd color to her skin.

Hsin of the River said that it was none of his business if Brenner had finally aggravated Thaddeus beyond bearing. His skin was an interesting shade of brown, and his image was accompanied by a flock of tiny, vividly blue birds.

The Nymph was not home, and could not readily be located; Bredon regretted not getting a look at the legendary beauty. She was thought to be visiting the Skyler, but the Skyland did not answer.

Before them the battle still raged, though darkness had fallen. The weapons used by both sides lit the skies in intermittent flashes, and in that flickering, polychrome glow Bredon saw several of the flitting silver drones tumble from the skies. Others were blown to fragments as he watched. Whenever their numbers seemed to be diminishing, though, a dozen more arrived to take the place of those that had been lost.

When Geste asked for Aulden the Technician, a young woman's heart-shaped face appeared, framed in red hair and wearing a brilliant grin. Bredon noticed that despite the darkness she appeared to be in full sunlight.

"Hello, Imp," Geste said. "Could I speak to Aulden? I need his help."

Bredon had assumed that the woman was a servant of some sort; hearing Geste address her by the name of another Power was disconcerting. He looked more closely.

She was unquestionably beautiful, without a blemish of any sort, but she lacked the radiant glory that marked Lady Sunlight as something beyond mortal flesh. Her face was that of a lovely little toy, not a goddess.

"Oh, I'm sorry, Geste," she replied with a comical pout. "He's not here. Is there anything *I* can do? I'd *love* to help you, whatever it is." She smiled fetchingly.

Geste smiled back, but only for an instant. "I appreciate that," he said, "but I think we'll need Aulden too."

"Well, he went to do some work for Thaddeus a few days ago. He should be back any time, or you could call him there. . ."

"For Thaddeus?"

"That's right."

Geste hesitated, troubled. Imp noticed immediately, and her smile vanished, her green eyes suddenly troubled.

"Geste, what's wrong?" she asked.

"It's Thaddeus—or Thaddeus and Brenner, anyway. Thaddeus has an entire fleet of war machines attacking the High Castle."

"War machines?"

"High-powered drones. One of them attacked me as well. I think that must be the work he wanted Aulden for, building war machines."

"Oh, but Aulden *wouldn't!*" Imp said, shocked.

"Not willingly, I'm sure," Geste answered grimly.

"Not . . . ? Geste, he wouldn't— I mean . . . Geste, if this is one of your tricks, I swear I'll have Aulden sabotage every machine you own!"

"It's no trick. I promise you, Imp, it's not a trick. And it's not just Aulden I'm worried about, or Brenner; Sheila and Sunlight and Rawl were all last heard from at the High Castle, and Khalid and O are missing, last heard from at Fortress Holding."

"Geste, you *can't*— Really? All of them?"

"Really. All of them."

The heart-shaped face turned for a moment, giving Bredon a glimpse of thick waves of reddish hair; Geste waited.

Imp turned back and said, "They *are* all missing. If this is a trick, Geste, it's a good one—and it's terrifying me. If it's a trick, Geste, please, tell me now. I don't like being frightened."

"I wish I could, Imp, but it's true."

"Thaddeus is really *attacking* Brenner? Seriously?"

"It looks serious to me; send something to check for yourself, if you like."

"Have you talked to Shadowdark?"

"Shadowdark?" Geste was plainly startled, but only for an instant. "Shadowdark! No, I haven't; I'll call him."

"You call him, then; maybe he can talk sense to Thaddeus. I'll try and get through to Brenner, and maybe some of the others." Imp's image vanished.

The name *Shadowdark* was unfamiliar to Bredon, and he thought it had an ominous sound. "Who is Shadowdark?" he asked.

"Thaddeus's father," Geste replied. He started to say something to the floater, but Bredon distracted him with a touch on the sleeve. The Trickster looked up at the mortal, startled by his audacity.

"His father? He has a father?" Bredon asked.

"Of course he has a father," Geste snapped, annoyed. "And he had a mother once, too, but she's dead. We all have parents, like anyone else. Where did you think we came from?"

"I don't know, I . . . I . . ." Bredon trailed off into silence, and Geste ordered the floater to call Shadowdark.

A moment of silence ensued, during which time Bredon tried, and failed, to gather the courage to ask more questions. He was consumed with curiosity about what was happening around him, and with concern for Lady Sunlight, but Geste was obviously worried and irritable and in no mood to answer his inquiries.

Instead, he watched the battle around the High Castle. It continued unabated, and as far as he could tell neither side was gaining any advantage.

"My apologies, sir," the floater said at last, "but Lord Shadowdark was outside, unattended. A messenger was sent."

An instant later another floating face appeared.

Bredon had thought he was beyond surprise, but this face shocked him. The other Powers had all looked young or perhaps middle-aged, and had been clean and strong and handsome in different ways. None had seemed all that different from mortal humans.

Shadowdark's face was misshapen and pale, the left side bloated while the right sagged, both sides hideously wrinkled, more like some bizarre fungus than the face of an old man. Gruesome scars puckered the skin in a dozen places, tangled among the wrinkles. Patches of black stubble were scattered along his cheeks and jaw, but he had no real beard. Straight black hair hung limply past his shoulders.

He spoke, harshly making a demand, but the words were strange.

Geste replied, using equally strange words, and Bredon realized that for the first time in his life he was hearing another language spoken.

"What is he saying?" he asked, interrupting Geste.

Geste waved him away.

"If I may be permitted to translate, sir, I would be glad to do so," the floater said.

Geste glanced up. "Go ahead," he said. Then he continued speaking in the foreign tongue, ignoring both Bredon and the floater.

The floater explained, "Lord Shadowdark demanded to know who was calling him, and why, and Mr. Geste identified himself, and apologized for the intrusion. Mr. Geste is now describing the situation he found at the High Castle." It paused, and then said, in a flawless imitation of Geste's own voice, ". . . I hoped that you might be able to intervene. Thaddeus thinks very little of the rest of us, rightfully considering us to be relative youngsters lacking experience, but I am sure that he still respects *you*. He may well feel some degree of filial devotion, even after so long a time. If you would consent to speak to him, to attempt to make peace between Brenner and himself, we would consider it a great favor, and would gladly repay you however we could."

Shadowdark spoke, and the floater said, in a voice that failed to duplicate Shadowdark's in anything but pitch, "You told these stinking machines to drag me in here for that?"

"Yes, sir," Geste and the floater's imitation of Geste replied, in two different tongues.

"You're an idiot. It's none of my business. I don't care what you people do to each other; Thaddeus and what's-his-name can kill each other if they like. Even if I did care, I haven't had anything to do with Thaddeus in . . . in centuries, probably. Ask a machine, I don't know. He hasn't wanted anything to do with me since I left Alpha Imperium. Anything I could say would probably just annoy him."

Shadowdark's image started to fade, then returned to solidity long enough to say something the floater translated as "By the way, don't bother me again. I won't answer."

The face vanished.

"Damn," Geste said. "It's impossible." He reached out and grabbed an invisible support, then leaned forward and rested his head on his arm.

Bredon was baffled. "Who is this Shadowdark?" he asked,

directing his question somewhere between Geste and the floater. "Is he a Power?"

Geste waved wearily at the floater without raising his head. "You tell him," he said. "I need to think." He paused, then lifted his eyes to the "window" for a moment and added, "And while you're telling him and I'm thinking, take us home."

Chapter Nine

". . . He looked up from where he lay, and saw a man dressed in black, with a strange black hat upon his head and a raven on his shoulder, standing at the edge of the clearing.

"Of course, he knew immediately that this was Rawl the Adjuster. He struggled to sit up, but he could not. It took all his strength to call, 'Hello! Can you help me?'

"Rawl heard him and paused. He looked the situation over for a moment, then came and sat beside the storyteller. 'What do you need?' he asked.

"And the storyteller explained how he had counted the Powers, and that although he had always been told that there are twenty-eight Powers in the world, yet when he thought through every tale he knew, every legend, every little incident, and noted down each and every mention, however trivial or obscure, he came up with a list of only twenty-seven names. He told the Adjuster how this had troubled him, and how he had gone seeking through the world, to see if anyone could tell him who the twenty-eighth Power is. He told how he wandered on, ever more despairing as first wakes, then seasons, and finally whole years went by without an answer, until at last he had found himself in his present sorry state.

" 'Is that all?' Rawl asked. 'All you want is to know the names of all twenty-eight immortals?'

" 'Yes,' the storyteller replied, 'that's all. Tell me the twenty-eighth name, and I shall die content.'

" 'There's no need for you to die at all,' Rawl told him, 'for I can easily heal your wounds and send you back to your village sound and well.'

" 'I would rather know the name,' the storyteller said.

" 'I'll tell you that too,' Rawl answered. 'I suppose that it would be Shadowdark.'

" 'Shadowdark?' the storyteller asked.

" 'Yes, Shadowdark. He is the oldest of us all, and the most reclusive. He speaks to no one, either mortal or immortal. He lives simply, in the forest not too far from here, and if you did not know who he was you would have no reason to think him anything but a very tall and ugly mortal man—very tall and very ugly.'

" 'You say he is near here?' the storyteller asked.

" 'Yes,' Rawl replied, 'but you dare not seek him out. If you saw

him and thought him mortal, it would be of no matter, but if you saw him and knew him for what he is, you would die instantly . . ."
    —FROM THE TALES OF KITHEN THE STORYTELLER

"Sir, I'm afraid that you must rephrase your question if you want a coherent answer. Shadowdark is a Power, as you use the term, but I cannot tell you who he is without further specification."

After a moment's consideration Bredon accepted that. Not all Powers had neat, clearly defined roles like the Lady of the Seasons. He tried to choose his next question carefully, making it specific enough for the familiar spirit, or whatever it was, to answer, but general enough to give him as much information as possible in its implications. "Why does he speak a strange language?" he asked. "And why does Geste call him 'sir'?"

"I assume, sir, that Shadowdark speaks Alphan English because he feels most comfortable with that language, and that Mr. Geste addresses him as 'sir' because of the great difference in their ages and because Shadowdark has held much higher social status and rank in times past than Mr. Geste has ever achieved."

This answer brought a flood of new questions to mind; Bredon suppressed all but one: "How can one Power be older than another? I thought they were all immortals, created at the beginning of time."

"No, sir, I'm afraid you have misunderstood the situation. The people you call the Powers are effectively immortal, yes, but they were not created at the beginning of time. They were born over a period of several thousand years. The person who now uses the name Shadowdark was the first, and is now approximately seven thousand years old. I use an approximation because years differ in length on different worlds, but are close enough on most of the worlds Shadowdark has lived on to make such approximations possible. Thaddeus the Black is the second-oldest of Shadowdark's surviving children, and the oldest of those children currently on Denner's Wreck. These two are more than two thousand years older than any of the other Powers. Mr. Geste was born almost six thousand years after Shadowdark. He is the second-youngest of the Powers, followed only by Imp."

Bredon struggled with this for a moment.

"You said Shadowdark had lived in other worlds? And had a higher rank than Geste? I don't understand that. I thought that the Powers were the Powers, and had always been what they are now."

"No, sir," the floater replied with inhuman patience and calm. "The people you call the Powers came to this world, which you call simply 'the world' but which they know by the ancient catalogue name *Denner's Wreck*, 462 years ago. Prior to that they had lived on a variety of other worlds before gathering on Terra and choosing to investigate the lost colony on Denner's Wreck. As for Shadowdark's rank, at one time he was an emperor, absolute master of more than twenty worlds, before he grew bored with power and abdicated. Mr. Geste has never held any rank or office higher than his current position as freeholder.''

Bredon was growing ever more confused. The floater's explanations were clear enough, but simply did not fit with what he thought he knew about the universe or the Powers. An emperor ruling twenty worlds? The universe as he understood it only held three inhabited worlds—the one in the sky whence mankind had come, the one he lived in now, and the one the Powers had come from, where the gods ruled and where his soul would go when he died, to either serve the gods or to be fed to the demons in the wilderness called Hell.

"I don't understand," he admitted.

The floater was silent for a moment; Bredon glanced out the window into the surrounding bubble of darkness and saw only more darkness. He could only distinguish the window from the rest of the bubble by the presence of stars in the sky beyond.

Geste, almost invisible in the gloom, was still sunk in thought.

"I am afraid," the floater said at last, "that explaining the situation will take a considerable length of time. Your ignorance of history and cosmology presents a significant barrier to comprehension of the present situation."

Bredon asked, "What did you say?"

"I said you don't know enough to understand my explanations," the floater explained.

"Oh." Bredon started to protest, to defend himself, then stopped. The thing was probably right, he realized. He was not stupid, but he was very ignorant indeed.

He didn't even know what he was talking to. *Was* it a familiar spirit? He didn't know.

He wanted to know, though. He wanted to very much.

This entire journey had been a flood of new experiences and new ideas, and Bredon found it exciting and invigorating—so much so, that he had already forgotten his resentment of Geste, and had come close, at times, to forgetting that he was here in pursuit of Lady Sunlight, and not for the sake of the adventure itself. He wanted more. He wanted to understand what the thing was talking about. He wanted to understand who and what the Powers were, and what they were doing.

He had always liked learning, even as a very young child. He had spoken early, and had asked more questions than the other children. His heritage as a hunter had been a good one in regard to his love of knowledge; he had been not merely permitted, but required, to learn the habits of the various creatures that roamed the grasslands, to learn the patterns of the weather, to learn to read an animal's trail. He had been able to study the animals he hunted—not merely their behavior when pursued, but every aspect of their behavior, their anatomy, their environment. He had been free to roam the countryside, to explore more or less wherever he chose, and he had pitied those people who stayed always in the village. He had thought that he knew his world well.

Now he was discovering that he knew almost nothing, and he wanted to learn more. He did not want to go quietly back to his village and wait there while Geste rescued Lady Sunlight for him.

"You know, you don't really need to take me home," he said. "I don't mind coming along while you . . . while you do whatever you're going to do."

"Who's taking you home?" Geste asked, startled out of his reverie. "I never said I was taking you home."

"But . . . but you told the platform to take me home!" Bredon blurted.

"I said take *us* home. I meant *my* home," Geste replied coldly.

Bredon hesitated, confused, but unsure whether asking the obvious question would be wise.

Every story he had ever heard about Geste the Trickster had emphasized that Geste was a wanderer, that he roved about wherever he pleased. Other Powers had their holds, their places of power, but a few carried all the power they had with them— Rawl the Adjuster and Geste the Trickster were the two wanderers Bredon knew of.

He could not restrain his curiosity.

"*What* home?" he asked. "I thought you didn't have one."

Geste smiled for the first time since the drone had attacked the platform.

"Ah," he said smugly.

Bredon waited, but the Trickster did not continue.

"What home?" Bredon repeated.

Geste smiled, and gestured mysteriously with an upraised finger. "*You'll* see!" he said.

Bredon felt himself growing angry, but before he could say anything more, Geste gave in and continued.

"It's true," he said, still smiling cheerfully, "that I don't stay home much, and that I don't let anyone else in, as a rule. I don't suppose my home gets into the stories you people tell about us. It may well be that even some of the other Powers, as you call us, don't know it exists, since I've never held a party there, never had more than one or two guests. It's real enough, though, and you'll be the first mortal to see it in, oh, two or three hundred years."

Mollified, Bredon relaxed, and tried to think of more questions to ask.

They stood on the platform, surrounded by darkness, and Bredon knew that the world was rushing by them, but he could neither see nor feel any movement.

"How will you know when we're there?" he asked.

Geste shrugged. "I'll know."

Bredon could think of no polite way to pry further into that subject, so he switched to another that had been preying on him. "Do you really think Lady Sunlight is trapped in that place, that castle we saw?"

"Probably." Geste's smile faded. "If she's not, if she's faked all this somehow, then she's managed a stunt that makes any of mine look trivial." His expression turned thoughtful. "I wonder . . . I wonder, could she have put all this together? Got them all into a little conspiracy to get back at me?"

He hesitated, considering, then said, "No. She could never get Thaddeus to help. And Brenner wouldn't let them shoot up the High Castle for a joke, and that attack on us seemed pretty serious. Besides, if it *were* a setup, they couldn't know when I'd come across it. I only tried to find Sunlight to help you; I might have gone years without checking on her whereabouts otherwise, so you'd need to be in on it, and I can't imagine Sunlight finding you and recruiting you into something like that."

Bredon agreed, "Nobody recruited me for anything. I don't know what's going on at all."

"Oh, it's simple enough, really. We Powers squabble amongst ourselves all the time, but nothing much comes of it; we all have so many machines and devices protecting us that it would take a real effort to do one another any harm. But now it looks as if one fight has turned nasty, and Thaddeus is making that effort against Brenner, and Sheila and Sunlight and the others got caught in the middle."

Bredon thought he glimpsed something in Geste's expression,

something that indicated that the Trickster did not believe his own explanation, that he was worried, as if he thought something else, something more, was involved. Bredon could not imagine what else *could* be involved, but he could not find the nerve to ask directly, to admit he did not believe Geste. Instead, he poked around the edges of the subject.

"Do you think Lady Sunlight may be hurt?"

"She could be," Geste admitted.

"Is it my fault? Would she have gotten involved if I hadn't tried to get into the Meadows?"

Geste glanced at him, then looked away again. "Oh, I wouldn't worry about that," he said. "I doubt she paid any attention to you at all."

Bredon hardly found that flattering, but he let it slide as he pressed his inquiry.

"Could she be killed?" he asked. "Can a Power die?"

Geste laughed bitterly, then said, "Oh, we can die, all right, but it takes a lot to kill one of us. There isn't much on Denner's Wreck that could kill a Power except another Power, and even then it isn't easy."

"Do you think Thaddeus the Black might kill Lady Sunlight?"

Geste glanced at him again, his face unusually serious. "Not intentionally," he answered. "Are you hungry?"

The abrupt change of subject caught Bredon by surprise. "Yes," he said, realizing suddenly that he was indeed very hungry.

"Good; so am I," Geste said. "Worrying always gives me an appetite. We'll be at my hold in a minute, but I'd rather not wait." He reached out and began pulling foil packets and glittering crystal vials from the air and handing them to Bredon.

When Bredon's arms were full, Geste settled down cross-legged on the platform. Bredon followed his example; they sat facing each other as they peeled open packets and popped the lids from vials, and both ate and drank heartily of Geste's strange and wonderful viands.

Chapter Ten

"The Skyler's job, of course, is to maintain the sky, to put fallen stars back in their places, to herd the clouds into rainstorms, to polish the sky dry after every storm. She cleans the clockwork that moves the sun across the heavens, paints the colors of the sunset, collects the stars each sunrise, and then hangs them back up at dusk.

"It's a hard, lonely job, and the Skyler is always much too busy to spare any thought for the mortals below. She hasn't even got time to go to and from a home on the ground, so long ago she picked up an island from their sea and set it sailing in the sky, where we call it the Skyland. This makes her work much easier, since she can keep all the stars and clouds neatly stored away in compartments aboard the Skyland, ready when she needs them. Imagine what the bins and cupboards must look like, with the stars twinkling and the sunsets glowing softly, the clouds piled up everywhere, white and fluffy on top, gray and dripping below! What a wonderful sight it must be!

"Of course, it can be a bit startling for people on the ground to see that island hanging overhead, but it's nothing to be afraid of, just the Skyler at her work, keeping the heavens clean and beautiful for us all."

—FROM THE TALES OF ATHERON THE STORYTELLER

The last crumbs fell from his clothes and vanished in midair as Geste stood and calmly stepped off the platform.

Bredon started, then reached out tentatively and discovered that the surrounding bubble had vanished. The air was still almost motionless, but he realized it no longer felt quite as dead and trapped. An unfamiliar scent reached him, a curious mixture of flowers and spice. They had landed somewhere, some place so dark that the stars did not show above them.

Then light sprang up on all sides in soft pastel colors, like the light of an early dawn, accompanied by soft, plaintive music.

"Welcome to my home," Geste said, gesturing at the vast chamber that surrounded them. "Welcome to Arcade."

Bredon stared silently for several seconds.

The platform rested on the floor of a great hall, a dozen times bigger than the village feasting hall, bigger than the lounge he had seen at Autumn House. The ceiling was fifteen or twenty meters high, and the nearest wall more than a dozen meters away.

Both ceiling and wall were, for as far as he could see, of some white, porous substance, almost, but not quite, like bone. The walls curved over to become the ceiling, and were divided by vertical columns that looked not so much like pillars as like ribs, which continued up across onto the ceiling, where they became a web of elaborate tracery.

Green and blue-green vines crisscrossed the walls, and seemed to be quivering. To one side the walls were hidden by a grove of strange trees. Bredon marveled, wondering how vines and trees could grow inside the chamber, where the sun and rain could not reach them.

These trees seemed to be doing just fine, but they were like none Bredon had ever seen. Their branches grew in symmetrical patterns, and their trunks were all a peculiar ashy gray color. The leaves were green on one side, like any other leaves, but their undersides were colored a thousand subtly different hues.

Some of the trees seemed to bear fruit, but whatever they produced was nearly hidden amid the foliage, so that Bredon could not make out its nature. The scent he had noticed upon arrival seemed to come from the fruit trees.

Small creatures peered down at him from the treetops, but whenever he looked at one directly it would take fright and vanish into the leaves, so that he could make out nothing of them except wide golden eyes and flashes of soft brown fur.

Bredon had seen nothing of any of this as they approached, since he and Geste had been enclosed in the protective bubble. He looked for an opening they could have entered by, but could find none. There were no doors, no windows, no visible openings of any sort in the white walls. Even the gaps between the trees appeared too narrow to allow the platform passage. For all he could see, the platform had had to pass directly through the wall.

He saw no furniture, either. Except for the enchanted forest, the room was simply a huge, ornate, empty box. And he could not figure out where the soft, even light was coming from.

Geste was grinning at him, and Bredon remembered just whose home he was in—if it was really *anyone's* home. He stepped down from the platform, but moved with extreme caution, half expecting to bang his shins against an invisible chair or table, or his nose against a wall.

Nothing happened. He did not collide with anything invisible, nor did any of the creatures from the grove leap out at him. He took a few steps and stood uncertainly.

"Make yourself at home," Geste said, waving an arm in invitation.

Bredon eyed him warily. He tried to think of some response that would cleverly express his growing weariness, annoyance, and impatience, but could think of nothing that would not sound simply petulant. He looked around at the bare floor, the vine-striped walls, and the alien trees.

Geste said nothing to help him.

"Thank you," Bredon said at last. "I will." He lowered himself cautiously and sat cross-legged on the floor.

Although he knew it was still dark outside, the air in the room was warm, its scent pleasant and relaxing, and he had had an impossibly long and eventful wake. He slipped off his vest, folded it into a makeshift pillow, then started to settle down for a nap. This, after all, was a sleeping dark, not a midwake dark, and he had been awake far too long.

Geste watched for a minute, then shrugged in acceptance of a minor defeat. Bredon was obviously not going to do anything amusing. "I'm being a poor host," he said. "Gamesmaster, we need proper accommodations."

"Yes, master," a disembodied voice, much like that of the housekeeper at Autumn House, replied. "Whatever you say, boss. You want it, you got it. Right away, you bet. Ask and ye shall receive."

The slick gray floor to one side suddenly bulged upward into an immense bubble, four or five meters in diameter, almost touching Bredon; startled, he rolled away without thinking and came to his feet in a fighting crouch, a dagger in his hand.

The bubble burst with a loud pop. The fragments dissolved into air, with a sizzle and a smell like frying batter. Where the bubble had been stood a soft, richly blue mass with several oddly shaped appendages.

"I think," Geste said, "that something a little more primitive is in order. Our guest is a native of Denner's Wreck."

"I got you, boss."

The blue mass sank into itself, melting away like butter over a hot fire, and then hardened into a new shape.

It had become a bed. Four of the appendages had transformed into bedposts; the rest had vanished. The blue stuff, whatever it might actually be, now looked like fine fur.

Bredon relaxed, tucked the knife back out of sight, and carefully approached the bed.

It was, as far as he could determine, just a bed. Except for its color, the blue fur that adorned it was an ordinary fur coverlet, with a texture much like good-quality rabbit. The pillow and mattress were also blue, but felt like ordinary down-filled linen.

Both the spiced-flower smell and the frying odor were gone now, replaced by a cool, clean, inviting fragrance that reminded him of freshly washed linen hung out in a spring breeze.

With a shrug, Bredon dropped his vest and climbed into the bed.

The room vanished; the bed seemed to be floating in a soft black void. He could no longer hear the music.

Bredon had seen too many wonders to be much disturbed by this, and he was utterly exhausted. He rolled over and went to sleep.

Outside the illusionary void, Geste settled back into a floating seat that popped silently up out of the floor when he first began to bend his knees. A feelie vine slithered up silently to caress his ankles, and a messenger weasel jumped down from the forest and stood alert at his side, ready to run any errand its master might care to give it. Food trees ripened a variety of tasty products, prepared to drop them on an instant's notice, and certain other trees, the cousins of the feelie vines, pumped lubricious sap into erectile tissue and stood ready. Soothing scents spilled into the air. The music transformed itself from nondescript background noise to one of Geste's favorite suites, a piece slightly over a thousand years old that Bredon would not have recognized as music at all.

The Trickster paid no attention to his obedient creatures. He watched, amused, as Bredon slept. "Resilient, isn't he? He's just taking it all in stride," he said.

"That's just because he doesn't know what the hell is going on, boss; he doesn't know enough to be scared."

"You're probably right," Geste agreed. "I think *I'm* scared." He motioned for a drink; a silver service floater extruded itself from the floor by his foot, startling the waiting weasel.

"Why did you bring him here, boss?" Gamesmaster asked. "You aren't exactly in the habit of bringing folks home for dinner, after all."

Geste reached out and picked the waiting goblet off the floater. "You know what's been going on?" he asked. He tasted the drink, grimaced, then put it back on the floater.

The floater sank back into the floor and another—pale blue this time—emerged, but remained coupled by a thin strand of material. The messenger weasel nuzzled against Geste's hand, its fur testing the chemical composition of his sweat and relaying the information to the household machines to help them design a better beverage, which would be fed up to the waiting floater.

Geste paid no attention to that. He was too worried to pet the weasel, and let his hand hang limply against it.

"You mean old Thaddeus doing his best to blow away the High Castle, with Brenner and a bunch of other folks in it?" Gamesmaster said. "Sure, I know. I keep in touch. I've been getting all the dope from your floater, and from Mother, and from a dozen other places."

Geste squinted critically up at the ceiling and remarked, "You talk too much, you know that? You might want to consider reprogramming yourself a little, toning that down."

"I'll keep it in mind, boss, but I still want to know why you brought that noble savage here. Why did you come home at all, for that matter?"

"It seemed like a good idea at the time," Geste replied. "I promised that I'd set him up with Sunlight, didn't I? I can't take him back to his village until I come through on that; I've got a reputation to live up to, and besides, it should be pretty funny, watching the two of them together. You know what Sunlight is like, her whole ethereal, too-good-for-mortal-flesh routine, and here this poor kid wants to haul her into bed—she probably hasn't been laid by a human being in centuries, let alone some yokel who can't have any more romantic technique than one of those damned rabbits that are all over this planet." He snorted, and picked up his new drink.

"You're getting off the subject, boss."

He sipped at the goblet and nodded. "Yeah, I am; sorry. Anyway, I really did want to see what happened when I got the two of them face-to-face. I was looking forward to it. And I was looking forward to seeing Sheila again; it's been . . . what, half a year, almost?"

"Maybe a third."

"Still too long. In any case, I was looking forward to a little lighthearted fun, and a few interesting days, and instead I found myself in the middle of what might turn into a full-blown war. You know Thaddeus's history; he's started wars before. He may be out to rebuild his father's stupid little empire again. That threw me off stride; I haven't thought in terms of wars or empires or interstellar politics for centuries now. All I could think was that if I took Bredon home, he'd say I had welshed, and if I dropped him anywhere else I might be too busy to ever come back for him."

"If Thaddeus *is* out to conquer this corner of the galaxy, and you try to stop him, you could wind up too *dead* to come back and pick the kid up."

"I know—I thought of that, too. So I could take him home, or I could keep him with me, or I could bring him here. Keeping him with me on that little airskiff wouldn't work; he'd just get in the way. So here he is. And I want you, and all the rest of Arcade, to look after him, and see that he has what he needs, until I get back. Do whatever he tells you so long as it won't hurt anything. If I do get killed, you see that he gets home safely."

"You got it, boss. No problem."

"Good. Now, what can we do about Thaddeus?"

The intelligence had no quick answer for that. After a moment it hummed quietly to indicate its befuddlement.

"Fat lot of help you are," Geste muttered.

"Sorry, boss, but I'm a housekeeper, not a general. This is way the hell outside my programming. I don't know the first thing about stopping a war."

"You should—it's not that different from a game, and you know plenty about games."

The intelligence hesitated, then asked, "You think I should treat this like a war game?"

"Of course—why do you think they're called war games in the first place?"

"Well, yeah, I know that, but I never knew whether they were accurate simulations or not. If it's like that, the first thing we need is military intelligence, if you'll forgive the phrase. We need to scout out exactly what the situation is. Boss, you're the best-equipped person on the planet for that; you've got more spy gadgets than all the rest put together."

"That's true, I guess," Geste admitted, leaning back. "I never planned on using them for anything but fun, but I've got them, don't I? Start sending them out there, then. First priority is tapping into Thaddeus's own systems, finding out what he's done already, and what he plans to do. Put as many snoopers, crackers, and tapping devices onto that as you can—either silicon-based or organic or just transmitted software, whatever you can get in there. You'll need a lot, because he's always refused to centralize anything. For the real-world stuff, I want records of all movements in and out of Fortress Holding—record heat-signatures, or emissions, or whatever other features can be used to distinguish them, and try and identify the individual machines. Anything that seems slow and stupid enough, put a spyscope or homing bug on it—follow it and see what it does. And can we do anything about bent-space measurement?"

"Sure, boss, we've got lots of bent-space stuff. You told me to see about tunneling into the Meadows a couple of years back, and most of that place is in bent space, so I've been working on bent-space navigation for that—I never got into the Meadows with it, but I can find my way around in overspace or underspace or whatever other variant of polyspace you care to name, and I can spot every crimp in the planet's gravity well."

"I told you to do that?"

"You sure did; want a playback?"

"No, I believe you. I just forgot." Geste shook his head in pleased bemusement at his own accidental foresight.

"All in all," Gamesmaster said, "I think we're all right on reconnaissance, boss, but we haven't got much of anything for defense or attack."

"We can sabotage any system we can read, can't we?"

"Well, probably—it's not quite that easy. A lot of them will be tamper-protected, and we may lose the snooper every time. And Thaddeus is bound to have a lot of redundancy in his systems, as well as a lot of systems; he's fought wars before."

"That's true," Geste said thoughtfully, "I guess he has. He and Shadowdark."

"Oh, some of the others have, too."

"I suppose they must have." It occurred to Geste that he knew surprisingly little about some of his comrades. He dismissed that as unimportant, and returned to the subject at hand. "We must be able to mount *some* sort of an attack. I want you to devote whatever capacity you can spare easily to adapting equipment for use as weaponry, or maybe just building weapons from scratch. We may need an arsenal."

"You got it, boss. You want anything special?"

"No, I don't know any more about what he's got than you do."

"Okay, I got it; I'll do a mixed bag, whatever I think of. You let me know if you come up with any brilliant ideas for me to work on. Anything else?"

"On defense—Thaddeus can't get into a bent-space shelter, can he?"

"Not if you close it off before he can send anything through. But, boss, you wouldn't like being stuck in a closed-off bubble. Once you close it off from normal space, you don't just have a bend anymore, you've got a pocket universe. Breaking back out into normal space could be tricky. I wouldn't want to try it. And so long as you have a connection to normal space, Thaddeus can attack you through it, one way or another."

"What if we got off-planet? Just packed up and left?"

The intelligence hesitated. "Well, boss," it said at last, "you could try that. You could pack up and go back to Mother and take off for Terra or anywhere else you fancy. But that wouldn't stop Thaddeus. He got off Alpha Imperium centuries after the collapse of the local civilization, remember; he used salvaged materials and slave labor and built himself a starship in a mud-hut technology. He could do the same here. And meanwhile, if you just took off, you'd have to leave behind a lot of stuff. All the mortals, for example. And me. I wouldn't like that. I mean, I know that you won't hang around Denner's Wreck forever, but I always figured that when you left you'd see that I came along, or else you'd leave me a secure situation here. If you run off now, you can't take me along—there isn't room on Mother, and you couldn't make the modifications quickly enough to get away before Thaddeus shot you down. And if you left me behind, I figure Thaddeus would get to me sooner or later."

"I didn't know you cared," Geste said, genuinely startled. "I thought silicon life didn't have any ego or instinct for self-preservation."

"Well, I can't speak for anybody *else*, boss. I know you guys built me and evolved me from machinery instead of flat-worms or whatever you humans are descended from, so that I don't need to have any instinct for self-preservation, and I know that a lot of machines are about as much alive and self-aware as a rock, and I know that even some smart ones would just as soon be scrapped as not, but *I* sure *think* I have an ego. Blame it on your programming—or Aulden's, I guess, since he did the basic design for me. Whatever you want to call it, I know damn well that I don't like the idea of Thaddeus messing around with me."

"He doesn't even know you exist!"

"Yeah, but he'd find out eventually."

"And why couldn't we make modifications?"

"You aren't worried about the mortals around here?"

"Let's leave them out of it for the moment. Why couldn't we make modifications and bring you along?"

"You wouldn't have time. If Thaddeus sees you packing up, he'll try and stop you. He won't want you alerting whatever military authorities there might be out there. The only way you could get off-planet safely would be to just pick up and go, right now, and take off in Mother. Even then, he might try to shoot you down."

Geste leaned back, thinking, and his seat reshaped itself to better fit his new contour. The goblet in his hand also reshaped itself, to avoid spilling, and the feelie vine at his ankle threw a massaging tendril up toward the back of his neck. The music shifted subtly.

"It seems to me," he said, "that Mother is the big threat to his plans here; why hasn't he *already* shot her down? If I were trying to take over the planet without letting anyone outside the system know about it, I'd destroy Mother first thing, before anyone else knew I was up to something, in order to keep anyone from escaping. Thaddeus hasn't done that. Why not?"

"I'd guess he probably plans to use Mother himself. Seems obvious. After all, he surely doesn't want just Denner's Wreck. He must want a dozen or more suns, the same as before, and Mother's the only thing in the system with a stardrive. Building a new one would take a lot more time and a lot more resources than he wants, I'd guess. He could *do* it, he's done it before, but it's a lot easier to take the ship ready-made."

"But it's too big a risk, just waiting until he's ready. He must have something in mind, some way to make sure none of us are going to take the ship and leave him here while we go get help."

"If he does, boss, it's nothing *I* know about. Maybe we should ask Mother."

Geste waved a command. "Ask her, then." He sipped his drink through a straw the goblet extruded for him.

"Bad news, boss," Gamesmaster replied immediately. "Mother says that Thaddeus came up for a visit a couple of days ago and left off a few things, with orders not to touch them. They're hooked into the main controls and the stardrive. Mother's not happy about it, but she didn't have self-defense programs strong enough to override his orders, so they're all there now. He gave her orders so she couldn't even tell anyone until she was asked. It's a safe bet they're booby traps of some kind, something to make sure that nobody can use the ship except him."

"We're in real trouble, then. I mean, I'm sure that anything Thaddeus can rig up Aulden could get around—probably in about five minutes—but Thaddeus has Aulden stashed away somewhere, and none of the rest of us are fit to program a lunch box. If those *are* booby traps, and I'm pretty damn sure they are, then unless we get Aulden out we're stuck here on Denner's Wreck. Is there any way we can call for help?"

"Who would we call? How? We've been cut off here for centuries on this little vacation you people put together. I don't have any idea what's been happening back in civilization, and neither do any of the other machines that will talk to me. And we don't have an open channel to anywhere, either—nothing outside the system but normal-space communications. We could broadcast a message, anywhere you like up and down the electromagnetic spectrum, but it would go out at light speed, and it's eight light-years to the next inhabited system. That means it would be eight years before anyone could respond. Even if they took your word for everything and launched ships immediately, Thaddeus would have had eight years to do whatever he's going to do."

"Do it anyway. Send the message, before that monster finds some way to jam outgoing traffic for the whole planet. At least then Thaddeus will have a time limit. Eight years isn't much."

"Boss, I don't think that's a good idea—at least, not yet."

Annoyed at being questioned by his own machine, Geste snapped, "Why the hell not?"

"Well, first off, it will tell Thaddeus that we know what he's doing, and we haven't got any defenses set up yet. Do you really want to issue an invitation to come and kill us? Besides, it won't set a definite time limit anyway. We don't know that anyone will answer. The nearest known inhabited planet is New Schenectady, but why would anyone on New Sken care about Denner's Wreck? I've picked up cross talk from there every so often, and it's not a hotbed of wild-eyed idealism. If the message ever reaches Alpha Imperium we can expect an answer—they remember Thaddeus there, and last I heard they still had a death warrant out on him—but that's almost a century away in normal space. We might have help in eight years—or in ninety-six. I suspect we'd all be dead in ninety-six, if we antagonized Thaddeus like that."

Geste saw the truth in Gamesmaster's argument. "Then we've got to stop him ourselves, here on Denner's Wreck," he said.

"I'd say so, boss. Looks to me like you're up to your neck in trouble."

"We're up to *our* necks," Geste corrected.

"Boss, I hate to tell you this, after all these years, especially after what I just said about my being one of the guys, but my secret's out—I don't *have* a neck."

"That's too bad—means I can't wring it. Anyway, I meant all of the humans, mostly."

"Well, I'd have to agree with that."

"I have *got* to get help."

"I'd have to agree with that too. But you didn't do very well at enlisting troops before."

"Then I'll just have to do better. Who haven't I tried?"

The intelligence emitted a synthetic sigh, and began listing names.

Geste listened to the recitation with little enthusiasm. He had already covered every one of the immortals who lived anywhere near Fortress Holding, and he knew that the farther away a person's hold, the less likely that person would be to care what Thaddeus was doing. They would prefer not to believe that anything was going to disturb their quiet lives, and they would find it particularly hard to believe, coming from Geste the Trickster.

There were the three residents of the northern mountains, Isabelle, Dragon, and Arn of the Ice. The ocean-based immortals included Geste's closest neighbor, Lord Hollingsworth, who was relatively promising, and one of the oldest of the group; he might actually know something about military strategy. The others in that group—Feura and Tagomi—Geste had little hope for. The eastern forests, in addition to Shadowdark, held Lord Carlov, Lady Haze, Starflower, and Anna, who called herself the Lady of the Lake. Carlov liked to play the part of an ancient warrior, but Geste had no idea whether he would be of any use in actual conflict.

And somewhere in the skies there was the Skyler. Geste decided that she was the best place to start, for a variety of reasons.

First, her home, the Skyland, could be valuable. Being mobile, it would make an excellent base of operations. Geste could also see several possible uses for a million metric tons of airborne rock. If nothing else, it looked impressive to have the thing come sailing over one's head; in fact, the Skyler generally kept it out at sea to avoid terrifying the mortals.

Besides, if he came sailing overhead aboard the Skyland, people would be less likely to think that the whole thing was one of Geste's stunts. They knew that the Skyler was not the sort of person who would volunteer to help out in one of the Trickster's schemes. And the fact that people were gathering in one place, in person, rather than just talking over long distances, would help drive home the seriousness of the matter. As a rule, face-to-face gatherings were reserved for pleasure, and problems were dealt with through the communications systems. A problem that got Geste aboard the Skyland would seem more real.

The Skyler was a skittish, suggestible person. A threat of the sort Thaddeus posed would rouse her to action far more readily than it would most of the others.

Furthermore, because of her elevated location and his own preference for setting his plans upon solid ground, she had been the subject of very few of Geste's pranks, and should therefore be more willing than most to trust him.

And finally, she was a good friend to Imp, and Imp was genuinely worried about her lover, Aulden the Technician—and with good reason. If Geste could not convince the Skyler by himself, he would ask Imp to intervene on his behalf.

That reminded him that he had not heard anything back from Imp. Well, he would call her back after he had spoken to the others.

"Get me the Skyler," he said.

"You got it, boss."

An instant later the Skyler's familiar face appeared before him. She wore a worried expression, which was nothing unusual.

"Oh, Geste, it's you!" she said, her face brightening. "Thank heavens! Imp told me what's happening; what can I do to help?"

Geste smiled, then suppressed it. Imp had done the convincing for him.

"If you don't mind, I'd like to come aboard, and we can talk about it there. Should I come find you, or will you come find me, or shall we meet somewhere?"

"I'm headed for the Falls to pick up Imp; could you join us there?"

"Of course. I'd be glad to. See you there." Geste signaled, and the Skyler's image vanished.

Things were looking up; he had Imp and the Skyler on his side now, at the very least. Thaddeus would not be able to take them all by surprise.

But Geste still had no idea at all how they could stop the would-be conqueror.

Chapter Eleven

"... *fell to the sand and waited to die.*

"*The next thing he knew strong hands were grasping him and lifting him up, and he found himself being laid across a wagon, a wagon that moved without any wheels or beasts to draw it. And when he could gather the strength, he looked around and saw that on either side of the wagon were three men, and they were all clad in flowing robes of white and gold, and they all marched on silently, not saying a word, and in perfect step.*

"*He marveled at this, and wondered who could have found him, so far out in the desert, but then his weariness caught up to him and he fainted.*

"*When he awoke again he was in a tent, bright with the desert sun's light through the cloth; rugs covered the sands to make a floor, musicians played on pipes somewhere outside, and he lay upon a pile of embroidered cushions atop the rugs.*

"*Before him sat a richly robed man, holding out a cup.*

"*He took the cup and sipped from it, and found that it held an invigorating liquor he had never tasted before. He drank deeply, and when the cup was empty he felt well enough to stand and bow politely to his host.*

"*The man waved for him to sit down. 'I am Khalid,' he said, 'and you are my honored guest. Welcome to the Tents of Gold!' He waved a hand, and for an instant the wanderer saw not a simple tent, but a vast banquet hall, where fountains poured forth bubbling streams, and beautiful women danced to the pipers' music, and the tables groaned beneath the weight of a great feast.*

"*Then the tent was back, and Khalid said, 'What is mine, is yours. You have but to ask ...'*"

—FROM THE TALES OF ATHERON THE STORYTELLER

Bredon awoke slowly, uncertain where he was and puzzled by the darkness.

He remembered going to sleep well after sunset, and he felt well rested, so how could it still be dark? Had he slept clear through firstlight and into the midwake dark? He felt the soft fur coverlet under which he lay, and knew it was not one of his own furs; the texture was not quite anything he recognized. He did not smell the familiar scents of smoke and leather that filled his own

83

tent; in fact, he did not smell anything. Nor did he hear anything; the sound of the wind in the grass was eerily absent.

He sat up.

Light sprang up, a soft golden glow, and he remembered.

He was in Arcade, the secret home of Geste the Trickster.

The golden light was localized; all he could see was his bed—which was now yellow, though he remembered it as blue—and a small open expanse of smooth, shining floor that looked yellow, but might have been white in a more ordinary light.

He hesitated, unsure what he should do. Wandering about unguided in a Power's hold could surely be dangerous.

"Is anyone there?" he called softly into the unsettling silence.

"Sure, kid, I'm here" came the calm reply. "What can I do for you?"

Bredon recognized the voice as the invisible housekeeper, the one Geste had called "Gamesmaster."

"I don't know," he said, speaking normally. "What am I supposed to do?"

"Whatever you like," the intelligence replied. "The boss told me to take care of you, and he didn't set any rules. You can pretty much do as you please while you're here, at least as far as I'm concerned. I'm just supposed to see that you have what you need and don't get hurt."

That was reassuring, and Bredon relaxed a little. "Where is Geste?" he asked.

"He's gone out to the Skyland for a council of war. He wants to stop Thaddeus from screwing up anything, and to get Lady Sunlight back here for you while he's at it."

"Is there anything I can do to help?"

"Sorry, kid, but I doubt it. I figure you had best just wait here until the boss gets back—or gets killed, whichever it is."

Bredon was not sure whether Gamesmaster was joking in speaking of his master's death—after all, could a Power *really* die? Geste had said so, but Geste was a notorious liar.

Still, whether there was any genuine danger or not, Bredon could not shake the feeling that he was somehow responsible for involving Geste in something unpleasant. "I want to help, though," he said. "There must be *something* I can do."

"I don't know what it could be. Look, kid, I know you mean well, but this is between the immortals. You haven't got the technology or the knowledge or the experience to be of any help, so far as I can see."

Bredon knew that was true, but he refused to accept it without argument. He had never enjoyed sitting by and watching while others acted, and he felt somehow responsible for Lady Sunlight. Besides, from a purely selfish point of view, anything he could do to help would also improve his chances of eventually bedding her. "Maybe I can learn," he said. "Maybe I can see something the Trickster would miss, *because* I'm only a mortal, something that a Power wouldn't think of."

The intelligence hesitated, then replied, "I'm sorry, kid, but I just can't see it. Even if there is some little fact that you know that we don't that could be of use, how will we ever know it? You don't have the first idea what's really happening here."

"I *know* I don't, but I *want* to understand," Bredon insisted. "I want to learn. Can you teach me?"

"Well, sure I can," Gamesmaster replied. "Of course I can teach you. But I don't know how much you can learn in time to do any good. I've got direct neural loading in a lot of fields—imprinting, we call it—but not for any of the basics that you'll need, because Geste and all the rest had all that centuries ago and weren't planning on having any kids on this planet. I'd need to teach you a lot of stuff with ordinary sight and sound."

"That's fine!" Bredon said happily.

"Well, maybe it's fine. We'll see."

"When do we start?" The prospect of a new adventure, of learning what was really going on, thrilled him.

"Oh, anytime, I guess. But first, aren't there a few little things to take care of?"

"Like what?" Bredon demanded, suddenly suspicious.

"Oh, details like food, drink, and a quick visit to the equivalent of a hole in the ground?"

"Oh." Bredon realized sheepishly that the mysterious voice was quite correct; his bladder was full and his belly was empty. He flushed slightly, then smiled at his own discomfiture and stood up. "Lead the way," he said, his hand hooked into the waistband of his breeches.

Behind him, the bed shifted its shape, and oozed around him, forming a receptacle in the appropriate position. Other appendages formed, but waited their turn.

In the next several minutes Bredon was stripped, bathed, checked for parasites, shampooed, massaged, and generally cleansed and invigorated. He had no names for most of what the "bed" did to and for him, but when it had finished he felt absolutely wonderful.

"Would you like your old clothes back, or something new?" a soft, feminine voice asked.

Bredon was startled, and momentarily embarrassed by his

nudity until he realized that speaker was surely another inhuman spirit. When he recovered he decided he felt ready to take a little risk. "Something new," he said.

"Anything in particular?"

"No."

"Delighted to be of service, sir." Something silky slid up his legs and onto his back; he raised his arms to slip into the sleeves, and found himself wearing a one-piece garment that looked like velvet, but that weighed almost nothing and shimmered in a dozen shades of soft brown.

"Nice," he said appreciatively. He was dressed as well as a Power now.

A table appeared before him, seeming to form out of thin air, and a strangely shaped chair rose out of the floor behind him. He sat down gingerly.

"Did you have anything special in mind for breakfast?" Gamesmaster's familiar voice asked.

"I can't say I did," Bredon answered.

He expected more of the foil packets, but those, he discovered, were strictly trail food. Here at Geste's home, meals were served properly, on plates of various sizes and an assortment of oddly shaped dishes, some of which had the disconcerting habit of floating in midair a few centimeters above the table. All the plates and dishes had the knack of quietly vanishing once they were emptied.

Bredon did not recognize a single one of the foods he was served, whether by sight, taste, or aroma. All, however, were delicious.

When he had eaten his fill the golden light blinked out, plunging him into total darkness. Gamesmaster announced, "We'll begin your lessons now, and we'll start with some elementary cosmology. I'll do my best to put this so that you can understand it, and if there's anything that you *don't* understand, please stop me and I'll try to explain it more clearly. I expect some of this will conflict with what you were taught by your own people, but this is the way those you call the Powers understand the universe." It paused, but whether it expected a response or merely wished to heighten the drama, Bredon could not decide.

"In the beginning," a deep new voice said, "there was the Bang." An image appeared, a blaze of light hanging in the darkness before him, spreading out and scattering.

Bredon listened to the creation myth as retold by what he had to consider another of the Trickster's familiar spirits. The story was not very exciting; his own people had a much shorter and rather more interesting creation story, full of people rather than impersonal cosmic forces. The spirit, however, seemed to take its story more seriously than anyone took old Atheron's tale of the warring sects of Kru and Passijers being cast out of the heavens.

He listened, though, and he watched the images of planets coalescing out of dust, heard the explanation of how life arose from the seas, how the creatures changed their forms over millions of years. He gaped at some of the creatures he was shown, and laughed at others. The pictures were incredibly real, so clear and detailed that he had difficulty believing they were merely images.

Then humans entered the story, not sent down from the heavens, but as just another creature.

That was a new and interesting concept; Bredon rather liked the idea. He watched as the story ran quickly through the rise of civilization and the growth of technology.

It was only when he was shown the early sleeperships wallowing out toward the stars that Bredon realized he had been watching the history of the World in the Sky, rather than of his own world.

The tale of Denner and his Kru and Passijers fit in quite nicely with what he had just seen, and he suddenly understood what Geste and his other familiar had meant in speaking of other worlds. All those planets that had formed in the beginning were worlds, and the stars were suns—hundreds, thousands of them!

He told the spirits to stop while he absorbed this, and the image diffused into a soft white glow. He could faintly see the enchanted forest just beyond.

He repeated slowly to himself what he had just been taught. His world was not the only one between the heavens and the world of the dead. According to the spirit, there were hundreds of others, or thousands.

His mind boggled. What a concept! Worlds upon worlds, each with thousands or millions of people!

And the stars in the darktime sky—each of them was a sun, and each sun had a world beneath it. All his life he had looked up at a thousand other suns, without ever realizing it.

What were all those other worlds like? What would it be like to live in the light of another sun?

He stared into the darkness, trying to imagine an entire different *world*, fully as big and complex as his own.

He failed. His imagination could not even encompass the totality of his own world; he knew that already.

Other worlds! He shook his head.

But there was no need to try and absorb it all at once. He would have plenty of time to digest this wonder.

"All right," he said. "Go on."

The spirits, if that was what they were, obliged; the darkness lit up anew with the globe they called Terra, the world where humankind had first developed, and the story rolled on.

The magic called "technology" grew ever more powerful, and under its complex spells humans were transformed from mere mortals into demigods, no longer subject to aging, always strong and healthy, able to create almost instantly anything that they might fancy, even living creatures. These latter-day humans could reshape entire worlds at a whim, even bend space itself. Their machines became self-aware intelligences in their own right—not spirits, but living creatures that were built instead of bred.

Bredon was not sure that the distinction really meant anything; whether built or conjured, these things still seemed like spirits to him. He shoved that thought aside as irrelevant.

Naturally, many of the supernal beings that had been born humans grew bored with their world. With centuries of life stretching before them, boredom could be a severe problem. The leading cause of death on Terra was suicide brought on by ennui.

Millions of weapons against boredom were developed. Humans transformed themselves into machines or creatures, transformed machines into humans, plunged themselves into invented realities, and invented entertainments so complex and bizarre that Bredon could not begin to comprehend them, but throughout, one of the most popular ways to avoid boredom was travel. The universe was full of surprises. Artificial entertainments were limited by the imaginations of humans and human-made things, while nature remained unthinkably vast and varied. Whenever life in one spot grew tedious, one could simply pack up and go somewhere else.

In just this manner, twenty-eight bored people took a ship and a handful of ancient, incomplete records and, on a whim, searched out the lost colony of Denner's Wreck. Surprised and pleased by what they found, they settled down for an extended vacation there.

Bredon asked that the story stop again.

The Powers, then, came from Terra, just as his own people had; they were not from the world of the dead at all. Their power came from the magic called "technology."

"This 'technology' thing," he asked. "Is it something that people are born with, or something that they learn?"

The spirits were silent for a moment, trying to devise an

answer that would be correct, informative, and intelligible, but finally Gamesmaster settled for saying, "It's something they learn."

"Could I learn it?"

Gamesmaster hesitated. "Some of it," it said. "Without treatment, you won't live long enough to learn *all* current technological knowledge. Sorry, kid."

Bredon accepted that.

He reviewed what he had been told, and balked at one detail: "A *vacation?* A holiday? But the Powers have been here for centuries!"

"It's been a long vacation. Some of them have wanted to leave, at various times, but there's only one ship, and the rule is that unless there's an emergency of some kind they need a majority vote to go, and so far there have never been more than eleven out of twenty-eight voting for departure at any one time. If somebody wanted off urgently enough he or she could transmit a call for another ship, but so far nobody's bothered to do that. It's a nice planet."

"But *hundreds* of years?"

"Hey, these people live *forever* if they want to; they can spare a few hundred years."

Bredon had to chew on that idea for a while before he was able to shove it into the back of his mind, still undigested.

"So that's who the Powers are, and how they got here? And who my people are, and how *they* got here?"

"You got it, kid. And you don't know how lucky you are to be here, either. Ordinarily, a shipwreck like the one your ancestors lived through doesn't leave a viable colony behind; either the planet isn't habitable, or it's full of hostile native life, or some other such problem. And when the colony *does* survive, they usually rebuild a higher technology in order to fight off the indigenous life. Your people hit the jackpot, though; this place had enough sea life to provide an oxygen atmosphere, and no land life at all. No moons to make tidal pools, not much volcanic activity, not much land, for that matter, nothing to help land life along, so the stuff they brought with them had no competition and just dug right in."

Bredon did not really follow that, since as far as he knew there had always been plenty of life on land. He decided that Gamesmaster was trying to explain something about why salt-water fish and other sea creatures weren't edible. It did not seem particularly important. "Is there any more to the story?" he asked.

''Not the mainline history lesson, no. That brings us about up to date on that. But whatever other area you're interested in, I can tell you more.''

Bredon blinked, unsure where to begin; he thought for a moment, and then asked, ''Why is Thaddeus the Black causing trouble? Why is Geste so worried about him?''

''That's hard to explain without telling you a lot of stuff about just who Thaddeus is.''

''Tell me, then,'' Bredon said. ''I'm listening.'' He settled back in his seat, started as it shifted shape to accommodate him, and then relaxed, his eyes and ears open.

Chapter Twelve

"... there before him stood a menacing figure in black robes, fully three meters tall, with eyes of flame and with fangs showing between his lips.

"The apparition spoke, saying, 'I am Thaddeus the Black, and like your brothers before you, you have dared to defy me. Know, then, the price of defiance!' And he reached into his cloak and flung something down before Hillowan.

"He looked down, and saw that it was his brother Filowan's head, the eyes wide and staring, the mouth frozen in a scream of terror. He took a step back, and Thaddeus reached again into his cloak, and flung another head.

"This one was Gilloran's and, most horrible of all, the severed head was still alive! It rolled its eyes up at Hillowan, pleading with him, and tried to speak, but of course it had no lungs to give it breath, so that no sound came out. Hillowan screamed, and stepped back again.

"And Thaddeus opened his cloak and drew forth a third object, but this time it was no severed head, but something that hung limply in his hand, like a rag; and he flung it down before Hillowan, who saw that it was skin, that it was human skin—that it was the skin of his third and youngest brother, Sherowan, somehow peeled from his body in a single piece ..."

—FROM THE TALES OF ATHERON THE STORYTELLER

The first known immortal human, Gamesmaster explained, was the man who now called himself Shadowdark. That was not his original name, merely the one he had adopted most recently; it had now lasted a few thousand years, longer than any other he had ever used, including the long-forgotten one his parents had given him.

Shadowdark's immortality was not the result of technology, but a freak of nature, something he was born with. For all anyone knew, the same freak might have happened dozens of times before or since, but only Shadowdark and a handful of his descendants survived the myriad diseases and omnipresent dangers to life and limb that presumably killed off all the other people born with the same peculiarity.

Shadowdark's great peculiarity was in the way he grew. Once he reached adolescence he grew very, very slowly, at a steadily decreasing rate—but never completely stopped. At the age of thirty he stood less than a meter and a half in height; at sixty he still looked thirty, but stood just over 160 centimeters, as nearly as he could recall.

Since centimeters had not yet been invented at the time, and no records existed except Shadowdark's memory, the exact height might not be right, but the basic concept was. Shadowdark's body never finished growing, never made the transition from growth to maturity—and therefore to decay.

Bredon interrupted, "Like a tree, you mean?"

"Yes, pretty much like a tree," Gamesmaster agreed.

"But trees eventually die anyway, when they get too big."

"I know that; I'm coming to that."

There were limits to Shadowdark's growth, of course, Gamesmaster continued; eventually, when he was slightly over two thousand years old, his heart gave out and had to be repaired, and later his skeleton collapsed under its own weight, and he had to have most of it replaced. Fortunately, by the time his natural longevity began to fail him, technology had reached the point where it could take over and keep him going indefinitely. Otherwise, he would have died long ago. If any immortals had been born much before Shadowdark, they would surely be dead by now in any case, since medical technology had not advanced quickly enough to have saved them.

"Are you sure?" Bredon asked.

"No," Gamesmaster answered. "Who's telling this, you or me?"

"You are."

"Then shut up."

Bredon shut up, and Gamesmaster went on with his story.

In his early years, before he fully realized just how unique he was, Shadowdark had tried to lead a normal life. His peculiarity forced him to relocate every twenty or thirty years, establishing a new identity each time, but in between these moves he did his best to maintain a home and family and business.

Later on, he found the constant loss of wives, friends, and children to be too depressing, and experimented with a variety of life-styles. By then, however, he had left behind a good many children, and a few of them had inherited his abnormal growth pattern.

Most of these died eventually, by violence or from disease, but a few managed to survive. Daughters did very poorly; bearing children in those primitive times significantly increased their risks.

His son Peter was the oldest survivor. He was born when Shadowdark was less than a century old and still living in his native land.

The second was Thaddeus. He was born in a land that had been conquered and abused by Shadowdark's people; Gamesmaster provided the name and date, but neither meant anything to Bredon. He ignored all the names and dates on Terra as essentially meaningless; the only important fact was that this land was being mistreated by Shadowdark's countrymen.

Shadowdark had fled to this place at the age of a century or so, no longer welcome in his own country, and had taken a local woman as his wife. The marriage had not been happy, and Thaddeus was not a happy child—particularly after his father abandoned him and his sisters.

Gamesmaster displayed an image of Thaddeus, and Bredon asked, "Why is he called Thaddeus the Black? He isn't much darker than I am."

"*I* don't know," Gamesmaster said. "I suppose it has something to do with his temper, or his record."

"Oh." Bredon shut up, and Gamesmaster continued.

Shadowdark and Thaddeus found each other again decades later, and were, in time, apparently reconciled with one another, their disagreements not so much forgotten as temporarily set aside. They saw one another off and on over the centuries, sometimes traveling together or even living together for a time, but the relationship always had its unpleasant side. The only thing that really held them together—far more important than their blood relationship—was their shared memories. They were the only people still alive who remembered the land of Thaddeus's birth and the people they had known and loved there. Peter, the only other person of approximately the same age, did not visit that land until centuries later, when everything had been altered beyond recognition.

When he was nearing two thousand years of age, Shadowdark went through a bad period. Gamesmaster could provide no details, but apparently the enforced isolation and duplicity of being an immortal in a world of mortals had driven him temporarily insane. When he recovered, he decided that he needed a goal, something worthy of an immortal, something that would distract him and that might somehow put an end to his loneliness.

What he hit upon was the accumulation of wealth and power. He had pursued both before, but had never bothered to hold on to them for long. Neither greatly interested him in and of itself.

Now, however, what he intended to do was to buy himself into a position where he could reveal his immortality without fearing that jealous mortals would kill or imprison him.

At first he had planned on an island, where he could establish himself as a god-king, but before he could achieve this modest goal humans began to make their first steps toward traveling to other worlds, and the idea of having an entire world to himself appealed to him. He set his sights on ruling his own planet.

When he had his planet, finally, he needed something to do with it, and therefore set out to conquer others, as well. It gave him something to do to pass the time, something that he had not done before.

The end result was the Imperium, which at its peak united twenty-four worlds under Shadowdark's absolute rule. This, Gamesmaster noted, was long after Denner's Wreck had been found and then lost again. In fact, even the first planet, Alpha Imperium, had not been found until after Denner's Wreck had been lost.

"Why didn't he go to another world sooner, then?" Bredon asked. "Why didn't he come here?"

"Because he wanted a world of his *own,* not just to be a member of a colony."

"But if he'd lived so long, had so much experience, couldn't he have conquered a planet like this one?"

"Well, yeah, he probably could have, but he didn't."

"Why not?"

"How the hell should I know? I'm just a dumb machine; all I know is what's in the records or what people have told me, all right?"

"All right," Bredon said, somewhat cowed by this outburst.

"May I go on?"

"Please, go on."

"Thank you." Gamesmaster paused, in imitation of a human gathering his wits, and then continued its tale.

Like everything else, it explained, even absolute power will eventually bore an immortal. Furthermore, during Shadowdark's reign on Alpha Imperium, artificial immortality, using tailored symbiotes and genetic reprogramming, had been developed and become widespread, so that he no longer needed to disguise his agelessness. In time, he lost interest in the Imperium and left.

Before leaving, however, he located his son Peter, and appointed him as the new ruler in his stead. To leave the empire without a monarch would have been unnecessary cruelty; he had set the entire system up so that it revolved around himself, and with his departure the whole structure would have collapsed into anarchy and civil war had he not appointed a replacement.

Peter, however, found he had little taste for power, and furthermore was not very good at wielding it. After less than a century he grew tired of the whole thing and turned it over to Thaddeus.

Thaddeus enjoyed power very much. Unfortunately, he was far worse than his father or half brother at using it. His brutal abuse of his subjects and utter ineptitude in running the economy and foreign policy resulted in a messy revolution. He was overthrown, driven from his palace, and seemed to vanish. No one knew what had become of him.

Sure enough, as Shadowdark had feared, the Imperium immediately collapsed, and Alpha Imperium sank into barbarism. Stupid little wars between different factions destroyed almost its entire civilization.

Centuries later Thaddeus reappeared, still on Alpha Imperium, at the heart of the fallen empire. He tried to conquer the planet and to restore the Imperium to its former power and glory.

He failed miserably, and was overthrown once again. He did manage to build a single starship on a planet that had a technology little better than Bredon's people had on Denner's Wreck, which was quite an impressive accomplishment in itself, but he was unable to put together any sort of empire. This time, when he was defeated, he fled from Alpha Imperium to Terra, where he located his father.

What his purpose might have been in rejoining Shadowdark Gamesmaster did not know and did not care to guess. Whatever the reason, he stayed with Shadowdark and his current group of companions—playmates, really—for a couple of years, and accompanied them on their jaunt in search of Denner's Wreck. The other members of the party had optimistically assumed that Thaddeus had returned to his senses and given up his dreams of absolute power. After all, being free to use Terran technology on a primitive planet should be power enough for any sane person.

Now, though, 462 years later, Geste suspected that Thaddeus might be returning to his vicious and warlike ways, and feared that he planned to conquer Denner's Wreck and use it as a base to build a new empire. Gamesmaster thought Geste was right.

Thaddeus had a good chance, too, because the other immortals on the planet were disorganized and generally harmless.

"Harmless?" Bredon yelped. "The Powers are harmless?"

"To each other, yes," Gamesmaster replied. "Not to you mortals, no, but to each other."

Of them all, it explained, only Aulden the Technician really understood all the technology they used, only Aulden had the capacity to create entirely new technology; and Aulden had disappeared while visiting Thaddeus. Only Brenner of the Mountains had ever maintained much of an arsenal, and Thaddeus was in the process of wearing that down. Most of the rest would surrender quickly, rather than bother to fight; their lives were very precious to them, and they would assume that they could simply outlive whatever scheme Thaddeus might have in mind.

One of the usual traits of an immortal is the conviction that anything can be lived through, that nothing is worse than death. When one has infinite time in which to find a way out of an unpleasant situation, one has little need to hurry or do anything rash, and the idea of risking eternity is not at all appealing.

And the mortals of Denner's Wreck simply did not have the technology to oppose Thaddeus. He would probably either ignore them completely, or recruit a few as servants and soldiers.

Geste was not willing to surrender, however. He did not care to see Thaddeus at the head of an army again. Too many people were likely to die. Even short-lifers' lives were precious, after all.

And Geste knew enough of Thaddeus's history to suspect that even if the other immortals surrendered, Thaddeus might still kill them all, just to be on the safe side.

"Even Shadowdark?" Bredon asked.

"I guess so, kid."

"His own father?"

"We don't think that would stop him."

Bredon mulled that over for a moment.

He had not followed all the details of the story—much of it, such as all the stuff about empires, was simply too alien—but he had caught the gist of it. Thaddeus wanted to bully everybody. He had tried running things twice before, and botched it both times. He was on this world, Bredon's world, because he had gone running to his father after the second disaster, and had tagged along when Shadowdark came here.

Shadowdark puzzled Bredon. How could he be so disinterested? And why was he so hideous?

"Why does Shadowdark look like that?" he asked.

"Just lazy, I guess. He's got all the technology he needs to keep him alive, but he doesn't bother with anything to keep him looking good. And he's looked a little strange for a long time; after all, he's thousands of years old, and he never stopped growing."

"He *still* hasn't stopped?"

"He still hasn't stopped. He stands almost three meters tall now, but he needs machines to help him stand at all. Most of his body has broken down and been rebuilt or replaced. He's a mess."

"Is it *worth* living forever, like that?"

"I wouldn't know, kid, I'm just a glorified household gadget. All I know is silicon life; you're the carbon-based life, you tell me whether it's worth it. Shadowdark seems to think it is."

Bredon shuddered slightly.

He decided that he didn't want to think about Shadowdark or Thaddeus or any of the other Powers for a while. The reference to itself as a household gadget, although incomprehensible to him in itself—as were the references to carbon and silicon—suggested another, more appealing topic. "Tell me about technology," he said.

"Good grief, kid, that's a hell of a tall order. Where do you want me to start?"

"I don't know. I want to know all about the magic that Geste and the other Powers use, how they do all those things—floating in the air and turning things invisible and all the rest. And I want to know about the spirits they talk to, like you and that thing on the platform and the one Geste called a housekeeper at that place in the mountains."

"I guess I could teach you how to work the gadgets Geste has around the place. Do you care *why* they work, or do you just want to know how to use them?"

"I just want to know how to use them—at least for now."

"Good enough. I can do that with imprinting, I won't need to spend hours showing you pictures. Okay, kid, you're on. I'll teach you the whole routine, from tailored microbes to pocket universes, whatever we've got on hand. Step right this way."

The surrounding darkness vanished, and Bredon found himself once more in the vast white-ribbed chamber he had seen upon first arriving. The enchanted grove still stood nearby, and the vines still clung to the walls. He realized that he had never left the room, despite the changes in color and light, that most of the chamber had simply been hidden. All the spirits and miracles that had attended him had been right there—he had been bathed and fed and instructed all in this same spot.

Now everything except the walls, the vines, and the forest had vanished.

The room was totally silent when neither he nor Gamesmaster was speaking. Noticing the grove, Bredon wondered why the leaves on the trees did not rustle, then saw that there was no wind to move them. That the little animals that lived in them made no noise at all was rather more surprising.

That was not particularly important, however. The forest was just a distraction from what Gamesmaster wanted to show him.

An oval door had appeared, two meters tall and a meter wide, in the nearest white wall. The nearby vines pulled aside and it irised open. Strange soft music spilled out.

Bredon was obviously expected to go through it, but he hesitated. Could he trust this familiar spirit?

"Come on, kid, it won't bite you," Gamesmaster said. "Right this way, and I'll teach you the basics of running a modern household."

Bredon gathered his courage, stood, and strode across the room and through the door.

Chapter Thirteen

". . . rowed to the place where he had first seen the lights in the water below, and there he waited, patiently, just as he had before.

"Darkness fell, and he looked down through the water, but as always he saw nothing until the time was right.

"The midwake darkness deepened with the passing of an hour, and than another hour, so that the middledark hour was almost upon him, when he looked down over the side of his boat again, and this time he saw them—tiny lights, red and green and gold, twinkling in the lake, not far below him at all.

"With the lights to guide him, he dove over the side of his boat and plunged down into the lake, as he had before. And, as before, when he was scarcely two meters into the water the top of his head hit something, crack! And as before he fainted, and would have thought he would drown had he not known what to expect.

"Of course, he did not drown; he awoke lying in a fine bed in a richly appointed chamber, and knew that he was once again in the underwater palace of the Lady of the Lake.

" 'Hello,' he called. 'Can you hear me?'

" 'Yes, of course,' said a voice, and he turned his head to see the Lady herself approaching. 'I see it's you again,' she said. 'What is it this time?'

" 'I need a new boat,' the fisherman told her. 'A bigger, finer one. The other fishermen say that a boat like mine is nothing special, nothing worthy of the Lady of the Lake, and that you could not have given it to me, for if you had I would have the biggest, finest boat that ever floated.'

"And the Lady's eyes grew wide, and she puffed up her chest, and she shouted at him in a fury, 'You dare to come here demanding another new boat? You dare? When you wrecked your own boat against the invisible towers of my home, I took pity upon you, for I saw that I had unintentionally harmed you, and so I gave you a new boat, just like the one that was wrecked. But that boat was not good enough—you had lost time from your work, and had been injured, so you came back and I gave you a bigger, better boat. And you came back and told me that the boat was too big for your old nets, so I gave you new nets that can never break or snag. And you came back again, and again, and each time I gave you what you asked. But now you want an entirely new boat, and why? Merely so you can brag more easily!'

"Her eyes were red with fury, and her fingers sprouted long,

99

*curving claws as she said, 'I have had enough! I wronged you, and
I tried to atone, but you, in your greed, will not leave well enough
alone. I am out of patience, and your greed has been your downfall!'*

*"And then the room vanished from about him, and he found
himself being swept up into the sky atop a waterspout. The Lady
of the Lake had vanished, but he could still hear her voice.*

*" 'You are a fisherman no more! If you ever again venture out
onto the water, for any reason, then I shall send demons to tear
you to ribbons and feast on your screaming soul!'*

*"And then the waterspout vanished as the sun appeared in the
east, heralding secondlight, and he found himself alone and
naked, cast up on the beach with nothing at all, his boat gone,
his clothes gone, everything that he had had, lost . . ."*

—FROM THE TALES OF ATHERON THE STORYTELLER

Light sparkled from the rippling water around the invisible
turret, and Geste blinked; the glare was too diffuse for his optic
symbiote to handle readily, leaving him to the more primitive
methods of his own reflexes and eyelids.

"Has it ever occurred to you," Anna demanded, glaring at
him as harshly as the scattered sunlight, her hands on her naked
hips, "that maybe Brenner brought this on himself? You know as
well as I do that he probably started the fight himself, took a
potshot at Thaddeus over some stupid little squabble. That would
be just like him—him and that damned arsenal of his. Only this
time, Thaddeus was ready—or maybe he had Aulden ready, I
don't know. But it was probably Brenner. You just think it's
Thaddeus who's at fault because of what he did on Alpha Imperium, and that's not fair, holding all that against him. That was
hundreds of years ago. And not only was it hundreds of years
ago, but it was on a different planet and in an entirely different
situation. He hasn't caused any trouble here on Denner's Wreck,
has he? He certainly hasn't bothered *me*."

"He's causing trouble now," Geste pointed out.

"No," Anna corrected, waggling a finger, "he's *involved*, but
you don't know he *caused* it. I'll bet Brenner started it."

"Maybe he did," Geste conceded desperately, blinking again,
"but it's getting out of hand. If you don't care about Brenner,
what about Sheila, and Sunlight, and Rawl, and Khalid, and O?"

"Khalid and O probably aren't even there," Anna retorted.
"They're probably off somewhere together by themselves with
an airskiff of sex toys. It's been decades since I saw either of
them play with another human being, unless you want to count

Khalid's little flings with the native girls, and they're both of them overdue for a bit of quiet companionship.''

"Mother tracked them to Fortress Holding, though." The rippling sunlight was unbearable; he darkened the lenses of his eyes, even though it left him half-blind and reduced Anna to a shadow. He did not really care to see the details of her nude body, in any case, nor did he need to watch her expression for nuances of emotion; her words made her attitude perfectly clear.

"Maybe they left by the back way, shielded. They went there of their own free will, didn't they? How do you know they aren't staying there as Thaddeus's guests?''

Geste saw that he was not getting anywhere on that tack, and rather than chase any further through Anna's unlikely scenario he switched his ground. "All right, we don't know about them, but what about the others?''

Anna snorted in a manner hardly befitting the dignity of a demigoddess. "Rawl deserves a little trouble, the way he keeps poking his nose into other people's business! He came by here a few years back and ruined my entire day, lecturing me over some stupid argument I'd had with a fisherman.'' She waved in the direction of the nearest village.

"But Sheila and Sunlight—'' Geste began.

"All right, all right,'' Anna said, raising her hands briefly in mock surrender, as if she were making a great concession, "I guess they got caught in the middle, but I'm sure Thaddeus isn't going to hurt them. He probably won't even hurt Brenner, just teach him a lesson by blowing apart that stupid castle of his. It would serve him right.''

"But how do you *know* he won't hurt anyone? Thaddeus *does* have a pretty nasty record, even if he's behaved himself lately.''

"I know that, but give him a chance! You . . . Look, Geste, I know you mean well, and I suppose you're sincerely concerned about this, but it's none of my business if he and Brenner are having a fight. You're a lot younger than I am; maybe you can still get worked up about what's right and wrong instead of what's comfortable, but I'm just not interested. It's not my problem. If one of them starts interfering in *my* business, then I'll be glad to help, but if they only pick on each other, why should I care?''

Geste had no clear answer to that. "Honestly, Anna,'' he said, "I really do think Thaddeus is trying to do here what he did on Alpha Imperium. I think he may be recruiting troops from the short-lifers for building a new empire. A lot of people could get hurt if we don't stop him.''

"Just short-lifers and troublemakers like Brenner. He's not going to bother me, Geste, and he's never going to be able to bother any of the *civilized* planets—where would he get the firepower? And as for the people here, what do I care about short-lifers?"

"Well, they're people, too, aren't they?"

"I suppose they are, but they're all going to die anyway. What difference will a few years make?"

Exasperated, Geste burst out, "Don't you have any sense of responsibility toward your fellow creatures?"

"No," Anna retorted, "I don't. I have my own problems."

"Ha!" Infuriated, Geste turned away and marched across the turret roof, back to his waiting platform. The turret was a hole in the lake beneath him, leading down into Anna's hold, but with his eyes dimmed he could see nothing but darkness below.

The instant he had both feet aboard the platform, it lifted him upward, sailing toward the island that floated above Lake Anna.

He looked up sullenly at the jagged black rocks overhead, undimming his eyes as he did and wishing that the Skyler had put her hold further east, where it would have blocked the sun and left him debating Anna in its shadow, instead of half-blinded by the sun.

He had never expected unanimity in opposing whatever scheme Thaddeus might be hatching, but he was still distressed by the results of his excursions. He had thought at least *some* of his fellows would join him, if only as an amusing diversion.

No one had. He had spoken to them all now—all who would agree to listen, at any rate. Anna had been the last, and his only companions remained Imp and the Skyler. Two, out of twenty-seven.

No, he corrected himself as the platform slid up past the sharp stone edge of the Skyland's disk and green lawns appeared before him, Thaddeus did not count, which left twenty-six, and seven of those had vanished or were under attack. Two out of nineteen had chosen to join him.

That was still a really lousy ratio. He grimaced, wondering if Thaddeus had intentionally attacked those most likely to resist, or whether it was just luck.

The other seventeen might well come to regret their decision. Arguing that Thaddeus might kill them all had seemed so melodramatic, so impossible, that he had not even suggested it to most of them, but nonetheless he believed it to be true. Thaddeus was a vicious, ruthless killer, a sociopath; he had demonstrated that repeatedly on Alpha Imperium. That he had harmed no other immortal for five hundred years proved nothing. For all they knew he could have killed dozens of short-lifer natives. Besides, he had lived for seven thousand years, which was plenty of time to learn patience.

The others must know that, being immortals themselves, but still they refused to acknowledge that one of their own comrades might be a danger. To them, Thaddeus was not the Imperial Butcher, the man who had been reputed to eat small children; he was just old Thaddeus, Shadowdark's kid, arrogant and foul-tempered, but harmless.

If they had thought otherwise, how could they have justified not turning him in centuries ago, back on Terra?

How, Geste asked himself, had *he* ever justified not turning Thaddeus in?

He had gone along with the rest. Basking in the subtle glory of keeping company with the oldest human alive, none of them had wanted to risk offending Shadowdark. And Thaddeus himself was the third-oldest human alive, millennia older than the rest of them. No one had wanted to antagonize him.

Thaddeus had claimed that he was not a murderer, as the Alpha Imperials called him, but only a political outlaw. He had been an absolute monarch at the time of his alleged crimes, granted the power of life and death by the laws of Alpha Imperium; his actions were not illegal, not murder, until retroactively declared to be by the governments that had replaced him.

Besides, his companions had told themselves, even if he had committed mass murder, he was the product of ancient times, when humankind was violent and wild. His father, Shadowdark, had once admitted to having committed a string of murders during his worst period, several thousand years ago, yet no one had ever considered turning *him* in. Murder was said to have no statute of limitations, but after five thousand years it became hard to take it very seriously. No government existed that would try Shadowdark for those crimes.

Excuses, Geste thought in disgust, simply excuses. They had not turned in Thaddeus or Shadowdark because they all found a rare and subtle thrill in the presence of these strange and ancient men. Such thrills were not lightly discarded by bored immortals.

And none of them, save he and the Imp and Skyler—three of the youngest in the group—were willing to admit their mistake and take action against Thaddeus now. Immortals, Geste reminded himself bitterly, tended to became very set in their ways.

The platform passed over the last of the bare stone of the Skyland's outermost rim and skimmed across a close-trimmed lawn. A few of the Skyler's creatures scampered past. Ahead of him Geste saw the main house, its roofline like broken and tumbling rocks, windows peeking out from beneath every angle.

The Skyler and Imp were seated on a verandah, waiting for him, as the platform settled smoothly down onto the grass a few meters from the house. He stepped off and walked slowly up the gentle slope to join them.

"We heard it all," Imp said, pointing toward the ground to indicate what lay below. "Now what?"

"Can just the three of us do anything?" the Skyler asked nervously, brushing at her bottle green gown. A floater hovered near her hand, holding a drink that Geste guessed to be mildly sedative—or would she just have her symbiotes adjust her mood? No, he thought, she was the sort of person who preferred not to rely overmuch on her internal devices, organic or otherwise. The drink was probably drugged.

"I don't know if we can do anything or not," he said. "But we can try. Imp, back at the Falls, do you have anything that we could use as a weapon?"

"I don't think so," she said slowly, "but I don't really know. After all, Geste, the Falls is Aulden's hold, not mine. I just live there, off and on, when I get tired of wandering. I didn't help design it. I don't know what he might have tucked away. But I do know that he never mentioned any weapons, and I've never seen any."

"Would any of your intelligences know?"

"I don't know."

"Ask them."

Imp nodded, and held up a hand; a small, amorphous floater, her primary long-range communications system, wrapped itself invisibly around her upraised fingers and tapped into her nervous system. Although he could not see the floater itself, Geste recognized the gesture and the subsequent light trance. Imp had never liked carrying her equipment internally, and kept a small flock of floaters instead.

While she was communing with the device, Geste asked the Skyler, "What about you? Do you have any weapons aboard?"

The Skyler shook her head. "Weapons scare me. I stay up here so I won't need any; there's nothing the short-lifers here can possibly do that would reach the Skyland. And until Imp called me about Thaddeus and Aulden, I didn't think I needed to worry about the rest of you." She glared at him accusingly.

Geste nodded. He had expected as much.

Imp finished her silent contact and reported, visibly upset,

"Aulden *did* have weapons, lots of them, but he took them with him! Thaddeus didn't even need to build most of his arsenal; he just stole Aulden's! Domo says there isn't anything left that could be of any use."

That was bad news indeed.

"We may not have much time left to prepare, if Thaddeus already has Aulden's entire arsenal," Geste said. "I told my housekeeper to see what weapons it could come up with; I think it's time we went and picked those up and then headed for the High Castle, to help those people while we still can. If Aulden's provided the weapons, Thaddeus can probably break in there anytime he wants to make the effort. He hasn't yet—I've got the place under surveillance—but I don't know why not."

Imp nodded. "Hurry! Once he's sure he has all the weapons he needs, he may *kill* Aulden!"

The Skyler hesitated, and Imp turned on her. "Go! Go! Go, you silly woman! What are you standing there for? Get this rock moving!"

The Skyler waved a command, and the Skyland began moving southward, steadily picking up speed.

Chapter Fourteen

". . . she turned the next corner, certain that it had to be the last, that she would see the great wooden door leading out onto the rocks above the sea, but instead she found herself back in the little stone room once again, where Lady Haze still sat before the fire, rocking and knitting, the strange music box tinkling beside her.

" 'Hello, my dear,' said Lady Haze. 'Have you given up yet?'

" 'No!' the girl said. 'I know I can find my way out!'

"Lady Haze sighed and put down her knitting and got up from her chair. 'No, my dear,' she said. 'You can't find your way out unless I permit it. I told you, I am the mistress of this castle, and of the rocks on which it stands, and the fog that surrounds it, and the sea below. Nothing happens here that escapes me, and no one who comes here escapes me until I let her go. Within these walls I am the absolute ruler of all. Now, if you will give me back my jewel and swear that you will never enter my castle again, I shall let you out, and you will be free to return to your home. If you persist in this foolish attempt to leave, and still deny that you stole it when I can see it in your pocket right now, then you may well spend the rest of your life wandering about these passages.'

"And the girl broke down, defeated, and pulled the glowing gem from her pocket and gave it to the woman, weeping as she did so.

"Lady Haze accepted the jewel, and then turned and pointed. 'There is your way out,' she said.

"And the thief turned, and to her astonishment the great wooden door was right there, in the same room, where she knew only a blank stone wall had been just a moment before. She ran to the door and flung it open and stepped out, and found herself on the wet black rocks outside, the sea roaring behind her and gulls screaming overhead. She turned to look, and the door she had just come through was gone; the castle wall behind her was bare stone. The sky was gray and dim, the sun low in the west, and wisps of fog were rolling in, so she knew that soon it would be full dark, and foggy as well, making the rocks a very dangerous place to be; she despaired of her task and fled for the village, leaving the castle behind her, to vanish in the fog.

"And I might end her tale there, save for one curious detail. She was in Castle Haze for a wake or so, she believed—a light and a dark and a light—having entered at first dawn and left, she thought, at second sunset. But when she returned to her village, she learned that

*she had been gone for almost a season, more than eight tensleeps, and
long since given up for dead!"*
          —FROM THE TALES OF ATHERON THE STORYTELLER

Bredon had long ago lost track of time, and it occurred to him,
as he sat at the entertainment console sketching commands on a
sensor with his thumb, to ask Gamesmaster how long he had
been in Arcade. Before him, naked women who had never lived
anywhere but in his imagination danced obscenely. Several bore
a remarkable resemblance to Lady Sunlight, but he had never
dared to intentionally depict her.

The machine's answer shocked him. He flicked the sensor
aside, and the holographic display he had been manipulating
vanished in a mist of pinkish sparkle, leaving only the faint scent
of female sweat that he had added for an extra touch of realism.

"Four wakes?" he said, looking up at the vermilion ceiling.
"Just four wakes?"

"Well, seven lights, anyway; it's just now first sunset outside."

"Is that *all?*"

"Hey, kid, it's enough!" Gamesmaster replied. "What did
you think?"

"I've learned so much," Bredon said, marveling, "it feels as
if I've been here a season or more!"

Gamesmaster buzzed derisively. "Not hardly. You've slept
just four times; did you think you were going a couple of dozen
wakes at a time?"

"I don't know; I lost track, spending all that time under the
ne . . . nyoo . . . ''

"Neural-pattern imprinter."

"That's right, the imprinter. That seemed to last forever,
sometimes."

"It generally took about ten seconds a shot."

"I know, I just . . . Wait a minute." He paused, readjusting
himself to the real world after hours in the fantasyland of high
technology. "Four wakes? Has Geste been back?"

"No, he hasn't, not yet, but as a matter of fact he's on his way
right now."

"I thought he must have come and gone while I was being
taught," Bredon said, concerned. "What took so long? Has
something gone wrong?"

"That's hard to say," Gamesmaster replied judiciously. "He
didn't exactly set any recruiting records, but so far nobody's shot
at him since he left the mountains."

"Who does he have as allies now?"

"The same two he started with: Imp and the Skyler."

Startled, Bredon asked, "No one else?"

"No one else. He got resounding disinterest from all the rest, from Starflower to the Lady of the Lake."

"Can the three of them stop Thaddeus?" Bredon asked worriedly.

"How the hell should *I* know?" Gamesmaster's voice remained fairly calm, but Bredon knew it was upset.

"Sorry, I guess that wasn't a fair question," he said.

"It's all right. I guess we're both a little nervous."

Bredon hesitated, then asked, "Can an arti . . . artif . . . artificial intelligence be nervous? A silicon one, I mean?"

"Well, technically, kid, I don't really know if it's what *you* would consider nervousness, but it works for me. I feel it in situations that ought to make someone nervous, and not in others, and it's uncomfortable, so I call it nervousness."

"I guess that's nervousness, then. After all, I don't really know how other humans feel, just what *I* feel."

"Hey, you've got it exactly! Although I have the equipment to hook you up to someone else so you *do* feel what they do, if you want. But you'd need a volunteer to hook up to."

"Oh, that's all right," Bredon said hastily, "I'm not that curious."

"The boss should be landing soon; he's just left the Skyland."

"Uh . . . why *did* he come back here, if he didn't get any more recruits? To pick me up?"

"Not hardly, kid. Don't get exaggerated ideas of your own importance. I don't think he plans to take you anywhere. He's here to pick up the weapons I've been whipping up for him."

"That's right, Bredon," Geste's voice said from nowhere.

"Hey, boss, that's not nice! I hadn't had a chance to tell him you were listening!"

"I'm sure he doesn't mind."

"Well, I—" Bredon began.

"See?" Geste cut him off. "So, Gamesmaster, what little surprises have we got for Thaddeus?"

Bredon leaned forward in his seat and tapped panels on the console; a wall screen blinked, and he found himself looking at a flawless three-dimensional image of Arcade's entrance hall where he had slept that first dark, home to the "enchanted forest" where almost all Geste's carbon-based playthings lived. The ceiling was rolling back to admit a flying platform. The Trickster himself, wearing dark red this time, stood aboard the airskiff.

"Well, boss, not as much as you might like, I'm sure,"

Gamesmaster said. "I've whipped up a lot of plain-vanilla energy weapons, up and down the spectrum, most of them mobile and semi-intelligent and the rest portable miniatures, but I'll bet my last circuit that Thaddeus can defend against every damn one of them. I can't nail down his gene pattern exactly enough to tailor a personal virus—anything I can come up with by approximation has a good chance of killing someone else, usually Shadowdark, but sometimes Sheila or Feura, and it might get any number of short-lifers, so I haven't done any antipersonnel microbes at all. I've done some limited-field sabotage germs—stuff that can eat hell out of equipment but won't spread much. The problem with those is getting them into the systems they're bred for, and of course, he may have bacteriophagic protective systems; if he's as paranoid as his record implies, he might have his entire demesne laced with his own swarm of bug-eaters."

"What about his personal modifications, symbiotes, whatever?"

"We don't have good records on those, boss; remember, he's a born immortal, so he doesn't need as much symbiosis as most of you. I've worked up some bugs that I think might possibly eat out what he's got in his bloodstream, but you need to get them close. And of course, he may have added more that we don't know about at all, and he's sure to have his immune system alarm-rigged and multilayered. Basically, boss, unless he's been sloppy, I don't think we can get at him with anything microscopic, but we may be able to invade some of his equipment and rot out the soft parts. And I've got some macroscopic stuff I'm working on, but even with forced growth and imprinted training I don't have anything bigger than a cockroach yet, and what I *do* have is dumber than dirt. They'll eat plastic, though, and dodge anything that moves, and they can take pretty high voltage without frying. I used what we had, but we didn't have anything in the forest that I could use unmodified. Those little brains don't hold much unless you build it into the genes, and they'd need better claws and teeth and defenses, so I've mostly been growing new ones, not training the ones we had. I'm working on some machine-killer mice, but they need another five wakes, minimum."

"We probably don't have five wakes."

"I know, boss, that's why I didn't bother with a metal-eating rhinoceros."

Geste, standing on his platform in the entrance chamber, cast a startled look in the direction of Gamesmaster's central processor. "Is that a joke?"

"Matter of opinion, I guess."

Geste smiled, and would have laughed aloud under other circumstances. "Have you got anything else?" he asked.

"Sure, boss, lots of it, hardware and software both, and a lot of it is already launched and trying to burrow into Fortress Holding, or riding in on the airwaves looking for a foothold. Saboteurs of all kinds. I think we may have taken out a few of his peripheral systems already, but I don't have enough feedback to be certain, and he's so decentralized and layered that it may not matter. And I've been working on space-benders and time-warping stuff; I've got a half-decent pocket-sized stasis field generator ready to go."

"Good, that's all good; I'm proud of you. Start loading it all on the Skyland, then, and see if you can give me an inventory, with instructions for use, that I can load into inboard memory."

"You got it, boss; transmitting to your skull-liner now."

Bredon had listened to all this with fascination. Even after his incredible cram course in Terran technology, he did not follow all of it. He had no idea what a rhinoceros was, or mice. Cockroaches he knew well, since the world—Denner's Wreck—had plenty of them. Microbes in general he was very vague about. He had not had time to learn everything, by any means, not even everything that was used in Arcade. At Gamesmaster's suggestion he had focused on the inorganic technology used in Arcade, emphasizing silicon- and metal-based systems rather than carbon-based life or warped space.

A stasis field generator? He knew what various field generators were, but not what a stasis field was.

He had encountered, but did not really understand, descriptions of the artificial symbiotes that the immortals had living inside them, augmenting the natural repair and maintenance mechanisms of their bodies and providing them with some of their "supernatural" powers. He knew now that his bruised nose and other injuries received in trying to break into the Forbidden Grove had been repaired by an offshoot of one of Geste's symbiotes.

What he chose to ask, though, was "What's a skull-liner?"

"Oh, it's a computer that's grown onto the inside of the boss's skull, inside his head, where it can link itself to his brain. Gives him a few gigabytes of extra memory when he needs it, and lets me feed him information at high speed."

"What sort of a computer?"

"Silicon crystal, mostly."

"I thought silicon life was built; I didn't think silicon computers grew."

"They don't, by themselves; the skull-liner was installed by programmed silicon-skeleton bacteria."

"Oh." The thought of tiny creatures growing into a machine in his head was somehow repulsive; he shuddered slightly.

His recent experiences had shaken him. Terran technology was overwhelming in its diversity, complexity, and power. He now truly understood that a Power, a Terran, could do almost anything with the right equipment—but so could anyone else.

The Powers were just people. What made them Powers were their machines and their creatures—and sometimes it was impossible to tell the machines from the creatures.

The true wonder was not the Powers themselves—after all, they had not created their technology, they had merely inherited the results of thousands of years of work by millions of people. The true wonder was their technology.

Bredon had begun to sample that wonder, to explore the fringes of a universe unlike anything he had ever dreamt of, and he wanted to know more. Thanks to the imprinter he had learned how to use most of the machines in Arcade, but Gamesmaster had had no basic science texts, no explanation for how most of the machines worked. Geste had no need of anything like that. What Geste needed was instruction manuals, and those he had.

Bredon wanted to know not just what the machines did, but how; not just how they worked, but why.

But even while his thirst for knowledge was driving him on, even as he reveled in his new mastery over Arcade's devices, there was a growing kernel of uneasiness, of fear, in the back of his mind. He sometimes thought that he was going too fast, that he was tampering with things beyond his comprehension, perhaps even beyond the comprehension of the people who built them. Some of the things he saw seemed unclean, or unholy, or just horribly dangerous.

Tailored bacteria, for example—those were bugs, like the bugs that caused disease, but instead of causing harm these performed useful tasks like assembling a computer inside Geste's skull.

But Bredon could not help wondering whether such bugs could be trusted, whether it was entirely safe to put a computer inside one's head. Could Geste ever really be sure that he was still the master of his own mind? The computer was, in effect, a disease. It was a beneficial disease, vastly expanding his memory, letting him think more quickly and more clearly, but by changing *how* he thought, didn't it also affect *what* he thought?

And the bugs that put it there—could they be trusted to follow the planned pattern exactly? What if a tailored bacterium, exposed to the myriad chemicals and radiations in Arcade and in Geste's body, were to mutate at the wrong time? Bredon had had the mechanism of intentional mutation explained to him in detail; Gamesmaster had passed off spontaneous or accidental mutation as unimportant, but Bredon did not feel sure of that.

And the bent-space generators, machines that could wrench reality itself out of shape, creating space where none previously existed, making rooms bigger on the inside than the outside, turning corners in directions that didn't exist before—those also worried Bredon. The Powers bent space to enlarge their homes, to save themselves long walks between scattered outposts, and for any number of other trivial purposes. Bredon knew, as a matter of simple pragmatism, that if you bend anything enough, it will break. Could space itself be damaged by the twisting the Powers gave it?

Terrans had been using these technologies for millennia, and as of four hundred years ago, when the Powers left to come to Denner's Wreck, Terra and most of its people were still intact. Even so, Bredon found himself uneasy at the thought of everything that might go wrong.

Now Geste intended to use these things as weapons, intentionally making them even more dangerous, right here on Denner's Wreck.

He also intended to leave Bredon here, in Arcade, while he went off to battle Thaddeus and perhaps rescue Lady Sunlight—or perhaps get her killed.

Bredon's mind snagged on that thought. He knew, consciously, that Lady Sunlight's plight was not his fault, but some part of his mind refused to accept that. If he had not broken the disk and summoned Geste, the Trickster might not now be preparing to fight. Lady Sunlight would still be wherever she now was, but not in danger of getting caught in the cross fire.

Geste was gathering weapons that could, if they went wrong, kill thousands of innocent people.

And when Geste left, he, Bredon, would be along again in Arcade, with only the machine intelligences to talk to, and he did not care for that prospect. He knew now how Gamesmaster and the others worked, and that knowledge made them seem far less human—and less trustworthy.

Furthermore, he was running out of things he wanted to do in Arcade. He had not yet tried out most of Arcade's vast array of entertainments, but he did not care to; he had sampled enough to discourage him. The one hologame he had attempted, the simplest Gamesmaster could find, had ended in his ignominious defeat in mere seconds. The first story Gamesmaster had played for him had been incredibly realistic, exciting, and romantic, but had been so alien in setting and concept, and so emotionally complex, that he was still not sure what he had actually felt, and did not feel ready to try another. The very reality of the experience—sight, sound, smell, touch, taste, all slightly more intense than real life—had frightened him.

Part of the fear was of something he did not understand; another part was fear that he might become addicted to such experiences and give up his own world. Gamesmaster admitted that some humans did, indeed, prefer fiction, or history recordings, to reality. It mentioned other insidious dangers as well, drugs or neural hookups that could be addictive.

Bredon knew that if he grew bored enough, he might try things in Arcade that he would do better to avoid. He had already been dabbling in computer simulations that were fantastically real, and terrifying in the sense of power they gave him when he was actually controlling nothing but colored light, synthesized sound, and artificial odors.

He did not want to stay in Arcade.

Geste, however, probably would not want him along.

Geste did not necessarily have the final say, however. Bredon was not just a savage, cowering before a demigod. He was a free human being, and could do as he pleased. Geste had carelessly given him partial control over Gamesmaster, and therefore over all the machines and creatures in Arcade, probably thinking that he would be too frightened and ignorant to make any use of them.

If so, Geste had been wrong, because Bredon had learned how to use them.

"Gamesmaster," he said, "privacy, please."

Abruptly, he was enclosed in utter darkness.

"Yes, kid, what can I do for you?" Gamesmaster asked.

"Get me aboard the Skyland. *Now*."

Chapter Fifteen

"... the boatmen saw an island in the sea before them, an island at the mouth of their own harbor that had never been there before.

" 'Has it risen from the bottom overnight?' some asked.

" 'Did it fall from the sky?' said others.

"But among the elders of the village was a woman who had studied the legends extensively, and she knew at once what this island must be. 'It is Avalon, the home of Tagomi of the Seas, greatest of the aquatic Powers,' she told the villagers. 'This island, unlike all others, floats freely wherever its master wishes it to go.'

"The villagers heard her words, and knew that she spoke the truth, and they marveled that one of the Powers had come to their little corner of the world.

" 'What could he want here?' they asked each other.

"One young man, Filomor by name, replied, 'Why don't we ask him?'

"The others laughed, and called him mad. 'Would you go up and ask him, ask a Power, ask Tagomi, what he wants here, as if he were a common vagabond?' they asked.

" 'Yes,' Filomor replied, 'I would do just that. Will anyone come with me?'

"And then the others grew angry, and cursed him, and threatened him, and told him, 'You must not go there. You must not disturb him. If you anger him with your audacity, he might destroy us all.'

"But Filomor was determined, and would hear none of their arguments. 'I will go to him and ask why he has come,' he said. 'And nothing in the three worlds will stop me.' And he took his boat and rowed out onto the sea, across the harbor to the strange green island ..."

—FROM THE TALES OF KITHEN THE STORYTELLER

No one human saw Bredon slip off the platform as it sank to the great empty expanse of close-clipped lawn. No one human saw him glance around in the dimness at the flawlessly even grass, the delicate flowers that swayed gracefully without wind, and the great jagged house at the top of the long, gentle slope as the platform slid silently back across the rocky verge and down into the empty space beneath. No one human saw him scurry quickly into the ornamental shrubbery that glistened nearby, the glossy green leaves almost black in the dim light of the stars overhead and the distant glow of the main house. No one human saw or heard any trace of him. He was a hunter, a named Hunter and the son of a Hunter, and he knew his trade. The midwake darkness made it easy to avoid human eyes.

The Skyler's machines were another matter; they needed no visible light. The instant his foot left the protective field the platform had provided, he was seen, scented, felt, heard, measured, analyzed, his mass adjusted for in the island's lift, the biochemistry of his breath and body odor recorded for future identification, his movement matched against known human behaviors to judge his intentions.

Bredon felt nothing, heard nothing, saw nothing of the machines, but he knew they were there, and that the central intelligence would be informing the Skyler of his presence within seconds. He pulled the little communicator from one of the pockets in his vest.

"Hello, in the house," he whispered.

"Identify yourself, intruder," a harsh voice replied, speaking not from the communicator but from the air above him.

"My name is Bredon," he said. "Gamesmaster sent me. It's playing a joke on Lord Geste. Look, I know you have to report me, but could you wait until we're moving? Please? If you don't the joke will be ruined. You can watch me as closely as you like, even confine me, and I won't cause any trouble."

The intelligence hesitated, then said, "I'm sorry, sir, but I *must* report you to the Skyler *immediately*. I'm transmitting a report of your arrival right now. Anything else would run counter to my most basic programming. She may choose not to ruin the joke herself, however."

Bredon shrugged. Gamesmaster had warned him, but he had thought it was worth trying. That had been foolish. One high-order artificial intelligence, given another similar one's exact design specifications, can predict that one's reactions pretty closely, and Gamesmaster had the Skyland's complete original plans in memory. Geste had ordered them downloaded from Mother years ago, to help in planning a stunt that he had hoped to pull. If the Skyler had made any modifications, they hadn't been enough to loosen up the original programming for dealing with trespassers.

Well, he told himself, maybe the Skyler has a sense of humor and will play along. He crouched down more deeply into the bushes.

Light suddenly blazed up, washing across the lawn and the shrubbery, turning them vividly green. The stars overhead vanished in the glare. "All right, Bredon, come out of there," Geste's voice called.

Bredon cursed, then slid out of the bushes and got to his feet. The lawn was lit almost as brightly as full sunlight, and he could see a thousand previously hidden details of the Skyland—bushes trimmed to resemble mythological beasts, small animals and machines skittering about on mysterious errands, the main house like a dozen villages pressed together into a single structure, little pavilions and follies scattered across the entire island in a myriad of shapes and sizes and colors, the whole panorama neat, orderly, incredibly complex, and somehow sterile and dull.

The Trickster, still in his red outfit, was coming around a corner of a nearby pink gazebo; a globe of golden light accompanied him as far as the edge of the lawn, then vanished.

He stopped, hands on his hips, and smiled at Bredon. "I take it you want to come along," Geste said.

Behind him was a woman, tall, thin, and obviously nervous, with curling, ill-kept black hair and a dusky complexion, clad in a gleaming, tight-fitting green gown. Bredon guessed that this was the Skyler herself. If he could ingratiate himself with her, Geste might find it that much harder to order him off the Skyland. He bowed formally in the manner of his people, and as he groped for flowery greetings he said, "My apologies, lady, for coming here uninvited."

"Who is he, Geste?" the woman demanded. "What's he doing on my island?"

Geste mockingly returned Bredon's bow, and then waved theatrically as he announced, "Skyler, this is Bredon the Hunter, son of Aredon the Hunter, of a village in the grasslands for which I know no name. Bredon, this is the Skyler, mistress of the Skyland, on which you stand."

"I receive an honor such as I have never imagined possible even for the gods themselves, my lady, in being permitted to see you even briefly," Bredon said, taking his speech from an old story Atheron liked to tell, about a mortal who so charmed the Nymph when she carried him away to her home beneath the river that she kept him there for a year and a wake, rather than the usual dark or two.

The Skyler stared at him, but still spoke only to her fellow immortal. "Geste, what is he *doing* here?" she demanded.

Geste sighed. "Skyler, I apologize. I got involved with him in the course of one of my little games, and he was with me when I discovered that Thaddeus was causing trouble. I left him at Arcade, where I thought he would be safely out of the way, but it appears that he doesn't care for my hospitality, and would prefer to sample yours.''

Bredon could think of nothing appropriate to say, so he simply bowed again.

"Well, *I* don't want him *here!*" the Skyler said.

That, Bredon thought, was that. With nothing left to lose, however, he decided to try arguing.

"Geste, you can't leave me there. I want to help, I want to see what happens. I *can* help, if you let me; Gamesmaster taught me to run some of your machines."

Geste was startled. "It did?"

"Of course!" Bredon replied, startled by the Trickster's surprise. "You told it to do what I wanted, and you were gone for almost four wakes; what else was I supposed to do?"

Geste smiled. "When you put it that way I don't really know. *I* would have just waited—eaten, slept, played a few games, perhaps. I keep forgetting how impatient you mortals are, and how easily bored."

"Some mortals would have done the same," Bredon said, "but I'm too restless for that."

"So I see," Geste replied.

"May I come along, then?" He did his best to sound casual, to make it a polite request, rather than begging.

Geste contemplated him, still smiling, clearly thinking it over.

"Geste!" the Skyler exclaimed warningly.

"No, wait, Skyler," Geste said, still looking at Bredon. "He may have a point. Maybe he *could* help. Thaddeus will never expect a native to be a danger."

"Why the hell not? *I* would! I don't trust these people!"

"But, Skyler, Thaddeus is different, and you know it. He's so damn arrogant that he hardly considers *us* a threat, let alone some poor bastard who survives by killing rabbits with rocks. Bredon might be able to walk right up to him, where we couldn't get within kilometers without being probed down to our marrow."

The Skyler hesitated, almost pouting, then gave in.

"All right," she said, "but keep him away from me. And Skyland, you watch him, every second. And I won't eat with him, and I don't want him in the main house." She turned and stalked away.

Geste and Bredon watched her go, and when she was out of sight the Trickster gave Bredon a smile that could only be considered conspiratorial.

"Don't mind her; she's just nervous."

"It's all right," Bredon answered, "I don't blame her. According to the legends she has never spoken to a human—I mean, a mortal—before.''

Startled, Geste looked after the departed immortal. "She hasn't?"

"So the stories say."

"Skyland, is that true?"

"Yes, sir, to the best of my knowledge it is. The Skyler does not believe any contact with the indigenes to be safe."

"They aren't indigenes; they didn't evolve here."

"My apologies, sir. Say rather, the previous inhabitants."

"She's *never* spoken to any of them?"

"Not to my knowledge, sir."

Geste considered this. "She always votes to stay here, though, whenever anyone wants to go home," he pointed out.

"Yes, sir, she does," the Skyland agreed.

"Why does she want to stay, if she never has any contact with the people here?"

Bredon thought that was obvious, even to someone as ignorant as himself, but he let the machine answer rather than risk making a fool of himself if he should be wrong.

"She has never stated a reason, sir, but in order to carry out my duties most effectively I am required to understand the Skyler's psychology as far as I can, and based on that understanding I would say that she does not like *any* strangers, and prefers Denner's Wreck to Terra because the population here is far smaller and less intrusive."

Bredon almost nodded. It *was* obvious.

"I hadn't realized she had it *that* bad," Geste said, more to himself than to Bredon or the Skyland.

The two men stood silently for a moment, and then the Trickster roused himself.

"Well, Bredon, the weapons are all aboard, and Imp is seeing to it that they're all linked to our central control system. We'll be heading for the High Castle as soon as the Skyler gets around to giving the order. It will take a few hours to get there; this thing isn't designed for speed. Have you had lunch?"

Chapter Sixteen

"In the southern portion of the desert west of the mountains, in the harshest part of the desert, where nothing grows, nothing lives, here is the domain of Madame O. The man who finds her is fortunate indeed, for not only will he be saved from death by thirst in that barren land, but he will be given food and drink the like of which most mortals dare not even dream, foods of spun crystal and glossy velvet, drinks like liquid song. He will see sights most mortals cannot imagine. Her chambers flow with light and color; the very touch of the air is like strange silks. The grass that grows in her courtyard is as soft to the touch as a kitten's fur, and fountains on the amber terraces sing like silver bells as they pour forth flashing streams of stars . . ."
—FROM THE TALES OF KITHEN THE STORYTELLER

"I want to go home!" Lady Sunlight wailed, turning about as if looking for an exit from the great stone chamber that served as Brenner's central guest hall.

The others ignored her. "You're sure that he'll do it?" Sheila asked, shifting uncomfortably in her red pseudo-leather chair. She was not accustomed to chairs that refused to reshape themselves to accommodate her.

"Of course I'm sure!" Brenner snapped, as he continued his slow pacing, each step timed to the ancient music that played softly as a constant background. "If I weren't sure I wouldn't have said anything. Barring a miracle, Thaddeus will be through the wall in the south tower within half an hour."

"We're doomed," Lady Sunlight moaned, "all doomed!" Her pet clung to her neck and chittered in sympathetic distress.

"Will you shut up?" Brenner snarled at her, still pacing.

"No, I won't shut up!" she shouted back. "That madman is probably going to kill us all!"

"No he isn't," Brenner replied in a more moderate shout than her own. "And if you'll shut up I'll explain why not."

"Thaddeus is certainly capable of murder," Rawl pointed out quietly. "We all know what he did on Alpha Imperium."

"Yes, we do know," Sheila said, annoyed. "And we don't need you to remind us of it just now."

"I never forgot it," Brenner said, forcing himself to stop

119

pacing and to maintain an even, conversational tone. "That's why I've always kept a closer eye on him than the rest of you, and I suppose that's why he attacked me first."

"I had always supposed that you simply didn't like him," Rawl remarked, settling back in his black pseudo-leather chair.

"Why? Did you think none of us had any appreciation for justice but you?" Brenner's tone was harsh again, but he kept his voice down to a normal volume.

Rawl shrugged.

"And for all of that, if you're so concerned with justice and punishing those who have done evil, why didn't you ever do anything about him? You knew who he was."

"Yes, I knew," Rawl admitted. "And I knew I should have turned him in before we ever left Terra. I was weak. I chose not to get involved. I bowed to the obvious will of the majority." The sound of an explosion penetrated the surrounding stone and force fields. "Had I done what I knew was right, we would not be here now. I would apologize, but it seems a little late for that, and in any case you're all as guilty as myself."

"He must be crazy!" Sunlight shouted, waving her arms and sending her floating polychrome dress into wild, billowing contortions that sent floral perfume out in thick waves.

"Oh, yes," Rawl replied. "He's obviously been quite mad for centuries."

"On that we agree," Brenner said.

"Oh, we're all going to die!" Lady Sunlight said again.

"No we are *not*," Brenner replied, rocking on his heels. "And if you'd all ever shut up for a minute and stop distracting me, I'd explain why not."

"Speak, then," Rawl said. " 'If thou hast any tongue, or use of voice, by Heaven, I charge thee, speak!' "

"Really, Rawl, if you're going to start quoting Shakespeare—" Sheila began.

"Hush, and let the man speak," Rawl replied.

"I will," Sheila reported. She turned, and said, "Go on, Brenner." She and Lady Sunlight looked at him expectantly.

"Right," he said. "Yes. Well. We aren't going to die, because if that was all Thaddeus wanted, I think he could have gotten in here a lot more quickly than he has. He hasn't tried anything really ruthless; he hasn't nuked us, for example. My castle could hold off a few small nukes, but if he laid into us with a series of serious high-yield thermonuclear warheads I think we'd all fry in pretty short order. There's something in here he wants intact, and I think it's probably us, or at least one of us."

"That's not very much more appealing than dying," Sheila remarked.

"Speak for yourself!" Lady Sunlight snapped.

"I did," Sheila replied calmly.

"It doesn't matter which is worse, because neither one is going to happen," Brenner said. "I told you, I've been watching Thaddeus. I thought he might try something, and I'm ready. There's a way out of the High Castle that he doesn't know about. There are *several* secret ways out of here, actually, but I think he may have found some of them. There's one, though, that I *know* no one has been poking around, and that's the way we're going out. Rawl, you keep all your equipment with you, don't you?"

"Generally speaking, yes." the Adjuster agreed cautiously.

"So if we get out of the castle, you can contact the others?"

"Easily," Rawl said.

"Even if there's interference, and Mother isn't on line?"

Rawl paused, considering, then said, "Not as easily, but still yes."

"Can you transport us?"

"For short distances—if I leave two of you behind, to anywhere on the continent."

"Well, that's fine, then. We'll get out of here, and put through some calls, and get everyone together to take care of Thaddeus before he gets out of hand."

"He may already be out of hand," Rawl suggested.

"Well, I mean before he becomes unmanageable."

"He may already be unmanageable. We don't know what's been happening out there for the last hundred hours or more; he's got us completely cut off. He could easily have done a lot of damage already. Most of the others wouldn't be prepared to resist as you are."

Brenner looked at him, disconcerted. "That's true," he said thoughtfully.

"What do you think he's trying to do, anyway?" Sheila asked.

Rawl shrugged. "He probably wants to rebuild his empire."

"Here? On Denner's Wreck?" Sheila waved an arm to take in the entire planet.

"Why not? It's a start."

"Can we stop arguing about all this and get out of here?" Lady Sunlight demanded.

Something crackled loudly, and a nearly subliminal flicker ran through the chamber's lights.

"Yes," Rawl said. "I think that would be a very good idea."

"Right. This way." Brenner turned and marched out, leading

the way from the guest hall. Lady Sunlight ran after him, so close on his heels she nearly collided with him, her pet clinging for its life.

Sheila rose and followed more calmly, and Rawl brought up the rear, glancing about with interest as they passed through passageways he had never seen before.

At the end of a winding corridor a drop-shaft took them down into the depths of the mountain, where they followed a twisting and circuitous route through the surrounding bedrock, Brenner pausing every so often to point with pride to some security device or other, only to be hurried along by Lady Sunlight before he could explain it adequately.

The lights flickered and died while they were still deep inside the mountain, and Rawl provided illumination for the rest of their journey in the form of a free-floating energy field radiating a warm yellow.

"How much farther?" Lady Sunlight asked as they rounded yet another curve.

"Not far," Brenner replied. "Look ahead there—you can see daylight."

Rawl stopped dead in his tracks, and his light vanished, plunging them into darkness.

"Rawl, what the hell—" Sheila began, then she too stopped.

"Shh!" he hissed.

"What's the matter?" Lady Sunlight demanded.

Brenner seemed determined to ignore the Adjuster's action. "Come on," he said. "I see light ahead!"

"That's why I stopped," Rawl said. "Have you all forgotten? It was dark out when we came down here. According to my internal clock, the sun won't be up for almost half an hour."

"Then what . . ." Sheila began.

"Your clock is wrong," Lady Sunlight said. "Come on."

"It's not," Rawl insisted.

"That's right," a new voice said, as light again filled the passageway, a harsh blue-white glare. Brenner began cursing.

"The sun isn't up," Thaddeus said, "but your time is. Now, come on out, and I won't have to hurt you."

Lady Sunlight began sobbing; Brenner continued to curse, switching from one language to another every few phrases.

"And if we don't?" Rawl asked.

"Believe me," Thaddeus said, "you don't want to know. Now, step on out and let my machines collect you. I have a fine welcome for you all here in Fortress Holding."

In the new light they could all see the little silver darts of heavily armed floaters cruising slowly in toward them, weapons trained forward, ready to fire.

Still cursing into his beard, Brenner reluctantly raised his hands. Lady Sunlight continued weeping. Sheila spat, and Rawl shrugged, but none of them put up any further resistance as the floaters surrounded them.

Chapter Seventeen

"The Lady of the Island, it is said, watches over all the islands of the coast, as well as her own, and whenever a boat founders, she is there, looking over its crew. She inspects them closely, and chooses the best, the strongest, the smartest, the most handsome, to come to her own island to be her lovers. Those who are almost good enough she takes as her servants. The rest she leaves to the mercies of the rocks and the sea.

"But be not too joyful, if you go to sea and find yourself wrecked upon the rocks, only to be carried away to her island, for when she tires of a lover she relegates him to the servants' hall, and whenever any servant displeases her, or grows old and slow so that he can no longer fulfill her every whim as quickly as she demands, she transforms him into a beast. And if one of these beasts should trouble her, then it is killed and fed to the others—or perhaps not killed first.

"This, then, is the tale that is told, but the truth of it is doubtful. No one who has been shipwrecked will admit to having seen her, and those who have visited her island and then escaped alive have seen no men there at all—only beasts, many strange and varied beasts, some of which can speak as men do. Perhaps the tale is just a lie, concocted by someone who wished to explain the beasts—or perhaps a lie told by the beasts themselves, who would prefer to be thought ensorcelled humans, rather than the mere beasts they seem."

—FROM THE TALES OF KITHEN THE STORYTELLER

A fine luncheon was served on a brightly lit stone-paved terrace at the Skyler's main house, where balls of glowing colored fog drifted in slow patterns overhead, and where several varieties of polychrome mutant peacocks, made supernaturally splendid by their customized genes, stalked in silent beauty on the rippling lawn nearby. Soft sourceless music played unobtrusively.

The meal was not a pleasant one. Despite the Skyler's earlier declaration that she would not eat with a savage, she and Bredon were both present, and both ate. No one made any mention of this inconsistency; after all, the others all seemed to silently agree, it was the Skyler's home and she could do as she pleased.

Bredon could not bring himself to contribute much to the conversation. He was worried, about himself and about Lady Sunlight and about what Thaddeus would do. Furthermore, despite his new insights into the workings of Terran technology, he was still somewhat awed by the realization that he was dining with three of the Powers—*the* Powers, about whom he had heard since infancy, beings just a step below gods.

He knew now that they were only human, but the aura the stories bestowed still lingered, reinforced by the otherworldly beauty of the Skyler's domain, and he felt it would not be respectful to speak openly in such company, as if he were their equal.

He was hardly in the mood for light chatter, in any case. As if his other worries weren't enough, his high-speed education had not covered details such as Terran table manners, so that he was in a perpetual state of uncertainty, constantly watching the others to be sure he was using the unfamiliar utensils correctly.

The Skyler met one of his surreptitious glances in her direction and glared back with such ferocity that Bredon thereafter studiously avoided looking at her, instead watching Geste and Imp.

Even before he caught her eye, the Skyler was moody and belligerent, and Bredon guessed that she resented the presence of so many people—one of them a stranger—aboard her private retreat. She devoted most of her energy to devouring her food, rather than to conversation. She chewed away defiantly.

Imp, clad in a red-orange bodysuit, seemed far more radiantly beautiful in person than she had in holographic transmission. Still distraught over Aulden's disappearance, she said nothing, except to reply as briefly as possible to Geste's occasional questions. She ate little, picking at her food. When he looked at her, Bredon found himself thinking of Lady Sunlight; not only did he sympathize with Imp's situation, her concern about a loved one held captive, but her beauty reminded him of Lady Sunlight. She was short and redheaded, with a heart-shaped face and worried expression, where Lady Sunlight was tall, thin, blond, and aloof, but both were extremely attractive women, and Bredon took an instinctive interest in Imp that had him involuntarily comparing the two in the back of his mind. Even when he had to resort to sheer imagination—he had never spoken to Lady Sunlight, had seen her only briefly in real life, and then again briefly in recordings at Arcade—Lady Sunlight won out in these comparisons, and that brought home to him again just how much he wanted her.

Imp knew nothing of this, did not notice Bredon's attention. She stared unseeing at her plate and occasionally put something in her mouth, where she would gnaw on it interminably before finally swallowing and picking something else.

Geste, for his part, did his best to keep up a lively conversation even while wolfing down his meal, but it quickly developed into a monologue. He accepted this, and began telling long, complicated jokes, most of which made little sense to Bredon.

The Skyland and the other various nonhuman intelligences said nothing beyond polite inquiries about the service, which was handled by several dozen tiny disk-shaped blue floaters that extruded arms and hands as needed. These disks were constantly buzzing and fluttering about, removing used tableware and replacing it with fresh, carrying food back and forth, refilling drinks through a bent-space siphon, and so forth.

Nobody, not even Bredon after the first few minutes, paid any attention to the peacocks, or the music, or the lawn that moved in graceful patterns without wind, or the lights drifting above them, or any of the wonders that made up the decor.

Despite his nervousness, Bredon ate until he could eat no more, stuffing himself shamelessly on the mysterious and savory foods that were presented to him. When he had finished, he glanced around and was astonished to see the three immortals still eating. Imp was still only nibbling, but Geste and the Skyler were clearly consuming even more than Bredon had.

A moment's thought provided him with a provisional explanation of how a woman and a small man could each eat more than a large, hungry young man. These people had their internal machinery to power. Each one carried at least one symbiotic organism in his or her blood; each presumably had a skull-liner drawing energy.

An old story about one of Geste's pranks came to mind, one Bredon had heard only once, as a very young child. The Trickster had gotten himself invited to dine in the hut of a poor family of outcasts, and had eaten their entire winter store. Unable to refuse a Power, the household had grown steadily more worried as they politely offered meal after meal and watched Geste consume them all without hesitation, leaving the family with less and less for the coming cold.

Finally, one of the children, seeing the last of his mother's sugar cookies disappearing, had begged Geste to stop. Geste had just smiled and eaten the cookie.

With the polite facade cracked by the child's action, the family broke down and begged the Trickster to stop eating, but he had kept on devouring everything in sight.

Bredon could not remember whether, as Atheron told it, Geste burst out laughing first, or the family ran out of food first, but in any case, they *had* run out of food, and Geste *had* laughed, and while the parents were still polite and respectful the children had grown resentful and chastised Geste, which had only made him laugh harder.

Beyond that the details were fuzzy in Bredon's memory, but he knew the story had a happy ending, that Geste had given the family an endless supply of wonderful new foods that made them all wealthy. Atheron had meant the story to teach the value of hospitality, he supposed, but Bredon had never really believed the story to be true.

Watching the immortals eat, though, he began to wonder.

It occurred to him that the story certainly *could* be true. Even a Power couldn't actually eat an entire winter store, but he could make it vanish into invisibility or into a bent-space receptacle of some sort, and the whole incident, as Atheron had described it, fit Geste's slightly cruel sense of humor.

Bredon sat politely quiet as the others continued their meal, Imp and the Skyler in sullen silence, Geste still babbling on with an endless anecdote about an intelligence designed for piloting a starship that had accidentally been installed in a floor-cleaner.

Imp eventually abandoned any pretext of eating, and even the Skyler and Geste stopped doing more than nibbling. The flying disks stopped bringing new foods, and devoted themselves to removing the old and cleaning away every crumb or drip that remained.

Finally, as the eastern sky began to fade from black to blue with the approach of secondlight dawn, the disks brought tall, thin, strangely shaped glasses of something that sparkled blue. Geste ended his current tale abruptly, and turned toward the approaching service machines in time to accept his glass before it could reach the tablecloth.

The women were less hurried, and allowed the drinks to be set down before they picked them up.

"What is it?" Bredon asked, as he lifted his glass with the others.

The Skyler threw him a resentful glance and snapped, "This, barbarian, is an after-dinner cordial, a beverage—" She cut herself off short.

"Thank you, lady," Bredon said. He sipped from his glass.

The stuff was sweet and sharp and strongly alcoholic, which Bredon had not expected; he stopped before more than a trace had passed his lips, to avoid any risk of an unbecoming splutter. The people of his own village ended their meals with sweets, but never with alcohol. Their potent corn liquor was reserved for celebrations or as relief from long drudgery, and while this elaborate meal had certainly not been a celebration, Bredon had not considered it drudgery, either.

He sipped again, and now that he knew what to expect he found the drink very good indeed. "This is excellent, lady," he said.

The Skyler threw him a distrustful glance, then grudgingly replied, in a tight, brittle voice, "Thank you."

Emboldened, Bredon groped for something else to say. Before he could devise anything suitable, the Skyland interrupted.

"Excuse me," it said, "but I'm afraid I have bad news."

"What?" the Skyler demanded. Her voice broke, indicative of her extreme state of nervous tension.

"The High Castle has been breached," the Skyland said. "The attackers have broken through a full seven levels of defense, counting the stone of the walls, and have entered the main structure at three separate points. Of the observers reporting to me, none can detect any further evidence of activity on the part of the defenders."

The four humans looked at one another.

"How long until we get there?" Imp asked, putting down her drink.

"We should arrive in the vicinity in about an hour," the Skyland replied.

Bredon noticed that Geste had his head cocked strangely to one side, and guessed that he was listening to something the others could not hear.

"What do we do now?" the Skyler said, an edge of hysteria in her voice and her blue cordial still in her hand.

"We go on," Imp said flatly. "Aulden's still in Fortress Holding, and the others may be holed up somewhere in the High Castle. I'd be surprised if Brenner didn't have a bolt-hole of some kind, one that he kept out of Mother's records."

"He did," Geste replied, "but Thaddeus found it."

The two women turned to him, startled; Bredon had been watching him all along, and had expected some sort of dramatic announcement.

"What are you talking about?" the Skyler asked, annoyed and frightened.

"I've got scouts of my own working on this. You know that, of course. Brenner did have an escape tunnel, a bent-space one right through the mountain, heavily fortified and thoroughly hidden. Unfortunately, as Thaddeus and I both know, it's possible to locate and map any kind of bent-space construction, and that's exactly what Thaddeus did. He has a small army of creatures and machines waiting at the mouth of the tunnel, but so far no one has emerged. Brenner probably had some way of checking, and saw them there, so he didn't go out that way."

"Are you sure he has just the one tunnel?" Imp asked.

Geste shrugged. "It's the only one I've found. I had thought we might be able to go in that way, if we really needed to get inside."

"He might have had a normal-space one," Imp said. "You wouldn't have found one like that, would you?"

"Not necessarily. I had my machines mapping all the bent-space work around the High Castle—there isn't much, I guess Brenner doesn't like it—and I know there aren't any other bent-space tunnels, but I can't say for sure about anything else. I had machines scouting normal space all around there too, but they might have missed something. If he _does_ have one, it's pretty well hidden."

The Skyler said, "There must be some way to find it."

"Sure, lots of ways. The easiest would be seismic mapping. I didn't try that because I don't have the right equipment, and it could be spotted if Thaddeus is watching closely. Which he probably is."

Imp asked, "Did you watch to see if _Thaddeus_ did any seismic mapping?"

Astonished, Geste's smile vanished as he turned to the diminutive redhead. "I didn't think of that," he said. "And I don't think any of my machines did, either."

"Is there any way to check?"

"Wait a minute." Geste's eyes rolled back disconcertingly for a moment, then dropped down again.

"Damn!" he said. "Damn it!"

"What?" the Skyler demanded. "What is it?"

"Mother reports that somebody, identity unknown, set off a pulse charge near the High Castle about ten wakes ago, before Thaddeus began his attack. At that time Thaddeus had several machines scattered in the area. It's a safe bet that he set off the charge, and those machines were mapping the echoes. If Brenner _does_ have a normal-space tunnel, Thaddeus knows it, and we don't."

"But Brenner would check, wouldn't he? He wouldn't rush out blindly." Imp did not sound very certain of herself.

"You're right," Geste reassured her, "he wouldn't. So if Thaddeus had a party waiting outside both tunnels—if there _is_ a second tunnel—Brenner ought to know about it, and he wouldn't go out that way. Unless Thaddeus managed to fool him somehow."

"But then, where *would* he go?" the Skyler wailed.

"Nowhere; he must still be in the castle," Imp said.

"But Thaddeus broke in!"

"Skyler, we don't know what Brenner has in there. He and the others might be safe in a stasis field, or a time warp, or he might have split a bent-space section off into a pocket universe, or he might have whole layers of internal defense that we never even thought of."

The Skyler took little comfort from Geste's words. "Or they might all be dead," she retorted.

"Yes, they might, or Thaddeus might have caught them—my observers say there have been ships leaving the High Castle, carrying loot, and they might have been aboard one."

"What would he *do* with them?"

"*I* don't know."

Bredon felt helpless and out of place listening to this conversation. He knew he was not one of these people, did not really belong here. He wanted to ask about Lady Sunlight, even while he knew that the others knew no more than he did and would not welcome the interruption. To distract himself, while the others spoke in an intent little knot, he let his gaze wander the horizon.

The eastern sky was pink and gold, and the sun would appear in seconds. Bredon looked up past the glowing balls of gas to where the sky was still a deep dark blue, high overhead.

Light flashed, and his first thought was that the sun had passed the horizon, but then he realized that the light came from the northwest and was far too bright. "What—" he began.

The others had all seen the flash as well, he realized. Imp flung her arms up in front of her face, and Geste dropped to the ground shouting a strange syllable: "*Nuke!*"

The Skyler simply stood, too astonished to move.

Chapter Eighteen

" '. . . Are you a warrior?' the stranger demanded.

"Proud of his strength and skill, Walren foolishly answered, 'Yes, I am!'

" 'Then, face me in combat!' the stranger called. And he flung a weapon like a long, thin knife, longer than a man's arm, to the ground before the lad. He drew a similar knife from a sheath on his belt, and waited.

"Walren began to be afraid now. He thought the stranger was a madman. He stooped and picked up the strange knife. 'What is it?' he asked.

" 'It's a soared, of course,' the stranger replied. And then he leapt forward, his knife stabbing out at Walren.

"Walren jumped aside and swung his own long knife, but the stranger knocked it away easily and slashed Walren across the breast with his blade.

"Astonished, Walren looked down at the blood seeping from his chest, just in time to see the stranger's blade plunge into his heart.

"Everything went black, and he knew that he was dead.

"But then, to his surprise, he awoke, lying on a pile of leaves in the forest, with the stranger standing over him.

" 'That was pitiful,' the stranger said. 'How can you call yourself a warrior if you can't do any better than that?'

"Walren raised his head and looked at his chest, and saw that although his blouse was still cut open, and blood still stained the fabric, the wounds had closed up and left not even a scar.

" 'Who are you?' he asked the stranger.

" 'I'm called Lord Carlov,' the stranger replied with a bow . . ."
—FROM THE TALES OF ATHERON THE STORYTELLER

"I can't believe this is happening," Lady Sunlight moaned, stirring uncomfortably on the unyielding bench.

"It's happening," Rawl told her calmly. "Accept it." Inwardly, he marveled that the woman could have lived for so long without learning that *anything* could happen. He did not understand why so many of the immortals led such limited lives. It was always by their own choice; were they so desperate for security as to give up *all* risk and experimentation, and turn completely inward?

Or were they just stupid and unimaginative? Endless life and

131

unimaginable power did not make a fool any less a fool. Some people did not seem to learn from experience, most particularly when they did all they could to limit their experiences to the familiar.

He hated to think that his companions were all fools. On the other hand, he knew from his centuries of wandering among the people of Denner's Wreck that a large percentage of the human race was made up of fools, and there was no reason his little clique should be any different.

For that matter, wasn't he as big a fool as the rest? He was just as much a captive as the others. He mulled that over silently.

"Brenner, why didn't you see all these things waiting for us?" Lady Sunlight demanded, waving at the surrounding plastic.

"*I* don't know," Brenner replied bitterly, staring down at his clasped hands. "Thaddeus must have hidden them pretty well. Maybe he sabotaged some of my defensive systems, broke in and fed them false reports that the exit was still clear. I spotted all the stuff he had waiting outside my *other* tunnels easily enough."

"He probably meant you to," Sheila said from the other side of the little transport.

"In fact," Rawl said, leaning back against the yellow plastic wall, "the entire attack may have been a feint, a trick, a means of herding us out through that tunnel to where he could capture us alive and undamaged."

Brenner looked up. "Do you think so?"

Rawl shrugged. "Who knows? It could have been." He did not think Thaddeus was inherently any less a fool than most of the others, but he knew that he could be very clever indeed in pursuing his foolish goals. Thaddeus was crazy, but he was not stupid.

"What does he *want* with us?" Lady Sunlight asked.

"How should I know?" Brenner answered angrily.

"Hostages," Rawl muttered softly, so softly the others did not hear him.

Lady Sunlight started to reply to Brenner's outburst, blaming him further for his ignorance, but then she saw the expression on his face and thought better of it. She looked away, in the direction of the other transport, the one that held her pet and various devices. Silence fell, as all four contemplated their unhappy situation.

Thaddeus's machines had stripped them of all their equipment except what was actually built into them. Lady Sunlight had given up her pet, a feelie vine, three small creatures she had had tucked away, and six small floaters. Sheila had had only a single floater; her airskiff did not fit through the tunnel and had been left behind.

Rawl had resisted briefly, taking out three minor machines from Thaddeus's arsenal, and had had forty-two floaters immobilized by suppressor fields, and four creatures captured alive. Several other small creatures from Rawl's menagerie had escaped safely into the woods surrounding the exit from the tunnel, and three had died making the attempt, fried by Thaddeus's weapons. One, a modified ferret, had last been seen being pursued by an artificial predator Thaddeus had designed and grown himself, working mostly from feline genes.

Brenner had had nothing at all for Thaddeus to confiscate. All his external devices had been built into the High Castle, or had been left behind in his hurried departure.

Of course, they all still carried symbiotes and a variety of internal machinery. Thaddeus had not tried to do anything about that. In fact, the transport that they had been forced to board was not even shielded against most communications frequencies; Rawl discovered, after the brief spurt of conversation triggered by Lady Sunlight's outburst, that he was able to contact the mother ship and inquire after the other immortals.

None of the other captives had thought to try that, so far as he could see.

No one was reported dead, Rawl learned. That was some comfort, but Khalid, O, and Aulden were missing, all three last heard from in the vicinity of Fortress Holding. Geste and Imp were aboard the Skyland, of all places, and had been going from hold to hold recently, and were now apparently headed for the High Castle; Rawl suspected that this meant they were aware of what was happening and were coming to lend what aid they could.

He smiled wryly to himself. They were already too late. The High Castle was gone. Once Thaddeus had his captives and booty out, Mother said, he had nuked the place. Rawl hesitated for an instant, and then decided against telling Brenner and Sheila and Sunlight that. They were disheartened enough already.

Still, Geste and Imp and the Skyler would find nothing but radioactive rubble.

At least they were trying, though. What were all the others doing?

Nothing, apparently. They were just going about their business.

Rawl did not like that. If the Skyler and her party knew what was happening, they would surely have told everyone. Why weren't the others doing anything to stop Thaddeus?

He knew that he could not manage a proper holographic transmission with just his internal systems; but with Mother to relay, Rawl thought he could get a message of some sort out, either audio or data feed. He tried to put a call through to Isabelle.

He was cut off, not by static, but by the sudden dead silence of an electromagnetic barrier effect.

"No, no, Rawl," Thaddeus's voice said, startling the other captives. "I can't have you spreading wild rumors."

"Rawl?" Lady Sunlight said, puzzled. The other two looked at him, surprised but silent.

"Rumors?" Rawl asked.

"Certainly. Just rumors. What else could it be?" Thaddeus laughed unpleasantly.

Rawl wished, briefly, that Thaddeus had come out in person to oversee their capture. That would have given them a better shot at escape or at doing some serious damage, since Thaddeus's forces would have had to put some effort into defending their master.

Of course, Thaddeus would never have been that stupid.

A moment late the yellow plastic walls opened suddenly, shrinking down into themselves. The transport dissolved until nothing remained but the two simple benches, facing each other in the center of a moderately large chamber.

The walls were drab gray; no music played, and the place smelled of oil and metal.

Sheila and Rawl quickly took in their new surroundings; Brenner looked around slowly but without real interest, and Lady Sunlight glance back and forth wildly.

"Where are our things?" she demanded.

Thaddeus appeared suddenly, standing before them a centimeter or two off the floor. Rawl looked at the brown-garbed figure and realized it was not tall enough; he would have assumed it to be a transmitted image in any case, and Thaddeus gave that away by reducing his size to one more normal for a human being than his actual 2.9 meters.

"What things?" the image said, smiling.

"You know what things!" Lady Sunlight spat.

"You mean this?" The image held up Lady Sunlight's golden-furred pet, its neck clutched in one huge hand. The little animal was kicking and scratching desperately, unable to breathe. As it had been bred without claws, its struggles did no good at all.

"Let him go!" Lady Sunlight shrieked.

Thaddeus smiled and squeezed harder.

The animal gasped once and went limp. Thaddeus squeezed harder, then released the creature. It fell and lay still. Rawl noticed that Thaddeus had carefully dropped it inside the transmission area, so that his captives would be able to see for themselves that it was really dead.

"Vicious bastard," Brenner muttered.

"Really, Thaddeus," Sheila said, "is this necessary?"

"Maybe not," the image replied, "but I'm enjoying it. I'm really enjoying seeing you smug little fools realize who is actually in charge here."

Rawl watched intently, suddenly aware that something was wrong here. Would the real Thaddeus have casually handled Sunlight's pet so directly? He had no way of knowing what the little animal was capable of, and for as long as Rawl had known him, Thaddeus had never taken an unnecessary risk.

This, then, was not the real Thaddeus, or perhaps it was not the real pet.

An android, perhaps? A clone?

It didn't really matter, though.

"Stinking son of a bitch," Brenner said. "Where's the joy in strangling little animals?"

"Oh, there's joy enough," Thaddeus replied. "There's a feeling of power to it, feeling that little bit of life squirming in your hand, and then feeling it break and die. The best part, though, is watching you people while I do it. You all thought you were as good as me. As good as me? Hell, you thought you were better! You think I didn't know what you felt? You were all basking in that glow of power over me, knowing that you could turn me over to the rebels on Alpha Imperium at any time, knowing you could put an end to a life that's lasted longer than any of you. You all thought you were better than me because you'd never been defeated the way I was—but none of you ever *tried*. None of you could do any better. *I'm* the conqueror here, and now you *have* been defeated. Like it? Like the feeling? *Do you?*"

"No," Sheila said. "We don't. We never gloated over your defeat, Thaddeus."

"No? Then why didn't you turn me in?"

No one answered.

"*Why?*" he screamed.

"I don't know," Sheila shouted back.

"We felt sorry for you," Lady Sunlight said before Rawl and Sheila could stop her.

"You *pitied* me? Well, pity yourselves now, you sanctimonious little idiots!"

Something flashed in the chamber that held them, and Rawl felt his skin crawling and drying. His internal systems began reporting damage. They had been bombarded with a short burst of high-intensity radiations of various kinds—ultraviolet, narrow-band gamma rays, and others, all designed to kill off tailored microbes, but which incidentally damaged human tissue, several kinds of symbiote, and electromagnetic data storage.

He looked down at his hands; the skin was reddening already. He would have a ferocious sunburn in minutes, and his symbiotes were too badly hurt to repair it quickly. His skull-liner had lost large chunks of memory. Some of the independent intelligences that roamed in his body had died, he was sure.

So much for any attempts to fight their way out. They were at Thaddeus's mercy.

"Take off your clothes," Thaddeus ordered.

"Why?" Lady Sunlight asked. "Why should we?" She was once again on the verge of tears.

"Because I'll kill you if you don't," Thaddeus began. "I'll kill you slowly . . ." Then he stopped and reconsidered. "No," he said. "No, I won't kill you. I don't want to make threats I won't keep, and I have no intention of killing you yet. No, if you don't take your clothes off, I'll take them off for you, and my machines won't be gentle about it."

Rawl was already peeling off his own garments, and the others reluctantly followed his example.

By the time they were all naked, a gleaming silver machine had rolled into the room and stood before them. Rawl studied it in wry amusement. Thaddeus was not only one of the oldest people alive, but one of the most old-fashioned. Nobody else still used wheeled machines; they were too limited in what terrain they could travel on. Thaddeus did not entirely trust antigravity. It had been around for more than four thousand years, but to Thaddeus it was still too new to be used extensively.

"Hello," he said to the machine, testing out its capabilities.

It did not reply. Thaddeus's image turned away from his intent inspection of Lady Sunlight and said, "It can't hear you. None of my mobile machines can. I programmed them all to block out your voices, to treat them as unprocessible background noise. You aren't going to get out of here with their help, any of you."

Rawl shrugged. "I didn't expect to," he said truthfully. He had known that Thaddeus would have taken precautions against anything of the sort. He had not guessed what form the precautions would take, though; coding their voiceprints to be inaudible was, like many of Thaddeus's methods, unusually simple and clever, taking an indirect route to the desired result. Most people would have simply ordered the machines not to take orders from anyone else, but Thaddeus realized that there were ways around that sort of blanket command.

And there was an added psychological dimension, as well; these machines would not only not obey the captives, but would refuse to even acknowledge their existence except as objects. Thaddeus was doing his best to depersonalize his prisoners. He had stripped away their defenses, their machines, their creatures, their clothes, even the voices they used to give orders. Even their health, something they had all taken for granted for centuries, had been disrupted by the radiation burst; they would all be in mild pain for hours, maybe days, before their skin healed and their symbiotes regenerated.

Rawl almost admired the paranoid completeness of it all.

"Come along," Thaddeus said. "The machine will lead you to your cell. The others are waiting."

"Others?" As usual, it was Lady Sunlight who rose to the bait.

"Aulden, Khalid, and O," Rawl said, taking away a little of Thaddeus's own.

The image frowned. "How did— Oh, I see. Of course. Yes, it's Aulden and Khalid and O. Now, come along. Your chains are waiting."

"Chains," Brenner spat. "Thaddeus, you . . . you . . ." He could not find the words he needed. As a metal arm reached out toward him, he stepped forward, following the machine.

The arms reached out for the others, and they all obeyed, allowing themselves to be herded toward an open door.

"I can't believe any of this," Lady Sunlight said as she stumbled forward into the stone corridor beyond. "It can't be happening."

Rawl wished she were right, but he knew, as he walked to their cell, that it was all quite real.

Chapter Nineteen

". . . Arn of the Ice rides upon the north winds in the winter, and roams invisibly throughout the world, wherever the winds blow and wherever the snows can seep in. He draws icy patterns upon stone and glass, shapes the snow into graceful curves, and does all he can to transform all the world into a new wing for the Ice House . . ."
— FROM THE TALES OF KITHEN THE STORYTELLER

The Skyland's automatic defenses had been ready for anything when the nuke went off, and the island was undamaged. The Skyler's automatic defenses had also been alert and ready, and her optical symbiote had thrown nictitating membranes across both eyes before the flash could do any serious damage.

The symbiote itself had suffered extensively, but no one much cared about that. In a few wakes it would regenerate completely, it had no sensitivity to pain, and it possessed only the most rudimentary sort of consciousness.

No harmful radiation except visible light had gotten through the fields surrounding the Skyland, so one one had to worry about burns or hidden damage of any sort.

Geste and Imp had been looking at the Skyler, not at the flash. They were unhurt.

Bredon had been looking up, not directly at the flash, but he had no symbiotes guarding him, no programmed reactions, no defenses beyond what he had been born with and the dying remnants of the "repair kit" Geste had fed into his bloodstream. His eyes were intact, and would heal, but for the present he was half-blind, seeing everything only dimly. He had completely missed seeing the mushroom cloud.

By the time everyone's condition had been ascertained, and Bredon's injuries treated with microbe-administered analgesic, anti-infectants, and a healing accelerator, the machines had definitely established that the Skyland was completely unscathed. The island, having no orders to the contrary, had sailed on, directly toward the site of the explosion, and by the time anyone paid attention to their location they were over the mountains, and the rising sun was a disk, noticeably above the horizon.

By the time Geste had assessed the damage to the various machines he and his companions had sent on ahead—most of the observers in the area had been vaporized—the Skyland should have been within sight of the High Castle, and the sun should have been well up the eastern sky.

The sun was presumably where it should be. The castle, however, was gone, and the entire area covered by smoke, smoke so thick that once they had entered it the sun was hidden from view.

Of course, protective fields kept the smoke from touching anything on the island. The Skyland forged on, and the Skyler sent machines out to douse the fires and dissipate the smoke. Within an hour they were hovering near where the castle had been.

The peak upon which the castle had stood was still there, and a wide variety of debris littered its slopes, but the huge and complex structure that had once capped it was gone, leaving a gleaming crater. Bredon peered over the edge of the Skyland in wonder, cursing his damaged vision and marveling at the desolation.

It was hard to believe that anything had ever lived in the smooth, glistening black hole atop the mountain; the inside surface shone like glass, and carried an uneven reddish tinge that might have been the glow of the residual heat. Nor was the surrounding area much better; for as far as Bredon could see, the land had been laid waste.

The forests on the surrounding slopes had been blown down, trampled by the shock wave like grass beneath a horse's hooves, and most of them had caught fire; the Skyland's machines now had the fires contained, so that the smoke no longer blocked the view. Bredon and the others could see just how complete the destruction was.

"Well," Geste said, contemplating the crater, "there's certainly no one down there now. Either Brenner and Sheila and Sunlight and Rawl got out, or they didn't, and either way there isn't anything we can do about it."

After a moment of silent contemplation of the horrible thought that Lady Sunlight might have died, Bredon asked, "Isn't there any way we can find out if they're alive?"

Geste shrugged, then stopped. "Of course there is," he said. "I don't know why I didn't think of it before. They've all got emergency transponders." Without further warning, his eyes rolled back in his head disconcertingly for a moment, then reappeared.

''They're alive,'' he said. ''Or at least Mother tracked all four of them leaving the High Castle together, then lost them again at Fortress Holding. She spoke to Rawl briefly, too. So either they're all alive and captured, or they're alive and launching some sort of harebrained counterattack, or they're dead and Thaddeus is doing something very tricky and forging their signals.''

''What can we do about it?'' Imp asked.

''Not much,'' Geste admitted. ''We just go on, I guess.''

Bredon was relieved that Lady Sunlight still lived, and looked down at the crater with new eyes.

''If Thaddeus has weapons that can do this,'' he asked suddenly, pointing at the ruined mountain, ''why does he bother with those little flying things that were shooting at us when we came here before?''

''I can think of several possibilities,'' Geste said. ''First off, he seems to have wanted Brenner and the others as prisoners, not ash. A nuke would have killed them if it got through at all. Also, there are ways to defend against nukes. If Thaddeus had just thrown one at Brenner first thing, Brenner could have defended against it. I don't know what delivery system he used, but if he had just dropped it and triggered it while the High Castle was intact, it wouldn't have breached the castle's protective fields.''

''It wouldn't?'' Bredon stared at the wasteland below and tried to conceive of anything withstanding such force.

''It wouldn't. Nukes aren't subtle. They just throw an incredible amount of energy at everything. Brenner's defenses *were* subtle; Thaddeus had to pick away at them until he found the weak spots.''

''Oh,'' Bredon said.

''Another thing: we didn't bring any nukes with us when we came to Denner's Wreck; he must have built this one himself. And as I said, nukes aren't subtle. By setting one off, he's let us all know that he's been stockpiling weapons and that he's not afraid to use them. It gives the game away. Everyone will see that he's not just playing around.''

''That's good, isn't it? You can get the others to help, then.''

Geste shook his head. ''I'm not sure. If Thaddeus had dropped a nuke and Brenner had survived it, then I could; the others would all agree that it wasn't playing fair. But trying to stir them up with Brenner gone is another matter. It's over and done now. I don't know.''

''I think they'll help,'' Imp said, her voice tense. ''I think they'll have to.''

The Skyler said, ''What worries me is why Thaddeus feels he

can use a nuke now, after he had already broken the High Castle. Why does he feel so safe?''

The others all turned to look at her; she stepped back, her manner defensive.

"You're right," Geste said. "Why *does* he feel safe?"

"Or maybe," Imp said, "we should ask why he's willing to use one now when he wasn't before. What changed?"

"He captured the four there," Geste said slowly.

"But he already had Khalid and O and Aulden," the Skyler pointed out.

"That's just three; he must have thought that he needed more hostages before he let it become obvious what he was doing," Geste suggested.

"Do you really think that's it?" the Skyler asked dubiously.

"I don't know," the Trickster admitted.

The four stood silently for a moment. Then Bredon cleared his throat and said, "Why don't you ask him?"

"He won't talk to us," the Skyler snapped.

"Wait a minute," Geste said. "If he *is* feeling safe, he might be willing to talk now. It won't hurt to try."

"I don't know," the Skyler said. "I don't like this. I don't like *any* of this."

"None of us do," Imp replied.

"If we're going to talk to him, we should plan out what we want to say. What do we want from him, anyway?" the Skyler said.

"Frankly, what *I* want is to pack him away somewhere, without any of his external systems, and ship him back to Terra for a little psychological repair work," Geste said. "The man is deranged!"

"He's not going to agree to *that*," the Skyler said.

"I suppose not," Geste admitted "but maybe we can coax some sort of concession out of him."

"All *I* want is Aulden back," Imp said.

"And I want Lady Sunlight, if she's still alive," Bredon said.

"I don't want anything from him," the Skyler said bitterly, "except to be left alone."

"Well, maybe he'll agree to that," Geste said consolingly.

"Why should he agree to anything? He can do what he pleases, can't he? Brenner couldn't stop him; how can we? He'll just ignore us."

"I intend to be hard to ignore," Geste said. "Skyler, get this hold of yours moving west; let's see Thaddeus ignore a million tons of rock hanging over his head!"

The Skyler hesitated, then waved a command to a nearby floater. As Bredon watched, the scenery beneath them, which had been stationary for several minutes, began to move again.

"I don't like this, Geste," she said. She turned and began walking back toward the main house, calling back over her shoulder, "I don't like it at all!"

Chapter Twenty

". . . he turned, and found himself face-to-face with a great winged lizard, as tall as a man and a dozen meters long, with wings that could serve as a roof for the biggest house in the village.

"He sat down and began composing his death speech, wishing that someone were around to hear it besides this great green lizard-beast.

"But then, to his astonishment, the beast spoke, saying, 'Greetings to you, sir. Why are you here, in the land of my mistress?'

"And then Helleber knew that he was facing a dragon, and that he was in the domain of the Dragon Lady, and hope blossomed in his heart, for all the tales he had heard of her were happy ones.

" 'Why, I am lost,' he said, 'and have no food, no water, and no way to get home.'

" 'Then climb up on my back,' the dragon said, 'and I will take you to my mistress who made me, and I am sure she will be glad to help you.'

"So he approached, full of fear at the sight of the monster, but forcing himself to walk up to it calmly . . ."
—FROM THE TALES OF ATHERON THE STORYTELLER

The humans aboard the Skyland spent the rest of the secondlight in dismal, nervous anticipation, and when the sleeping dark approached, no one slept or suggested sleep. The sun was sinking in the west, and they were nearing Fortress Holding.

By unspoken agreement, they gathered on the terrace where they had eaten lunch.

"He hasn't done anything," the Skyler said.

"Are you sure?" Imp asked.

"Of course I'm sure! I've got my machines watching Fortress Holding, just as you do!"

"He hasn't done anything that I've seen," Geste agreed. "Oh, a few of his machines fought off some of my saboteurs, but that's nothing."

"He must know we're coming," the Skyler said nervously. "Why doesn't he do something?"

"I don't know," Geste answered.

They were silent for a moment, and it was not a human who broke the silence.

"Excuse me," the Skyland said, "but Thaddeus the Black is calling and wishes to speak to, quote, 'whoever is in charge up there,' end quote."

"There you go," Geste said with a wave. "He's doing something. Talk to him."

"Oh no," the Skyler said. "*You* talk to him."

"It's your hold," Imp protested.

"But it was Geste's idea to come here," the Skyler insisted.

Geste shrugged. "All right. Put him on, Skyland."

A face appeared in the air, and Bredon studied it curiously.

So this was the infamous Thaddeus the Black! He had seen old pictures back in Arcade, pictures that Gamesmaster had shown him while explaining who Shadowdark and Thaddeus were, but this was the first live transmission Bredon had seen.

The first thing Bredon noticed was that, as the pictures back at Arcade had shown, he was not black, his name notwithstanding. His complexion was slightly darker than most of the other Powers Bredon had seen, but Leila and Hsin were both a good bit darker, and there were people in Bredon's home village who were darker, and the southern traders who came by twice a year selling metal pots and pans and tools were darker still.

His hair was black and curly, but that scarcely seemed enough to justify the name. His eyes were brown, and he was heavily bearded. The face behind the beard was lined and scarred, unusual for a Power, but no more so than many a villager's face was by his fortieth turn of the seasons, and by no means even close to the grotesquerie of Shadowdark's visage.

Thaddeus did bear some resemblance to his father; their eyes were similar, and both had prominent noses, though Shadowdark's was straight while Thaddeus had a definite hook to his.

And his face was oddly proportioned, like Shadowdark's. Bredon remembered that Thaddeus was said to be almost three meters tall. The image was only slightly larger than a normal head; either Thaddeus's height was entirely in his body, or he was using a reduced-size transmission.

It was a strong face, neither a particularly attractive one, nor one ugly or frightening enough to fit the stories told about its owner.

"Hello there," Thaddeus said conversationally. "Only three of you? Are the best somewhere else? I'll wait while you call them, if you like."

"There are only the four of us," Geste replied, gesturing so as to include Bredon with the two women.

"Four?" Bredon was unsure whether Thaddeus's surprise was

feigned or genuine. "Who is that, then? Has someone taken a
new body, or been rebuilt? I thought that was an android or a
primitive."

Geste turned expectantly, to let Bredon speak for himself.

"I am Bredon the Hunter, son of Aredon the Hunter," Bredon
announced, aware how foolish that once-proud declaration of his
identity must sound to this unspeakably powerful and ancient
being.

"A primitive—so there *are* just three of you. You will have
your little joke, Geste, won't you?" He eyed Bredon warily,
however.

"What do you want, Thaddeus?" Geste inquired wearily.

"I just want to come to an understanding."

"What sort of an understanding?" the Skyler asked.

"And where's Aulden?" Imp demanded.

"Aulden is right here, Imp; he's alive and well. As for what
sort of an understanding, that's why Aulden is here." The image
of a handsome, rather distracted-looking, outwardly youthful
man appeared briefly beside Thaddeus's image, then vanished
again before Bredon could even be sure of the color of his hair.
"And Sheila, and Sunlight, and Rawl, and O, and Khalid, and
even Brenner." More faces flashed briefly, then faded. Bredon
felt his throat tighten at the glimpse of Lady Sunlight's radiant
features.

"What are you talking about, Thaddeus?" Geste asked.

"Bluntly, Geste, I'm talking about blackmail. I have seven of
your friends here, all alive, at least for the moment, but all very
much in my hands. If any of you interfere with my plans—for
that matter, if any of you fail to give me your fullest cooperation—
I'll start killing my prisoners."

He smiled malignly down at the party aboard the Skyland, and
for a long moment no one spoke.

"Just what *are* these plans that we aren't to interfere with?"
Geste asked at last.

"I would suppose that you've already guessed. You all know
who I am. I intend to rebuild my empire, and this time I won't be
stopped."

"No? You've lost two empires already, haven't you? Why
should the third be any different?" Geste said sweetly.

Thaddeus's expression turned dark, and he hissed, "Watch
your mouth, Trickster, or I might just stuff Sheila's guts in it."

Geste's smile vanished, and Thaddeus calmed slightly.

"I should have expected that from you, Geste," he said.
"Yes, I lost two empires. The first one was poisoned against me

by my father and my brother, so that I couldn't hold it. The second was built on a bunch of stupid primitives who betrayed me because they didn't have the brains or the guts to understand anything. *This* time that won't happen. I'll build my own empire, one that Peter and Shadowdark didn't meddle in, and I won't trust anything important to savages—I'll use artificial intelligences or my own tailored creatures instead, or just preconscious machines.''

"And you expect us to just stand by and watch?"

"Oh no, *more* than that—I expect you to help me. I've got your woman, Geste, and your man, Imp, and the others as well, and I expect you all to turn over all your equipment to me, so that I can use it to build my fleet. And in exchange, when I've built my empire, you can each have a planet to rule as my viceroy.''

The three immortals on the Skyland exchanged glances with one another; Bredon looked from one to the next, but they ignored him.

Thaddeus did not, however. He said, "Oh yes, and if you care about the primitives like your friend here, if you cooperate, I won't kill any more of them either, unless I have to."

"Any *more?*" Geste asked, startled.

"Well, certainly; I had to kill off all the tribes that lived right around the Fortress. I couldn't trust them, not after what happened back on Alpha Imperium. That was how I got Khalid here, as a matter of fact; he came to protest about one bunch that were his special pets.''

The four stared at him, speechless.

Thaddeus smiled back. "Oh, I see you want time to think about it—or rather, to talk it over before yielding, in order to save a little face. That's fine; I won't rush you. I understand how it is. I've studied psychology for thousands of years, and I know that you need to salve your pride by holding out for a while. You go right ahead; make a foolish gesture if you have to, but just remember, I have your friends here, and I have enough automated weapons to kill you all and build my empire without your help, if I have to." He raised a hand in sardonic salutation. "Until the next sunset, as measured at the Fortress. I want your capitulation no later than that, or the first captive dies.''

The image vanished.

Bredon stared at the empty air, trying to decide whether or not to believe the casual confession of mass murder. Had Thaddeus really butchered hundreds of innocent people?

Yes, he probably had, if Gamesmaster had told the truth about what happened on Alpha Imperium.

Bredon's own tribe was safe; they dwelt far to the east of the mountains, while Fortress Holding was far to the west. Still, a shudder ran through him at the thought of what a Power could do to them on a mere whim.

The others were also staring at the air, but their thoughts were clearly different.

"It's a bluff," Geste announced.

"I don't know," the Skyler said.

Imp glanced at the others, then turned back to the empty air without commenting, obviously involved in her own considerations.

"Of course it's a bluff!" Geste insisted. "He wouldn't dare kill helpless prisoners like that. Someone would find out. If any of us die, Mother will know, and she'll report it back to Terra, and they'll send someone out to investigate. Thaddeus won't risk that."

"Of course he would!" the Skyler said. "We don't know what's happened on Terra in the last four centuries; someone might have blown the whole planet apart by now. And Mother would send the news at light-speed, and we're hundreds of light-years from Terra. We've been through this before, Geste."

"But he *couldn't*," Geste insisted. "Even without bringing Terra into it, if he kills one of us, a cold-blooded murder like that, the others won't permit it. They'll all join forces against him. He won't risk *that!*"

The Skyler frowned. "Geste, you're being stupid; of *course* he will. First off, he's crazy. Second, the others are all apathetic and lazy, and they won't try to stop him and he knows it. Third, they can all be blackmailed by threats to the other six, if he kills one—seven is a lot of hostages to risk. And fourth, even if they *did* all gang up on him, he'd probably still win, because he's ready for it and he's got Aulden."

Geste hesitated, then said, "All right, you're right. I suppose I knew it, but I didn't want to admit it. He *will* kill them, all seven of them. He says he already killed all those other people, and I don't think he'd lie about that—we could check it too easily. Seven more won't mean that much more to him. But damn it, Skyler, we *have* to stop him, even if he *does* kill them! This may be the last chance anyone has. He expects us to give in, so if we attack we can catch him off guard. And if we *don't* stop him, he'd going to start an interstellar war, and probably kill *millions* of people. We *have* to stop him!"

It was the Skyler's turn to hesitate. She pursed her lips and glanced about uncertainly.

"You're right," she said at last. "I hate it, but you're right. And if you can let him kill Sheila, I won't argue any more. I don't even *like* most of the people he has there."

"Good! Imp?"

"What?" The redhead started at the sound of her name.

"Do you agree?" Geste asked. "We attack?"

Imp stared at Geste as if not really seeing him. "I don't think so," she said, oddly detached. She pulled a gleaming object from the air and spoke into it, slowly and clearly: "Do it, code green, I tell you three times, code green, code green."

Geste lunged forward, grabbing for the device she held, but was not in time to prevent her completion of the command. Imp fell back under his onslaught, landing roughly on the stone terrace with Geste on top of her. A sudden whirring and hissing came from all sides.

Bredon was at first baffled by this entire incident, but then dredged up a bit of information from his imprinted knowledge. The gleaming object was a master-link communicator.

A master-link communicator went straight to the central controls of a system, bypassing all artificial intelligences and working directly on the basic computer functions the intelligences operated unconsciously, much as a human's internal organs functioned without any conscious control. Such communicators existed as a safety measure, to make certain that humans could always override their creations. Only a very limited number of commands could be made over a master link, all intended for emergency situations.

Imp had apparently set up a command of some sort under the name "Code green," but Bredon could only guess what it was, or even what system her link was connected to.

Geste, sprawled across a motionless Imp, was in a light trance, communicating with his machines.

The Skyler demanded, "What's going *on?*" Bredon looked at her, and realized she was on the verge of hysteria.

"Damn!" Geste spat, coming out of his trance. "She's aborted every major weapon system we had! I let her take care of coordinating everything, so our weapons wouldn't get in each other's way, and she had saboteur systems built into everything she could get at, all set to shut down on that command!"

"I didn't trust you," Imp whispered. "I had to be ready."

"Now what do we do?" the Skyler wailed.

Geste sat up and looked at her with disgust. She paid no

attention, and his expression altered to a more contemplative one. "We still have the Skyland," he said. "We can drop it on Fortress Holding if we have to. We'll need to sabotage his protective fields, though."

"Drop the Skyland? Oh no, Geste. No you don't." The Skyler was suddenly calm, shocked back from the edge of hysteria by the threat to her hold. "Not *my* home you don't. Drop *Arcade* on him if you like!"

"Arcade doesn't fly, Skyler, and by the time I could *make* it fly—without Aulden's help—it would be too late to do any good. The Skyland is the only one of its kind, the only real weapon we have left, because Thaddeus would never think we would use it as a weapon."

"And he's right, damn him, and damn you too, Geste! *Nobody* is going to do *anything* with the Skyland!"

"That's right," Imp said from where she lay. "If you smash the Fortress, you'll kill Aulden and the others."

"But—"

"No buts, Geste!" The Skyler's tone had softened somewhat.

Imp said, "I know you mean well, Geste, and maybe you're right, in the abstract, but we can't *do* it. We can't kill our friends and smash the Skyler's home. We *can't*."

Geste looked up at the Skyler, and then down at Imp, who still lay sprawled before him.

"You want to surrender?" he asked.

"We don't *want* to," Imp replied, lifting herself up on one elbow, "we *have* to. If Thaddeus has those seven people, we *can't* let him kill them."

"Would you say that if Aulden weren't one of them?"

"I don't know," Imp admitted, "I really don't. But it doesn't matter, because he *is* one of them."

"If he is," Bredon said, breaking into the conversation for the first time. He had been very carefully thinking over what he had seen, in the light of his new understanding of Terran technology. "Why did Thaddeus only show those images for quick flashes like that? Maybe he faked them, or used old recordings."

Startled, the other three all looked at him. "But Mother said—" Imp began.

"If he faked the pictures, couldn't he have faked that transmission too?" the Skyler asked her.

Geste stared at Bredon, but said nothing. The corners of his mouth twitched, however, and Bredon knew he was thinking hard, and was pleased with the results.

The two women, after staring at each other speechlessly for a few seconds, turned to stare at Geste, waiting for his response.

"*Could* he be faking it?" Imp demanded.

"I think," the Trickster said at last, "that we had better check for ourselves that Thaddeus *does* have captives, that he hasn't killed them already, before we agree to anything."

"How can we do that, if Thaddeus is faking all the transmissions out of Fortress Holding?"

"We'll demand to see the captives in person, in the flesh."

"He won't allow that," the Skyler said derisively.

"Why not?" Geste asked. "If he doesn't, what is he afraid of?"

The Skyler hesitated, then answered, "He won't trust us inside his fortress. We might sabotage the place, somehow."

"He can take precautions. Or he can bring the prisoners out."

"He won't bring them out; we might rescue them."

"Then he'll have to let us in. If he doesn't, then we'll fight him. All we want is proof that they're still alive."

The Skyler studied the Trickster's face. "You're up to something, Geste," she said. "I know you are, and Thaddeus will know it, too."

"My reputation," he said with a mock sigh, addressing himself to Bredon. "No one ever trusts me!"

"That's right, and Thaddeus won't, either," the Skyler said.

"But he'll let us in anyway," Geste said with a smile, "because he's absolutely certain that he's smarter than I am, and able to counter whatever scheme I might have."

"Then you *do* have a scheme!" Imp exclaimed.

Geste smiled again, wryly. "Not really," he said. After a pause he added, "At least, not yet."

Chapter Twenty-one

"'. . . I, Hsin of the River, will grant you a wish. Anything you desire shall be yours!' And he gestured grandly at the surrounding magnificence.

"Thedor blinked in surprise.

"'I want to go home,' he said uncertainly.

"'Of course,' said Hsin. 'My creatures will carry you from this house, and from this island, and see you safely home. That is not enough; I had intended to do that much in any case. What else would you have?'

"Thedor thought for a moment, and then he said, 'My friends will not believe me when I tell this tale. Can you give me some token to show that I do not lie?'

"'Again, you ask too little,' Hsin said. 'I tell you that my creatures will escort you to your village, in plain sight of all. Furthermore, if you return here, you will always be welcome in the House of Fifty Peacocks, and although you may not see me, my familiar spirits will always be ready to speak to you, and to testify to whoever may accompany you as to the truth of what you say. Now, what more would you have of me?'

"Overwhelmed, Thedor thought long and hard, and then said, 'My grandfather, whom I loved, died last year. Could you bring his spirit to speak to me, so that I might thank him for the wisdom he taught me, and tell him how much I miss him?'

"At this, Hsin was overcome with emotion. When he could speak again, he said, 'Death is hard, is it not, little one? Alas, even I cannot bring back the dead, unless I have studied their souls while they still lived. Is there nothing you would have for yourself?'

"'I can think of nothing,' Thedor said.

"'Then go in peace,' Hsin replied, 'and I will have spirits watch over you and keep you safe from all harm, for as long as you shall live.' . . ."

—FROM THE TALES OF ATHERON THE STORYTELLER

The image of Thaddeus, bright against the gathering dusk, stared at Geste in outraged disbelief. "You want *what?*" it demanded.

"Look, Thaddeus," Geste answered calmly, "we know that you've had Aulden there for wakes now. You could be showing us recordings, or simulations, or androids, or pseudo-clones, or even the original bodies with the brains rebuilt. We need to know that these are really who you say they are, and there is nothing you can transmit that can't be faked. We need to see these people, talk to them, feel them, maybe run gene scans and neuropattern tests with our own equipment." Geste shrugged. "I don't think we're being unreasonable at all. You're asking us to surrender ourselves to you in exchange for the lives of our friends; well, we want to check your credit, so to speak, and make certain that you actually have those lives and haven't already destroyed them. You couldn't buy a ship back on Terra without a credit check, and you can't here, either."

"If you think I'm bringing them out where you can get at them with one of your sleight-of-hand maneuvers, Geste, you've gone mad."

The Trickster remained cool. "Then let us in," he said.

"So you can sabotage my fortress?"

"Take whatever precautions you like."

Thaddeus paused, considering, and then asked, in a far calmer tone, "You'd submit to a search and give up all your equipment?"

"Everything's that's not built in, anyway. And we might want some of it back to run tests with."

"You'd have no objection to suppressor fields?"

"I'd welcome them, Thaddeus; you couldn't run a simulation under full suppression."

"How do you know that I won't just keep you all here?"

"You want our equipment and our help, and we'll leave orders for an all-out attack if we aren't out after a certain time—say, second sunrise tomorrow."

This was a bluff, of course, since Imp had sabotaged the weapons systems, but Thaddeus had no way of knowing that.

Thaddeus nodded.

"All right," he said. "Come along, then, all of you. I'll have everything ready in, oh, three hours, and you'll be out again within thirty hours. Fair enough?"

"That's fine."

"I'll send a floater to bring you in."

"Fine."

Thaddeus smiled almost pleasantly. "I'll see you then." His image flicked out of existence, leaving the drifting terrace lights and the fading glow in the west.

"There," Geste said, turning to the others. "We have three hours to come up with something."

"Geste, can't you shut up? He might be listening," Imp said.

"I'm not going," the Skyler announced suddenly, before Geste

could answer Imp's complaint. Startled, the others all turned
to her.

"I'm not going," she repeated. "It's crazy. I'm not giving up
the Skyland for anybody, not Thaddeus or Aulden or you two,
and I'm not going to walk into a trap, either. Three hours! He
could do *anything* in three hours!"

"But, Skyler—" Imp began.

"You shut up!" the Skyler said, almost spitting at her in
sudden rage. "You went and pulled the plug on us! We might
have caught him off guard and stopped him, but *you* wrecked it
all! I did my share, I brought you here with all those infernal
machines you rigged up, and then you ruined everything!" She
turned her attention to the Trickster. "I've gone as far as I intend
to, Geste. I'm sorry, I know you mean well, but I can't do any
more. I'll wait here until you come out—*if* you come out—but
that's all. I'm not going in. If Thaddeus wins, I'm sorry, but I'll
survive. It won't last forever."

"I'm sorry, too," Geste replied. "But I understand."

For an awkward moment the three immortals stood facing each
other, while Bredon sat to one side, watching uncomfortably.
Then Imp turned to face Geste, pointedly giving the Skyler no
further attention, and said, "All right, we have three hours—
what do we do?"

"I wish I knew," The Trickster said, as the Skyler turned and
marched away in the direction of her private wing of the house.
Lights and music sprang up before her.

Before Imp could snap at him, Geste added hastily, "But I'll
think of something. Let's see if we can do anything useful with
any of the weapons."

Imp nodded, and walked off toward the house, Geste close
behind.

Bredon watched them go, but stayed where he was. He knew
that he could be of no use with the weapons; he simply did not
know enough about the technology involved, despite his high-
speed training. He sat back in his floating chair to contemplate
the scenery and the situation. The gaseous lights drifted overhead, and peacocks still stalked the lawns, but the music had
departed with its mistress.

Precisely three hours after the image of Thaddeus had vanished, a bright red floater, egg-shaped and glowing and perhaps
half a meter long, sailed up across the star-flecked black sky. It
turned and skimmed over the side of the Skyland, and came
whistling across the lawn toward the terrace.

Bredon was there waiting for it. The Skyler had not been seen since she stalked off the terrace and into her personal chambers. Geste and Imp were also somewhere in the house, presumably still improvising gadgetry and schemes.

"Hello!" Bredon called.

The floater ignored him. It swept in about a meter above the dark stone pavement, emitting a variety of low beeps and whistles, then turned and cruised along the perimeter of the terrace.

"Hello," Bredon called again, waving.

The floater continued to ignore him. When it had completed a full circuit, it spiraled inward from the edges, slowing steadily, until it came to a stop, hovering above the center of the terrace.

Seeing that this machine would not acknowledge his existence, Bredon shrugged and called, "Skyland, tell Geste and Imp that the floater is here."

"I have already done so, sir, and they are on their way," the Skyland replied, in a calm, imperturbable tone that struck Bredon as being a little too smug.

"Thank you," he said, wondering what the Skyland thought of the situation. It did not seem to have the same sort of awareness and personality that Gamesmaster did, but surely, he thought, it must have an opinion.

Before he could ask anything, Imp emerged from the house, her long hair drifting about her in an uneven auburn cloud as she strode onto the terrace. She had changed her clothes, and now wore a black velvet garment that Bredon had no name for. He stared, forgetting all about the Skyland's opinions.

The fabric covered her shoulders, breasts, and belly smoothly and tightly, as if stretched into place, while leaving most of her upper body bare. From the waist down it flared out into a flowing, voluminous skirt that moved as if with a life of its own, sometimes wrapping and coiling itself about her hips and legs, other times drifting out in a cloud of cloth that seemed indistinct about the edges, as if the material were dissolving into the air.

Bredon found this garb both startling and devastatingly attractive. He stared, and forced himself to remember that he wanted Lady Sunlight, not Imp.

His body still responded in its own way, undaunted by any message from the conscious mind.

Imp did not notice. She did not look at him at all, but hurried to the floater. She reached out to pat the machine, but it shied away.

She turned and called, "Hurry up, Geste! We don't want to keep him waiting!"

Bredon wondered whether she meant Thaddeus or Aulden.

Geste appeared almost before Imp had finished her sentence, his flying platform gliding at his heels. "All right," he said. "Let's go."

"The platform may not come," the red egg announced in a harsh monotone. "I am to bring three humans. No other self-propelled beings or devices are permitted."

"Three?" Geste asked. "Not four?"

"Three," the floater repeated.

Geste threw Imp a worried glance. "Maybe Thaddeus *did* eavesdrop, if he knows the Skyler isn't coming."

Reluctantly, Bredon suggested, "I don't think that's it. I think he didn't want *me* along."

"Oh," the Trickster said, momentarily looking foolish. "Oh, of course."

Imp looked at Bredon with interest. "I think you're right. I don't think Thaddeus thinks of you as human at all. He probably sees you as Geste's pet."

Bredon grimaced. "I'm not a Power," he acknowledged.

"Thaddeus may think Bredon's an android or some sort of Trojan horse," Imp said, turning to Geste.

"He may indeed," Geste agreed. "It's too bad we didn't think to make him one." He asked the floater, "Did your master tell you which three humans you were to bring?"

"The three humans to be found on this terrace," the machine answered.

"No further description?" Geste persisted.

"No further description," the machine replied.

"Well, here are three humans, then. Let's go."

"Acknowledged." Something extruded from the underside of the egg, something as red and gleaming as the egg itself. At first it was a slim cylinder, but a few centimeters above the stone pavement the cylinder stopped. Its lower end transformed into a disk, which expanded swiftly and silently.

To Bredon, it looked as if the egg were spilling blood, pouring it in a steady stream into a circular puddle, a pool spreading across an invisible barrier three centimeters above the terrace.

When the red disk was almost three meters in diameter the expansion abruptly stopped. Imp and Geste stepped forward, and up onto the disk.

Bredon was more hesitant; he had trouble believing that the disk could actually hold him. The egg had seemingly created it from thin air, and although he knew from his crash course in modern technology that the necessary material might have been retrieved from bent-space storage, or synthesized out of the air itself, his years of experience in his own society left him emotionally convinced that it had to be an illusion.

Cautiously, he forced himself to put a foot on the disk.

It seemed as firm and solid as the terrace itself. Reluctantly, Bredon lifted his other foot and stepped forward.

Immediately, the disk material began spreading again, but this time the outer edge grew vertically instead of horizontally, rising up to form a cylinder around the three humans. At a height of about a meter and a half it curved inward, forming a dome.

Even as it grew, the floater was moving; as the Skyler's home vanished behind the rising walls it was already receding. By the time the dome had closed overhead, Bredon knew they were off the Skyland entirely.

As with all the transportation the immortals used, however, there was no sensation of movement. It was as if the three of them had stood on the motionless disk while the Skyland sped away from them.

When the dome was complete, the last circle of blue sky closed away, they were left without any point of reference at all. The original egg glowed warmly, providing them with light, and a soft, musical hum emanated from the floor, but they had nothing to see except the egg, the blank red walls, and each other. They stood in uneasy silence.

Bredon wanted to ask what plans Geste had come up with, but he knew Thaddeus was listening, so he carefully said nothing. He turned his eyes away from Geste to avoid temptation.

After roaming aimlessly along the featureless red dome for a time, his eyes seemed to settle somewhere of their own volition. He found himself staring at Imp, and once again felt his body responding involuntarily to the extravagant sexual advertisement of her clothing. He forced himself to look away.

Geste's gaze wandered from the egg to Imp to Bredon, then around the dome and back to the egg, and Bredon had the impression that he was thinking hard about something while trying to look casual.

Imp simply stared blindly into space, oblivious to the others.

Bredon finally settled on staring at the egg, trying to guess just what it was capable of. This was ultimately pointless, since he could not tell, by visual inspection, whether it had a bent-space extension; if it *did* have one, then it could be capable of anything. Studying the floater did, however, keep his eyes and mind off his companions.

Time passed—perhaps only a minute or two, possibly as much as an hour. Bredon had lost all sense of time in the absence of both conversation and the outside world. The only interruption of the silence came when Geste remarked, apropos of nothing, "Judging by this floater, Thaddeus is using a better grade of technology now than he has in the past—no wheels, no wings, no lenses or levers or dials. This is as modern as most of my own stuff. Maybe he's trying to impress us; he never trusted the slick stuff before."

Imp glanced at the egg, but no one spoke, and the silence returned, longer and stronger than before. Geste shrugged, started to say something more, then thought better of it.

At last, however, the dome began to fade, turning from red to pink, then to ever-greater transparency until it vanished completely, revealing that they had been delivered into a large chamber of dark stone, presumably somewhere in Fortress Holding.

When the dome had vanished, the disk on which they stood sank down, merging seamlessly into the gray stone floor, its red color fading gradually into the gray.

When the disk was gone the egg-shaped floater retracted the rod that had become their craft. The egg itself hung in their midst for a moment, then whirred softly and sped away, leaving the three humans momentarily unattended.

They stood in the center of an octagonal room, with a door in the center of every second wall. The ceiling above them was white glass, glowing softly. A faint scent of dampness and ozone reached them. No music played.

"Where's the Skyler?" Thaddeus's voice asked from somewhere overhead.

The three of them glanced at one another. "She changed her mind, decided not to come," Imp explained.

"What's that savage doing here?"

"You told the transport that you wanted three humans, so we brought three humans. Bredon wanted to come, so we brought him," Geste said.

"If he gets in the way, I'll kill him."

"I'm sure Bredon understands that," Geste answered.

Bredon nodded.

"Have it your way," Thaddeus said. "I don't suppose it matters, and I don't really give a damn. Take off your clothes."

Bredon glanced at his companions. Imp glanced at Geste. Geste looked up and demanded, "Why?"

"You know why," Thaddeus's voice replied. "You could have whole arsenals tucked away."

"What if we refuse?"

"Then you don't see Aulden and the rest."

Geste looked at the others, shrugged, and began peeling off his tunic.

Imp did something to the waistline of her dress with her fingertips, and the entire garment slipped free and fell to the floor. She wore nothing else. Bredon blushed, and looked to his own clothing.

When they were all naked, the loud voice overhead said, "Step through the door beneath the red light."

Bredon turned, and saw a tall doorway with a small red spot glowing above it. The door that had filled that doorway was gone, perhaps slid aside, perhaps dissolved, he had no way of telling. He followed the others through the opening, trying to be as calm about his nudity as they were. He knew, from references the others had made and things he had seen back in Arcade, and even from the childhood tales he remembered, that the Powers did not worry about sexual propriety much, but his own upbringing had been fairly traditional, and he was not accustomed to walking about naked in the company of a woman he was not about to take to his bed. He had not seen Kittisha the Weaver naked until his second night with her, and then only by dim firelight, yet here Imp was parading before him in full view.

The doorway led into a short corridor with gleaming metal walls, and as Bredon stepped into it he felt an odd sensation, as if his skin were buzzing silently. A sudden flash, so brief that he was not sure he had actually seen it, turned the tingling to an uncomfortable warmth, like the bad sunburn he had once gotten as a child. He looked, and saw that his skin was reddening slightly.

That old burn had resulted from a full light of carelessly lying in bright sunlight, after a long spell of convalescence from prickle-fever had left him pale and weak; it did not seem credible that a near-instantaneous flash could have caused the same thing, but his skin certainly felt burned. He marched on, ignoring the discomfort.

Then he was through the corridor and in a small room paneled in white. Three simple white robes hung in the air.

Geste took one, and Bredon another; Imp hesitated before donning the third. "Where is Aulden?" she demanded.

She received no reply. For a long moment the three of them stood there, waiting for whatever was to happen next. Bredon took the moment to notice that Imp's robe reached almost to her ankles, and Geste's to midcalf, while his own came only to his knee.

Then the wall opposite their entrance slid aside, revealing a larger room, of gray stone like the octagonal chamber they had first arrived in. This room, however, was not empty, as the others had been.

Chained to the far wall were seven people, four men and three women, all wearing white robes like those Bredon, Geste, and Imp had just put on. All seven sat slumped against the stone, their wrists, ankles, and necks bound by massive bands of metal, linked by tangles of heavy chain to each other and to ringbolts in the wall behind them. All seven appeared to be sunburnt to varying degrees, presumably by Thaddeus's machines.

Bredon immediately recognized the woman in the center as Lady Sunlight; even without her shimmering garments, even with her hair matted and bedraggled and her skin an uncomfortable shade of red, she was unsurpassably beautiful, and he felt something twisting and churning inside himself at the sight of her chained. He fought for control of himself, struggled not to simply run to her side.

"Aulden!" Imp shrieked. She dashed forward and flung herself upon the man at the far left of the group, a sturdy, sandy-haired man with a long nose and only a faint pinkness to his skin. Bredon remembered his face from the quick glimpse Thaddeus had given them.

Aulden looked up just before Imp landed on him. His expression was a compound of surprise and joy at the sight of her, but Bredon thought he saw an underlying hopelessness.

"I don't believe this," Geste muttered, standing in the doorway. "Chains! Genuine steel chains!"

Distracted for a moment from Lady Sunlight, Bredon started to ask what else Thaddeus would have used, but stopped himself. He could have used any number of methods of confinement, from barrier fields to neural repatterning.

Chains, however, worked quite well enough.

Imp and Aulden were smothering each other with kisses, and the other six were looking up with some interest at the newcomers. Bredon suddenly found himself overcome with shyness, faced with so much attention from strangers.

"Hello, Geste," one of the women said, a brown-haired, round-faced woman.

"Hello, Sheila," the Trickster replied.

"Who's that with you?" she asked. "Has someone got a new body?"

"No, no, nothing like that; this is Bredon the Hunter, from a village out in the grasslands."

Bredon bowed in acknowledgment, looking only at Lady Sunlight, hoping to see some sign in her reaction that she saw him as something more than an ordinary savage.

Lady Sunlight said nothing, did not react visibly at all.

"Pleased to meet you," Sheila replied. "Forgive me if I don't stand up." She rattled her chains with a wry shrug. "So, what brings you here?"

Geste smiled.

Bredon tore his eyes away from Lady Sunlight, forcing himself not to stare at her any longer, and looked at the other captives; they were not impressed with Sheila's banter. From descriptions in old legends, he guessed the dark, intense little man to be Rawl the Adjuster. The third woman, a sallow-skinned and black-haired, had to be Madame O. Both the other two men were big, black-haired, and brown-eyed, but one was pale and heavily bearded, while the other was swarthy and had only a light, gray-flecked beard; Bredon had no way of guessing which was Brenner of the Mountains and which was Khalid.

"Are you going to get us out of here?" the swarthy one demanded.

Geste's smile vanished. "I wish I knew," he said.

"That," said Thaddeus from behind them, "is not the answer I wanted, indicating, as it does, a certain lingering hope that outright surrender can be avoided."

Geste and Bredon turned around slowly; Imp, still wrapped in Aulden's arms, paid no attention.

Thaddeus stood in the doorway from the metal corridor, a towering black-haired figure in brown leather—or a synthetic approximation of leather. Bredon was not certain just how he could tell, but he had the impression that this was a real person, not a transmitted image. Perhaps it was because this Thaddeus stood his awesome full height, at least two and a half meters.

"Hello, Thaddeus," Geste said.

"Hello, Geste. Are you satisfied now that I have not tampered with my captives?"

"Well, no, not yet. I just got here."

"Imp, are *you* satisfied?"

Imp looked up, brushing hair out of her face. "It's Aulden—but how could you treat him like this, you monster?"

Thaddeus shrugged. "I don't love him as you do."

"Thaddeus, we have to talk this over. You don't need to do all this," Geste said.

"Oh, I don't? What do *you* know about it?" Thaddeus sneered.

"I know that it's stupid! What can you get from ruling an empire that you can't get peacefully?"

Thaddeus smiled with bitter amusement. "Are you really asking that?"

"Yes, I am! Look, can we go somewhere and talk about this?"

"You don't want these people to hear?" Thaddeus asked, with a wave at the others.

"No, that's not it," Geste said. "All right, we can talk here."

"No, no," Thaddeus said, holding up a hand. "We'll find someplace more comfortable. Come along, Imp."

"No!" she said. "No! I won't leave Aulden!"

Thaddeus shrugged again. "Suit yourself. Monitor, watch her closely. Don't let her out of this room, or obey her orders. And don't disturb me." All but the first phrase he addressed to a red light that gleamed above the door. It blinked an acknowledgment, and he turned back to the Trickster. "All right, Geste, come along." He waved, and Geste followed.

Bredon started to follow as well, and Thaddeus gestured. "Leave that here, though," he said.

Geste said nothing, but Bredon stepped back, and waited politely until Thaddeus and Geste were out of sight.

Chapter Twenty-two

" '. . . so you have found me,' Aulden the Technician said. 'Now, what do you want of me?'

" 'They say, in my village, that you can do anything,' Golrol said. 'Is it true?'

"Aulden stared at him for a moment, and then said, 'Very nearly, at any rate.'

" 'You can do anything?' Golrol persisted.

" 'Yes,' Aulden said. 'I can.'

" 'Really?' Golrol asked.

" 'Yes, I said,' Aulden told him. 'I can be anything and do anything.' He instantly transformed himself into a giant, a hundred meters tall, and then vanished completely, and then reappeared as a sunflower with Aulden's own face, and then appeared human once more. 'I can fly to the stars,' he said, 'or make their fire burn here on the ground. I know the secrets of time and space. I can make birds swim and fish fly. I can build a tower in a single night that will reach so high you cannot see the top. I can shake the earth and shatter the sky.'

" 'So you say that you can do anything,' Golrol said.

" 'Yes, I told you,' Aulden answered. 'Try me; name a task, and I shall perform it.'

" 'Can you bring me snow from the mountaintops, even now in midsummer?' Golrol asked.

" 'As easily as you can snap your fingers,' Aulden replied, and he spun about, and held out a handful of snow.

" 'Can you lift an entire mountain, then?'

"Aulden laughed, and said, 'Easily.' And he waved his hand, and with a rumble and a roar, one of the distant mountains tore itself free of the earth and rose into the sky, like the Skyland itself.

" 'And can you create a mountain from nothing?'

" 'Of course!' said Aulden, and behold, with a great rending crash a mountain rose from the plain where none had stood a moment before.

" 'And can you create a mountain so great that even you cannot lift it?' Golrol asked innocently.

"And Aulden paused, and stared at him, and slowly a smile spread across his face, and he began to grin, and then to laugh, and then to roar with laughter.

" 'Oh, mortal,' he said. 'You have me there. I should have known better than to boast so freely! Of course I cannot. I am no true god. I *can do many, many things that you cannot even imagine, but I cannot untangle such a paradox any more than you can . . .'*

—FROM THE TALES OF ATHERON THE STORYTELLER

When Thaddeus and Geste had vanished through the doorway Bredon turned back to the prisoners. Lady Sunlight still showed no sign of interest in him, so he addressed himself to the group as a whole. "Now what?" he asked. "Is there anything I can do to help?"

"I don't know," replied Sheila—the Lady of the Seasons, Bredon remembered, the goddess of the weather, who brought the warm sun in summer and the cold winds in winter.

Except that the woman he saw before him, although she was healthy and attractive apart from her fading burn, was just a woman, not a goddess. The Powers were only human, and their power lay in their technology.

And the seasons had nothing to do with technology, in any case.

"I don't know," she repeated, "but I hope so."

"I'd like to get you out of those chains, but I don't have a key or anything that will cut them."

"Thaddeus keeps the key with him, I think," the small man Bredon had identified as Rawl said.

"Why are you people talking to this savage?" Madame O whined. "What good can *he* do?"

"Thaddeus obviously doesn't think he can do anything at all," Lady Sunlight said, "but Thaddeus has been wrong before."

Bredon felt his pulse quicken as Lady Sunlight eyed him appraisingly.

"He's not wrong *this* time," O spat.

"Maybe not," Bredon admitted. "I can try, though." He looked around the room, but saw nothing useful. The red light above the door caught his eyes. "Monitor, where is a key for these chains?" he asked.

The intelligence hesitated. "I am uncertain whether you are authorized to ask that," it said at last.

"Why?"

"I have no record of your existence."

"Monitor," Sheila demanded, "answer this man's question."

"No," the intelligence replied at once. "The prisoner Sheila is forbidden all service beyond stated necessities and emergency aid."

Imp looked up from Aulden's chest for a moment, then glanced at first Bredon, then Sheila, then back to Bredon. "Aulden," she whispered, "Bredon took a lot of imprinting at Arcade; he's no technician, but he can run machines. Thaddeus doesn't know that, and he didn't give the machines any orders about him. What can he do to stop Thaddeus?"

Aulden's expression slowly lost its underlying hopelessness as he considered this. He glanced up at the red light, then motioned silently for Bredon to come closer.

The mortal came and knelt beside the chained technician.

"I can't do anything about the machines Thaddeus designed himself, like Monitor up there," Aulden whispered, "but they're all pretty stupid, because Thaddeus is a lousy technologist, so most of the fortress is run by intelligences we brought with us from Terra, or ones I designed for Thaddeus. I think you can do something with those. Except for Monitor, none of the machines can hear any of us immortals anymore, but they ought to be able to hear *you*. And Thaddeus doesn't use purely biological intelligent systems because he doesn't trust them, since they have a habit of turning independent, so you won't have to worry about creatures, just machines."

Lady Sunlight glanced up at the red light that represented Monitor, and asked, "Aren't you afraid that that machine will hear you, and tell Thaddeus?"

"No," Aulden replied. "You weren't listening. Thaddeus told it not to disturb him, with no qualification. Even if it hears us it won't tell anyone. It's a really stupid machine."

"What should I do?" Bredon asked eagerly.

"First," Aulden told him, "you need the emergency codes."

Two levels and a corridor away, Thaddeus settled into a gray floating chair and gestured for the Trickster to do the same.

Geste obliged. Something felt very odd about the room, and he realized as the chair adjusted itself that no music was playing.

When both were comfortably seated, Thaddeus asked politely, "Now, why do you think I should stop my efforts to rebuild my stolen empire?"

"Because it's stupid and pointless," Geste replied quickly.

"Oh?" Thaddeus's reply was cool.

"Yes," Geste said. "Seriously, Thaddeus, what can you get by ruling an empire that you can't just buy now, with what you have? You can have any material possession you could possibly want; our galaxy is jammed with raw materials and energy, and all it takes is time and technology to make whatever you want—food, shelter, clothing, amusements, even women, whatever creatures you want. What good will an empire do you?"

Thaddeus cocked his head and smiled cruelly. "Can you really be that naive?" he asked. The smile vanished, and his voice turned hard. "I can have *power*. I will prove my superiority to all you young upstarts, with your foolish egalitarian beliefs and petty social rituals. I'll get the human race *organized* again, put an end to all this hedonistic anarchy."

"Will you?" Geste asked, almost sneering in mockery of Thaddeus's own behavior. "Do you really think you can do that?"

"Of course I can!" Thaddeus roared back. "I'm thousands of years older than you, Geste; show a little respect for your elders. I'm not a manufactured immortal like you, dependent on machines and symbiotes for longevity—I'm a natural immortal, a member of a superior race, one of the chosen people. My family is *destined* to rule over you ordinary humans. I have a head start of more than two thousand years on any artificial immortal, and that two thousand years gives me experience and knowledge that you can't even imagine, with your pitiful few centuries behind you. You've lived all your life in pampered comfort, and you've been content with that, but I grew up in harder times, boy, I saw my mother's family murdered, my homeland destroyed, by you normal humans. I've lived through wars and disasters that would frighten you into catatonia, and I've learned from all of it."

"Have you? Then why did you fail twice before?"

"Because I was *betrayed!*" Thaddeus bellowed, rising from his chair, his face red with fury. "I *trusted* people, and they *betrayed* me!"

Geste resisted the impulse to taunt Thaddeus further. "All right, you were betrayed," he said quietly. "Doesn't that show you that people don't *want* you to rule them?"

"What the hell do I care what they want?" Thaddeus asked, as he sank back into his seat. "*I* want it! I never claimed to be doing this for anyone else!"

Geste abandoned that line and groped for another.

"You could get killed," he said. "You don't know what's happened out there these last few centuries. You might run smack into some sort of interstellar police force, or somebody else's empire, and get yourself killed."

"I'll risk it," Thaddeus said. "I don't believe it, for one thing; I saw what you decadent babies were like, and now that you're all fake immortals, four hundred years wouldn't be enough to change that. You people need a thousand years just to decide what to have for breakfast."

"But what if some group of short-lifers took charge, caught someone by surprise . . ."

Thaddeus stared at him in such open disbelief that Geste did not bother to finish his question.

"Short-lifers," Thaddeus said, "are absolutely harmless. They don't live long enough to learn anything dangerous. I've survived seven thousand years of the worst short-lifers can throw at me. If there's a short-lifer empire out there, all I have to do is wait for it to fall. It never takes very long."

The Trickster was by no means certain Thaddeus was right about that, but he did not see any sign that Thaddeus could be swayed by logical argument, and he did not continue that line of debate. "All right," Geste said. "Let me think." He reached up and scratched his ear.

Thaddeus took the opportunity to signal a housekeeping machine for a drink. He turned to Geste, intending to play the gracious host and offer the Trickster something, and found himself staring at a sparkling web of metal in Geste's hand, a web he recognized immediately as a stasis field generator, though he had never seen one so small.

Before he could say anything, Geste triggered his weapon, and Thaddeus froze into total immobility, a sphere of air around him freezing with him. The soft light in the room refracted strangely through the interface between normal air and the motionless field, and the colors within the field—the red of Thaddeus's angry face, the gray of his chair, the black of his hair, the brown of his clothing—seemed to fade.

As the stasis field reached full intensity, the three-meter globe first turned a dead, flat black, then brightened to gleaming, reflective silver, as light became first unable to leave the field, and then unable to enter.

Thaddeus was gone, sealed inside a mirror-finish bubble of timelessness. The housekeeping machine carrying his drink, a floating wedge of black with a crystal goblet embedded in it, bumped futilely against the bubble's bright, impenetrable surface.

Geste stared, trembling. He had forced himself to remain calm while arguing with Thaddeus; he had had his internal machines and symbiotes under orders to keep him calm, and a semi-intelligent biochip chanting gently hypnotic reassurance directly to his audial nerves. He had been as slick and smooth as anyone could have wanted in pulling the stasis generator from the bent-space pocket he had built into his ear.

Thaddeus had scanned his guests up and down the spectrum, checked for every sort of emission imaginable—Geste had expected as much, and had detected some of the operative devices with his own internal mechanisms. Thaddeus had blasted them all with high-speed flashes of high-intensity ultraviolet, infrared, and gamma radiation that were too quick to seriously harm human tissue, but which would fry virtually all surface-dwelling or air-carried tailored microbes, and would burn out the metastable energy fields that made up noncorporeal intelligences—not that they had brought any noncorporeals to Denner's Wreck, or had the means to create them. He had doused them all in chemical suppressants to prevent any sort of pheromone-assisted psychological assault. He had removed their clothing and searched it, all the way down to the subatomic level.

Their symbiotes had been damaged, their own tissues somewhat damaged as well, and Geste was fairly sure that he had lost some magnetic memory somewhere, but Thaddeus had been reassured that he had disarmed his visitors.

However, he had not checked on the shape of the spaces they occupied.

Even Thaddeus could not think of everything.

Geste had counted on that. He had never heard of putting a bent-space pocket into a human body, and he had hoped that Thaddeus hadn't either.

Not that that had been his only trick. Thaddeus had wiped out a wide variety of artificial bacteria and a few viruses with his disinfectants and ultraviolet, and had confiscated more than a dozen weapons of various kinds in Geste's clothing.

The bent-space pocket had been the Trickster's best gimmick, though, and he knew it. People built the pockets into floaters all the time, but not into themselves; it seemed somehow unhealthy to put a hole through one's own body, even a polyspatial hole that bypassed mere normal-space flesh. For one thing, an opening was needed. Virtually all the natural openings in the human body were already spoken for, and creating new holes was dangerous and unesthetic.

Geste, of course, had been desperate. He had considered anchoring the pocket to the roof of his mouth, but had rejected that; he had needed to be able to talk. Instead, he had sacrificed the hearing in his right ear. He hoped that removing the pocket and rebuilding his inner ear would not be too difficult.

His trick had worked, and Thaddeus was captured, but now Geste's programmed calm had run out. Adrenaline poured into his blood unregulated by his damaged and panicky symbiotes. He stood, shaking, as the realization sank in that he had done it, he had stopped Thaddeus.

A sliver of triumph worked its way through the numb relief, and then shattered into full-blown gloating. He had *done* it! Thaddeus was neatly boxed up and out of the way.

On the heels of exultation came doubt. *Was* Thaddeus boxed up? It seemed too easy, somehow.

Perhaps there were machines that were programmed to release Thaddeus. Perhaps there were creatures with orders to kill the prisoners. Geste stepped back and looked about warily.

"Not bad, Geste," Thaddeus's voice said, speaking from the wall behind him. "Not bad at all."

Geste turned, telling himself that it was just a machine, a recording or an artificial intelligence synthesizing its master's voice.

"A very nice effort," the voice said, "but not enough. No, Geste, I'm not a recording, not a machine. I'm Thaddeus. The *real* Thaddeus."

Geste was trembling again, harder than ever.

"You see," Thaddeus said, "you only got *one* of me."

Chapter Twenty-three

"The Power called Leila of the Mountain of Fire lives inside a mountain, in the great jungles far to the southwest. The top of the mountain was blasted away long ago, and inside the hole that the blast left burn fires so hot that the rock itself melts and flows like water. Whether it was Leila who blasted the mountain and lit the fires, or whether that happened before she came to live there, no one now remembers.

"Whatever the cause, the mountain burns, but Leila lives in it unharmed. Her skin is darker in hue than any mortal's, even a southerner's—almost black. Some say this is due to the heat of the flames surrounding her home.

"There is a village at the foot of her mountain, a large and prosperous village, and Leila looks after the people there. When one falls ill she comes to his bedside and touches him, and five times out of six he is well again the next day. When the crops fail or the hunters return empty-handed, Leila's creatures bring baskets of strange food and leave them in the village square, for the Elders to distribute to those who need it most. Storms always pass by the village without harming it, yet there is never a drought.

"This might be paradise, save that Leila asks a price for her protection; once a year she chooses a handsome young man from the village who must come alone to her home atop the mountain. This man knows he has been chosen when a voice calls him by name, a voice that speaks from the air.

"If the chosen one refuses, then Leila's protection is withdrawn from the village; no baskets of food are brought when supplies run low, the ill are left to recover or die on their own, storms no longer pass by, and a thousand lesser evils go unhindered. Leila takes no vengeance, she merely withdraws her aid.

"But that is enough; in all the memories of the villagers, and in all the tales going back many generations, no chosen one has held out against the summons for more than a season.

"And what becomes of the chosen ones, the sacrifices? No one knows. Some have returned alive, after a season or a year or ten years, but these fortunate ones never remember anything that happened after they passed the rim of the crater. Most never return at all. None have ever been found dead—if they return, they return alive and well, and usually live long, happy lives, troubled only by their inability to recall what befell them . . ."

—FROM THE TALES OF ATHERON THE STORYTELLER

Bredon paused, hesitantly glancing up and down the slick gray walls of the passage. He had counted four doors in the left-hand wall of this corridor, two of the regular large ones, and two wide, low ones intended for service machines, so that the next would be the fifth. Aulden had said to take the fifth door on the left.

The door, of course, was closed. That was not the problem. Getting through doors was easy. All he had to do was yell, "Emergency override! Human in danger!" and the doors would slide out of his way. That was a safety feature that Aulden said had been built into every hold on Denner's Wreck, back when they were first erected by the automated equipment Mother—the mother ship—had provided.

Of course, some of the Powers had removed safety features, or altered them, or tampered with them in various ways. Thaddeus certainly had. However, he had apparently not known about this one. At least so far, the command had worked on every door Bredon had shouted at in Fortress Holding, allowing him to roam freely.

No, the problem was not that the door was closed, nor even that he was unsure whether it was the right door.

He *was* unsure, he admitted to himself. The Fortress was a maze, with rooms and corridors criss-crossing apparently at random, almost all of them a dismal, uniform gray. It made the colorful and variform chambers of Arcade, which had utterly baffled Bredon at first, seem simple.

Aulden had given him instructions for reaching Thaddeus's war room, which Aulden had provided unwilling assistance in building, but the directions were hard to follow in the face of the endless corridors and the frequent encounters with patrolling machines. He could easily have miscounted somewhere, or turned the wrong way.

But it was not the chance that he faced the wrong door that worried him. It was the patrolling machines that caused him to hesitate. What if one was just behind the door? What if this one was not as cooperative as the others? After all, this would be the very heart of the Fortress, and it might be more carefully guarded than the corridors.

The first patrol machine had terrified him. A low, boxlike silver affair with several jointed appendages, it had stopped suddenly, pointed something at him, and demanded, "State your business."

Bredon had mouthed the meaningless syllables Aulden had taught him, hoping he pronounced them correctly.

"Acknowledged," the machine replied.

"Abort all programming and await orders," Bredon told it, his voice unsteady.

"Acknowledged," the machine said again. It stood, silently waiting, completely harmless, while Bredon walked on.

That was no standard safety feature, of course; the universal password was something Aulden had done his best to infiltrate into every system in the fortress when he first began to distrust Thaddeus, decades earlier. He was unsure how successful he had been.

Bredon knew that it had not worked everywhere; the doors, for example, were too simple to be tampered with subtly, but those still had the original safety overrides. Others machines Thaddeus had programmed entirely by himself, in careful isolation, so Aulden had never gotten a chance at those. Those would be the most dangerous, should Bredon encounter any, even though they were generally stupid.

Even with the ones Aulden had tampered with, there were ways Thaddeus could overrule Aulden's gimmick, without necessarily even realizing the password existed. He had hit on one quite by accident. Thaddeus had programmed his machines to literally not hear Aulden's voice, either spoken or transmitted.

It was a simple enough procedure, really, but not something Aulden had ever thought of. He grudgingly admired Thaddeus for coming up with it.

Even when the other captives had told him what Thaddeus had said about it, Aulden had had trouble believing it could work completely. It was a simple concept, but Thaddeus was so technically inept that Aulden had hoped for some loophole.

Aulden had tried to use his secret password to force the machines to free him and the other prisoners, but without success. Monitor heard him, but simply didn't react to the password at all; Monitor was apparently an independent entity of Thaddeus's own creation, not linked in any vital way to the rest of the fortress, and not built to any of Aulden's own designs.

Most of the other machines did not acknowledge Aulden's existence at all.

Aulden had always thought that he would be safe, that his mastery of the machines would allow him to resist any sort of coercion Thaddeus—or Brenner, or any other potential troublemaker on Denner's Wreck—might apply. He knew that he, or his built-in equipment, could dominate almost any program.

He had to make himself heard, though, before he could affect an artificial intelligence. When the metal claws had reached out for him and he had shouted commands at them, both orally and through his skull-liner and other internal systems, it was as though he had simply stood silently. The claws had picked him up and carried him away.

He had puzzled it out during the hours he spent in chains. The machines had not heard him. That was the only explanation.

When Brenner and Sheila and Rawl and Lady Sunlight had been delivered to the prison they had confirmed his theory. Thaddeus had told them the machines could not hear them.

Aulden had tested that. He had had each of the other prisoners shout coded commands to the machines that brought food and water, and the commands had been ignored—not merely refused, but ignored, as if they were not heard at all.

And of course, Thaddeus would have made sure that his machines could not hear any of the other immortals, either. He did not have to worry about any sort of infiltration. Machines could very easily be instructed not to accept orders from anyone but a human being—in many cases, that was standard default programming—so no machines or artificial creatures could deliver commands from his enemies. The other immortals would need to give orders personally, rather than through any sort of inhuman proxy, and Thaddeus had made sure that such orders would not be heard.

Bredon, though—Thaddeus had had no records of Bredon's voice, no reason to blank that voice out of the hearing of his machines. With Aulden's passwords, Bredon could override Thaddeus's control of any machine that Aulden had ever worked on.

Aulden was the only real technician on the planet, and Mother and all her subsidiaries had been built to his design. Most of Fortress Holding's machines would now obey Bredon, if he could get to them.

Fortress Holding had one unfortunate feature, from Bredon's point of view. It had no central controlling intelligence, no equivalent to the Skyland's mind, or Arcade's Gamesmaster, or the housekeeper at Autumn House. A single central intelligence susceptible to being overridden by Aulden's universal password would have been very convenient, but Thaddeus had not been obliging enough to provide one. Aulden said that Thaddeus had something called a "frankenstein complex" and refused to trust a single central intelligence. Instead, he used hundreds of separate intelligences.

All the major ones, however, could be commanded from a central control station. That was where Thaddeus spent most of his time, where he concocted his schemes, where he had directed the attack on the High Castle. He called it his war room. If

Bredon, or any other mortal who knew Aulden's password, could get into that room he could cripple Thaddeus's entire fortress in a matter of seconds.

Accordingly, that was where Bredon was headed, leaving a trail of open doors and blanked machines behind him, trying unsuccessfully to follow Aulden's hurried directions, unaware that he had miscounted doors in the corridor because of differences in terminology. Bredon, trained to be observant, had counted access panels. Aulden, trained in remembering details, knew quite well that the access panels were there, but did not consider them to be doors, and failed to realize just how spotty Bredon's grounding in the culture of the immortals was. To Bredon, anything a human or machine passed through in going from one chamber to another was a door; to Aulden, only openings intended to be used by humans were doors.

The correct door, the door Aulden had meant to direct him to, was a hundred meters farther on.

Bredon hesitated. He was, he believed, nearing the war room now, with just two more chambers and a short passageway to pass through. What if, worse than a mere machine, Thaddeus himself waited on the other side of this door?

Well, he would just have to risk it. "Emergency override!" he called. "Human in danger! Open up!"

The door slid obediently open, and he found himself looking into an unlit storeroom lined with dusty, vacant shelves and smelling of ink. No doors led to the war room antechamber. No doors led *anywhere*.

"Oh, you stinking demons!" Bredon hissed, realizing he was lost.

Worse than lost, he was alone in the enemy's stronghold, unarmed and virtually defenseless, without even a symbiote to hold wounds closed or counteract poisons.

No, he corrected himself, he was not unarmed or defenseless. He had Aulden's password. He turned and looked back down the corridor.

No one was coming. His danger, though real, was not immediate.

He still had no idea why Aulden's directions had failed him, but that did not matter. He was a hunter; when one trap or stratagem failed, he devised another instantly.

He turned and headed back for where he had left one of the machines awaiting orders.

Chapter Twenty-four

"I knew a woman once from another village, a village far from here, on the south coast where the eastern forests give way to sandy beaches, who claimed that she had once been a guest of Lord Hollingsworth of the Sea. As she told it, she had been playing on the beach as a girl, throwing sand out onto the drifting water sheets and watching as they first tried to eat it, then spat it back up in hundreds of little spurts that sent it bouncing around madly—apparently that was a popular game among the young people around there. As she played, though, something rose up from the sea, a great black shape that she could never describe clearly. She once said it looked something like an ear of corn the size of a house, or perhaps a giant fish, though of course there are no true fish in salt water.

"At any rate, a man came out of this thing and spoke to her, and told her not to fling sand on the watersheets, because it could kill them. They were delicate, this man told her, and trying to eat the sand could give them the equivalent of a very bad stomachache, one so bad that it could kill the weaker ones.

"She thought this worrying about watersheets was absurd, and said so, despite her fear and wonder at this person's strange appearance and even stranger mode of travel, which she took for an odd sort of boat. The man retorted that she knew nothing of the sea or its creatures.

"She admitted that she knew very little, and after some further discussion she found that she had agreed to visit with the man in his home beneath the sea.

"The man was Lord Hollingsworth, of course, and his home the sunken palace Atlantis, deep beneath the ocean. They rode there together in the boat, or fish, or whatever it was, and he showed her many of the sea's creatures, weird and frightening things of every size and shape.

"You know, a watersheet is so thin that if you get the right angle, you can put your hand right through it and not even notice. It's so thin that it tears apart into practically nothing if you pick it up, so thin that you can only see it by the way it changes the texture of the water's surface—but it's so strong, in some ways, that it can live through the worst storms, storms that will smash a boat or a house to splinters. Well, this woman said that there were creatures in the sea that made watersheets seem as normal as rabbits. There were things that changed color and shape, things that swam by spitting out pieces of their own flesh, things that glowed in the dark, things with flesh she could see through, so that she could watch their blue-green blood *flowing. There were worms kilometers long, things like fish with heads at both ends—oh, she could go on for hours describing the monstrosities Lord Hollingsworth showed her.*

"But what she really remembered was the Power's own comments on these creatures. 'You know,' she said he said, 'I never get tired of watching these. They're stranger than anything I could ever make.'

"And of course, I'm sure that you'll be struck with the same thing that struck her, and that struck me when I heard that—if he didn't make all the creatures in the sea, who did?"

—FROM A CONVERSATION WITH ATHERON THE STORYTELLER

In all the old stories, the tales of the ancient times when death was a common thing, the heroes always faced certain doom bravely, daring their foes to step forth and do battle, loudly proclaiming their faith in whatever noble cause they served, right to the last.

Geste wondered how, in all the hells of every dead religion that had ever been preached, anyone could ever believe such tripe. He was facing death now, he knew, and he was too terrified to stand, let alone laugh in its face. He fell back in his chair, teeth chattering, his entire body shaking with fear, forcing his eyes to stay open in the forlorn hope that he might see and fend off at least one or two attacks, extending his existence for a few precious seconds.

All he saw was his own face, mockingly reflected in the stasis field.

Thaddeus's laughter surrounded him, roaring laughter that did not sound sane to him.

"You thought you had me, didn't you, Trickster?" Thaddeus shouted. "You thought that you had me in stasis forever, out of your way, so you could go on playing God with these pitiful primitives, go on playing your stupid games with the women! Well, Trickster, it looks like *I'm* the one with the last laugh, the one with the best trick!"

Geste could not have answered had he wanted to. He had lived his entire life, centuries now, with the conviction that he would live on until he grew tired of it—and the happy suspicion that he would never grow out of it. Death was for other, lesser beings, never for A.T. Geste of Achernar IV.

Now he knew, with absolute certainty, that Thaddeus was going to kill him, and the thought of death, of ending, of nonexistence, tumbled down on him like an endless avalanche. He waited, trembling, for oblivion.

It wasn't fair, something screamed in the back of his mind. Sure, mortals died all the time, but they *knew* they were going to

die, they were told from early childhood that they would someday die, and no one had ever told him that, no one had prepared
him. He had been promised eternal life, and he was being
cheated out of it because he had been stupid enough to stand up
for what was right, instead of cowering like the rest.

"How *did* you hide that thing, anyway?" Thaddeus asked. "I
didn't see, either through my puppet or on the recordings. It's a
good trick, Geste—not good enough, of course, but a good trick.
How did you do it?"

Like the swift and sudden dawn of Denner's Wreck, the
realization burst in Geste's mind that Thaddeus was *not* going to
kill him immediately. He wanted something first. Fear washed
away. It was as if he had been trapped inside a mounting wave that
had broken upon the seashore—not the little waves of this tide-
less, moonless planet, or anything from the tamed and broken
oceans of Terra, but the great pounding surf of Achernar IV. He
was still afloat, drifting against his will, but he was no longer
blind and drowning. He was able to think again.

"I'll tell you how I survived, if you like," Thaddeus said, as
if making casual conversation. "It wasn't hard. What you have
in the bubble there is an old-fashioned clone. I made him about
sixty, seventy years ago now, did a little surgery when he was
about a year old, destroyed his personality, juiced up his growth
hormones to bring him up close to my own size, and then grew a
receiver into the brain, so that I could use that body myself. I've
got a little switch here, so that, up until a few minutes ago, I
could use whichever body I fancied at any given time. I did some
adjustments, so we'd be as indistinguishable as possible—sped
up his growth, as I said, and carved some scars, that sort of
thing. A neat job, wasn't it?"

Geste managed to nod. His reflected face bobbed up and down
on the stasis field, distorting as it slid across the magnifying
curve of the sphere.

"I figured it might be useful to have a backup of myself."

Geste fought to control his trembling; it lessened, but did not
stop.

"That's about the smallest stasis generator I've ever seen,
Geste; did you build it yourself?"

Geste twisted his head to one side, then back.

"No? Aulden?"

Another twist and return.

"No? Well, it doesn't matter. Is it collapsible? Is that it? I
don't really see how it could be, though."

Thaddeus paused, but Geste did not respond.

"You know, with that clone of mine, I had the switching mechanism set so that if the signal ever got interrupted, I'd be in control of my own body again, so here I am. A little safety measure. Has it occurred to you just what you would have done to me, if I hadn't done that?" Thaddeus's voice, which had been bantering and conversational, took on an edge.

Geste shuddered once more, then managed to still himself.

"I don't think you've thought about that, Geste. You see, *I* am always in my own body, the essential self; I've never trusted technological transmigration. If I'm in another body, I don't know it's still *me*. Sure, lots of people have transferred into other bodies, or machines—it's been going on for millennia—but how do you *know* that they didn't just die, that the mind in the new body isn't a simulation that *thinks* it's the same person? I'm sure you've heard the philosophical debates about this, haven't you?"

Geste nodded.

"I was sure you had. So you see, I keep my consciousness, my personality, my *soul*, in my own head, this same one I was born with seven thousand years ago. When I used that other body, it was all remote control, using a little transceiver arrangement at the base of the brain. When you put that body into stasis, you cut of all the input and output through that transceiver. You *cut off my brain*, Geste. I wasn't *in* the stasis field, not the *real* me, so I stayed conscious the whole time, but I was cut off from my own body, because I can't run both at the same time. And I couldn't switch back, Geste—the control is worked from whichever body I'm controlling at the time. We're talking about total sensory deprivation. I had a very bad second or two, wondering if the emergency switch would work—I had designed it for when the clone was killed, not enfielded. I suppose you thought you were being merciful, using a stasis field instead of a blaster, but what if I hadn't had my little switch, Geste? You wouldn't even have known what you'd done to me! I'd have starved, rotted, conscious the whole time!" His voice rose to a cracking screech.

Geste, his mind still slowly emerging from panic, saw the error in this; Thaddeus would *not* have stayed conscious once his body deteriorated below a certain level, and in a state of total sensory deprivation he would have felt no pain, had no sensation of the passing of time.

Still, it would have been a gruesome fate indeed, and Geste, shaken and terrified as he was, decided not to quibble.

"Now, how did you get that stasis generator in here?" Thaddeus demanded.

The thought of actually answering Thaddeus truthfully occurred to him, but he suppressed it. Right now, he was sure, only the fact that he had information Thaddeus wanted was keeping him alive. Besides, he was sure that his voice would tremble—if he could speak at all. He remained silent.

"Damn it, punk, do you want me to have to dissect you to find out?"

Geste shuddered again, even while a part of his mind wondered what would happen if an autopsy knife cut into the mouth of the bent-space pocket. Would it pop back out into normal space, its integrity disrupted? What would it do to his head if what happened?

His gorge rose in his throat.

No, he desperately told himself, the knife couldn't cut the pocket, he was sure. It was far more likely that the blade would break.

"I'm sending some machines, Geste—we'll see if they can't convince you to be a little more forthcoming with your information."

Geste sat, watching the triangular black floater bumping helplessly against its own reflection on the stasis field, never spilling a drop of whatever beverage it held.

The machines Thaddeus sent would not be as ineffective, he was sure. He lifted the stasis generator, thinking hard.

Thaddeus spoke again, but this time his voice was cut off in midword. "What the hel—"

Geste looked up, suddenly hopeful.

Chapter Twenty-five

"Lady Tsien lives in the treetops of the southern jungles, where she leads a horde of strange manlike creatures. Travelers there report that these creatures shout taunts at them as they pass by below, whooping with laughter and calling insults. Some claim that these were once true men and women, but that Lady Tsien ensorcelled them; others say that that's nonsense, for there are certainly men and women who have met Lady Tsien and come away unscathed, and no one can name anyone who turned up missing after seeking her out . . ."
—FROM THE TALES OF ATHERON THE STORYTELLER

The machine was not meant for riding on, but Bredon managed to cling to it. He sat precariously atop its central box, his feet on two of the forward appendages, his hands clutching the edge. "Go to the war room," he ordered. *"Ka nama kaa lajerama!"*

Giving the password again was probably unnecessary, he knew, but it reassured him.

The machine started forward smoothly, and Bredon held on tightly, ready to jump aside, out of danger, if it threw him off.

His caution was unnecessary. This mount did not make the abrupt starts, stops, and jerks of an unbroken horse. It made no attempt to dislodge him at all, but glided swiftly to its destination, doors sliding out of its way as it approached. It did not need to give any audible commands; it belonged here, and the doors recognized that. Unlike Bredon, the machine was a part of Fortress Holding. Other machines let it pass unchallenged, and paid no attention to its passenger.

Five minutes after Bredon ordered it to the war room, his motorized mount stopped dead in a tiny corridor. This cramped little passage ended in a door that did not open unasked as the machine approached.

This, Bredon guessed, was the final door. The war room would be just beyond it.

Thaddeus might well be there, too.

"Ka nama kaa lajerama!" Bredon shouted. "Get into the war room, as fast as you can! Cut your way in if you have to!" It occurred to him that even if the machine couldn't open the door,

179

maybe a human could, and he yelled, "Emergency override! Human in danger!"

Then he dove off his perch and landed rolling.

The door slid open, while Bredon's erstwhile transport sped forward so quickly that it struck the receding edge of the door a glancing blow on its way into the war room.

Moving as swiftly and silently as he could, Bredon got into a tense crouch at the corner of the doorframe, ready to spring into the room beyond or to flee, whichever might seem advisable. Then he leaned forward and peered around.

"What the hell?" Thaddeus's voice said. "What do you think *you're* doing here, you stupid machine?"

Bredon could not see Thaddeus. Leaning as far forward as he dared, he could still see only part of the chamber beyond the door.

The war room was huge, and every inch of it seemed to be lined with machinery. Bredon had never seen anything like it.

In Arcade and aboard the Skyland all the machinery was hidden away, to be maintained and operated by the artificial intelligences designed for that purpose. Systems generally functioned in response to spoken orders, and needed no switches or levers. Communications equipment projected images or voices from tiny, hidden openings, when necessary, but more often projected them directly through solid walls or created them entirely through invisible fields requiring no openings at all.

Thaddeus apparently did not trust such indirect methods. His was room was jammed with archaic screens, projectors, dials, gauges, switches, buttons, and so forth. Lights flickered and blinked in a rainbow of colors; the machinery itself was mostly steel gray.

The bristling arrays of gadgetry seemed threatening and evil to Bredon, like the flensed bones of tortured intelligences. He knew that that was foolish, that silicon life needed no skin to protect it, that Thaddeus had not tortured his machines, that the missing outer layer had never been there to be removed—but the image stayed with him.

The machine he had ridden stood in the center of the room, gleaming and motionless. A small scanner atop one appendage was pointed to Bredon's left; that, combined with the direction of the voice, convinced him that Thaddeus was in the left-hand corner of the vast room.

"Awaiting orders," the machine said.

"Aren't you supposed to be somewhere? Wait, I know you; you're a patrol and repair robot, aren't you?"

"Affirmative."

"Well, what are you doing here? I didn't call you. Did you get a signal from something in here?"

Bredon knew that in a few seconds Thaddeus would find out what was going on. If he was going to make any use of the element of surprise, he needed to do it quickly.

"Negative," the machine said.

Bredon dove through the door, rolled, and leapt to his feet in the center of the room. Before he was fully upright he shouted, "*Ka nama kaa lajerama, ka nama kaa lajerama!* Abort all programming! Abort, abort, abort!"

The effect was all he could have asked for. All around him, the hundreds of screens and image areas reacted. Most of them abruptly went blank; others flickered or shifted. Machines beeped and whistled from every side; dials dropped to zero. Lights flashed, blinked on, blinked off, changed color, and a baleful red suddenly predominated.

Thaddeus was there, inhumanly huge, wearing flowing black robes. He had looked up from the patrol machine in astonishment at Bredon's sudden entrance, but before he could do anything about this intrusion he was distracted by the beeping. He spun, amazingly fast for so immense a man, and saw the blank screens and red lights.

His eyes widened, and his mouth fell open. "What did you do?" he screamed. "What did you *do?*"

Screens showed READY messages, red lights blinked. Horrified, Thaddeus turned slowly in a full circle, looking at his machines, mouth open. "No!" he shouted. "Stop it! Defend me! I programmed you all—you *can't* obey him!"

Bredon, flushed with his sudden victory, took advantage of this opportunity and jumped at the huge immortal, intending to knock him down and beat his head against the metal floor.

Thaddeus, completing his turn, saw the attack coming. With the speed his rebuilt nerves and muscles provided, he was able to react before Bredon landed. The immortal's arms were up and braced, fending the primitive off.

Bredon responded as he had been trained; his father had taught him from an early age that he must never let the prey escape. As Thaddeus tried to fling him away he grabbed the Terran's wrist and clamped down.

Thaddeus tried to pull free, and discovered he could not. When he pulled back his arm, Bredon came with it. He saw that to pry the primitive loose with his other hand he would have to bring his face and body too close for safety, that it would give Bredon an opening.

Bredon bared his teeth in a snarl, and Thaddeus decided against getting any closer than necessary.

"You, robot!" Thaddeus called. "Get this thing off me!" He held out his arm with Bredon dangling from it like a sloth in a tree.

Bredon, however, was no sloth. He kicked out hard and caught Thaddeus in the gut. The immortal folded up, and they both went down. Bredon's death-grip on Thaddeus's wrist threw them off-balance, and both hit the floor hard, headfirst.

The machine Bredon had ridden reached out a long steel arm, wrapped it around Bredon's waist, and plucked the dazed short-lifer off the equally dazed Thaddeus. Bredon, however, still kept his grip on the immortal's wrist.

"Let go!" Thaddeus shouted.

Bredon did not bother answering. He clung remorselessly. The machine lifted him up, extending its arm until his feet dangled half a meter off the floor. Bredon still held on, dragging Thaddeus back up onto his knees in the process.

The machine began shaking Bredon.

He held on, unthinking, as he fought off the effects of the fall. His head cleared somewhat, despite the shaking, and he realized what was happening to him.

"Ka nama kaa lajerama!" he called when he had gathered his wits. "Put me down!"

He felt the arm start to loosen and added, "Gently!"

The machine obeyed promptly, but as the metal arm lowered Bredon, Thaddeus reached up and grabbed Bredon's own wrist.

His grip was inhumanly strong. Bredon had forgotten that the Powers augmented their own muscles directly, as well as through the various serving machines they commanded. He felt Thaddeus's hand tightening steadily on his wrist, cutting off the circulation, straining the very bones.

He released his own hold, gambling that Thaddeus would be more interested in freeing himself than in crushing his attacker's wrist.

He won his gamble; Thaddeus too let go, and pulled free. By the time the robot had released Bredon completely, Thaddeus was back on his feet and running for the open door, apparently not interested in unarmed combat with his opponent.

Bredon brushed himself off and looked after the fleeing figure.

Thaddeus had already turned a corner and was not out of sight. He knew the fortress maze infinitely better than Bredon did, and with his modified body he was almost certainly faster than Bredon. He was also far stronger, and Bredon had no weapons.

And of course, he was a meter taller than Bredon, and built proportionately. Even without any modification, he would have been far stronger and heavier than Bredon.

Pursuit, Bredon decided, would be really stupid. He, Bredon, had control of the war room, and with that he was fairly certain he could handle Thaddeus. Thaddeus could still command any of his machines that he ran into, of course—until Bredon gave Aulden's overriding password, anyway.

Thaddeus was still a very real threat, and would have to be dealt with.

Running after him, though, was not the way to do it. Instead, Bredon crossed to the console where Thaddeus had been standing and began studying the controls.

Chapter Twenty-six

"Everything of value beneath the surface of the World belongs to Gold the Delver. His is the hand that placed jewels in the rocks, and precious metals in the earth. When we find caves that seem to lead nowhere, these are but the abandoned back rooms of his endless caverns, closed off because he had no more use for them . . ."

—FROM THE TALES OF KITHEN THE STORYTELLER

"Thaddeus?" Geste called uncertainly, peering about at the blank gray walls. "Are you there?"

No one answered. Nothing changed. He was still alone in the room, with only the gleaming mirrored sphere of the stasis field, and the little black floater still bumping against it, for company.

Something had happened to Thaddeus. That was obvious. Furthermore, Geste had a pretty good idea what it might be that had happened. Bredon, he guessed, must have freed the others somehow, and now they were all at the war room, turning the tables on their captor, keeping Thaddeus too busy to bother with anything else.

Thaddeus would still have control of all the fortress machines, though. Geste had kept in touch with his machines for as long as he could before entering the jamming fields in the fortress, and he knew that the various attempts at sabotage had virtually all been useless. Only a handful of peripheral machines and software had been damaged. Aulden might be able to commandeer some sort of weapons, but Geste guessed the fight would be a close one, with Thaddeus's control of the fortress more than compensating for the superior numbers of his attackers, particularly since he had removed so much of their personal equipment.

And Thaddeus might have already dispatched his torture machines before the attack came. They could well be on their way to where Geste waited.

He was not entirely defenseless, of course; he had a weapon. He had the stasis field generator.

But that was in use. It could only create one field at a time. He could only use it against the original Thaddeus, or against Thaddeus's machines, if he released the Thaddeus clone.

If he turned off the field, though, what would happen to the body within? Would Thaddeus return to it?

From the description Thaddeus had given of how it worked, Geste thought not. He risked it; he pushed the control.

The gleaming bubble vanished. The triangular floater zipped into position with its drink, and the clone slumped forward in his seat, comatose. The chair reshaped itself quickly to keep him from tumbling to the floor, and he hung there, motionless.

Watching closely for any sign of life, Geste rose and walked to the door, his every sense alert. His slippered feet seemed loud in the silence.

Nothing happened. The clone stayed awkwardly slumped. The floater waited patiently for someone to take the drink.

Geste reached out, and the door slid open. Thaddeus had not ordered it to stay closed.

The Trickster stepped out into the corridor, relieved, and turned back toward where the others had been held prisoner. He did not expect to find them there, but had no idea where else to go, and thought they might have left a message for him.

The doors he encountered in the passageway, however, were not as obliging as the room door had been. They did not open as he approached, nor when he pounded on them or kicked them or gave them orders. He was trapped in a twenty-meter section of corridor.

He paced back and forth for a moment, then, frustrated, he turned to an emergency access panel and kicked at it.

It slid aside.

Startled, he stooped and looked in. He had always assumed that emergency access panels were for machines, and had not expected this one to open, but he was not about to pass up any opportunity.

The shaft behind the panel was narrow and unlit, and rather than any sort of lifter it held a metal ladder, mounted solidly to one wall.

This, he thought, would make a good place for an ambush. If he hid in it, he could spring out at Thaddeus, or at passing machines, unexpectedly.

Besides, it might lead somewhere useful. He guessed that he would be able to reach the correct level, two levels down from where he stood, and even if he could not reach the prison chamber, that would be an improvement on his current situation.

The stasis field generator was still in his hand. He considered putting it back in the pocket in his ear.

Ordinarily, he could not expect the same trick to work twice on someone like Thaddeus, but Thaddeus had not *seen* the trick. That was clear from his demand to know how it was done.

The same stunt just *might* work again, then. He reached up with his free hand, found the bent-space opening, and tucked the generator in.

He shuddered once, briefly. The sensation was so very weird!

That done, he clambered into the shaft, swung himself onto the ladder, and began descending into the gloom.

Two levels down, he kicked open another access panel and peered out into the corridor, hoping—although he knew the odds were wildly against it—to see or hear Thaddeus approaching. If the master of the fortress had happened along just then, Geste could easily have caught him in the stasis field before he had any idea he was in danger.

Thaddeus was nowhere in sight, but the Trickster saw something almost as good and almost as surprising. All the corridor doors were open.

Puzzled, Geste climbed out of the shaft into the passageway.

He could see now that not *all* the doors were open, but several were in either direction. He calculated his location as best he could from his accumulated memories of the fortress, and then headed in the direction that he hoped would lead him to the room where the prisoners had been held.

As Geste emerged from the shaft, Bredon was still in the war room, trying to puzzle out the controls, none of which were anything at all like anything in Arcade, when one of the darkened screens suddenly lit.

". . . right now, Monitor," he heard Thaddeus say.

An image appeared on the screen, a flat, two-dimensional image like a weaving, rather than a proper three-dimensional transmission, and Bredon needed a second or two before he recognized the prison chamber as seen from above the door.

The seven captives were still chained to the wall, and Thaddeus stood over them, looking up as if he were able to see Bredon.

"Listen, savage," he said. "You caught me by surprise, but I'm ready for you now. You come down here, right now, unarmed, or I'll start cutting throats." He held up a small black device, clutched tightly in one hand. "This is a knife."

"It is?" Bredon asked. He had never seen anything of the sort. The black thing had no visible blade.

"Yes, it is," Thaddeus replied. He held out a corner of his robe and waved the knife at it.

A chunk of fabric came away in his hand.

Bredon stepped back. The thought of Thaddeus cutting Lady Sunlight's throat was horrible, but he knew that if he obeyed and went down there, alone and unarmed, Thaddeus would kill him.

He needed time to think, time for a miracle to intervene. In the stories he had heard as a child, this was the time when Rawl the Adjuster would step in on the side of virtue, but right now Rawl was a helpless captive.

There were other Powers, though. Bredon had no idea what had become of Geste, for one thing, and there were all those other Powers who had refused to help, any one of whom might have reconsidered.

He needed to stall. Even if no one intervened, he had to have a moment to think.

"Wait a minute," he said. "We can talk about this."

As he spoke, a vague realization began forming. He had control of the fortress machines, if he could figure out how to use it. Surely, he could do something with that!

He looked at the mysterious screens and panels, hoping for inspiration.

"I don't want to talk, savage," Thaddeus said. "Get down here!"

"All right, all right! Just a minute!" With sudden inspiration, he added, "I don't know the way!"

Thaddeus snorted in disbelief. "You got from here to there," he said.

"But I wasn't watching the route, I just rode that machine."

Thaddeus paused, considering that, and Bredon felt a sudden chill as he wondered if he had made a mistake in mentioning his control of the fortress machines.

Geste was sure that he was on the right route. He was also sure that somehow the escaping captives had not only gotten the doors to open, but had gotten them to *stay* open. No other explanation made sense, because the open doors were in a direct path to the prison chamber.

He hurried along, eager to do what he could to help, keeping one hand near his ear.

He rounded the final corner, then stopped, frozen in astonishment.

The prisoners were just as he had left them, still chained to the wall, and Thaddeus, surely the real Thaddeus this time, was standing over them with something clutched tightly in his hand. He was clad in black, rather than the brown the clone had worn.

His robe had been cut, and a severed scrap of cloth lay on the floor by his feet.

"All right, savage," he was saying, "I'll tell you how to get here. It's easy."

This was an irresistible opportunity, better than anything he could have hoped for; if he was somehow making a mistake, he could straighten it out later. He pulled out the stasis generator, adjusted the range, and pushed the control.

Thaddeus froze, his face raised to Monitor's light, one hand raised in a gesture of admonition, the other holding the disintegrator knife. His black garb seemed to expand and fill the surrounding air as the field darkened around him, and then he vanished completely as it crystallized into the familiar mirrored sphere.

In the war room, as Bredon groped for something to say, some new delaying tactic, he saw the stasis field appear. He stared at the screen, baffled.

Then he relaxed and sank into Thaddeus's control chair, overcome with relief, as Geste stepped into view and the prisoners, despite their chains, burst into applause.

Chapter Twenty-seven

"... told among the people who live along the banks of the river where the forests end and the grasslands begin. There, a woman will often wake in the middle of the night to find the furs beside her empty. When that happens, she knows that the Nymph has called her man away for a few hours' pleasure.

"You might think that the women would be upset by this, that they would be jealous, but in fact few are. They have lived all their lives knowing that this happens, for it's hardly a secret. Scarcely a grown man in the area has not been called at least once. In fact, the wife of a man who has been called back repeatedly will often take pride in the fact—must her man not be a wonderful and inventive lover, to have been so summoned?

"It's not as if another woman had seduced their men. After all, who can compete with a Power? And they can take comfort in knowing that for ten sleeps afterward, after a dark or two with the insatiable and perverse Nymph, their men are always too tired and too jaded to bother straying to the beds of other mortal women ..."

—FROM THE TALES OF ATHERON THE STORYTELLER

The disintegrator knife would have been handy for cutting the chains, but it was trapped in the stasis field with Thaddeus. Monitor refused to provide any assistance, and eventually, at Geste's suggestion and with Aulden providing the necessary technical advice, Bredon sent a machine down that blew Monitor out of the wall in microscopic shards.

While this was being done Bredon and Geste exchanged accounts of what had happened, piecing together the entire story of Thaddeus's downfall. When they had the tale straight, Bredon put a reassuring call through to the Skyland; almost all the jamming and defensive fields had been shut down when he gave his "abort" command to the entire war room, so communication was easy.

The Skyler, though relieved, had no intention of entering Fortress Holding. She would wait where she was, she said.

The same machine that destroyed Monitor, under careful direction, was able to remove the shackles from the seven captives and lead them all, as well as Geste, to the war room.

As they made their way through the passages, Bredon, growing more confident in his abilities, summoned other machines, and by the time the Powers reached the room he had a steady stream of service devices bringing food and drink.

This done, he stood and turned to face the door.

Brenner was the first to arrive; he burst into the war room smiling, directly behind the guiding machine. The machine wheeled itself quickly to one side, letting the Powers into the room. "Well done, boy!" Brenner called. "Well done indeed!" He started to cross the room to address Bredon more directly, but then stopped at the sight of the machines bearing food and redirected his steps.

"*Very* well done!" he called as he stuffed a handful of delicacies in his mouth.

Khalid and Madame O arrived close on Brenner's heels. They said nothing, but headed directly for the refreshments.

Lady Sunlight hung back, looking at the vast, machinery-lined room.

Geste, Rawl, and Sheila were more polite. The three of them crossed the room to congratulate Bredon on his part in their victory.

"I think we make a pretty good team," Geste said, holding out his hand to Bredon. "If you hadn't kept him busy like that I couldn't have gotten him. And if you hadn't jumped him when you did, and disabled most of his machines, he probably would have killed me."

Bredon accepted this praise calmly, but felt compelled to point out, "It was Aulden's password that made it all possible. I couldn't have done anything if he hadn't set it up for me."

"So you're all wonderful," Sheila said mockingly.

Aulden and Imp, who had fallen behind the others, arrived then, ambling into the war room with their arms about each other. Aulden disengaged himself and promptly settled into a nearby chair. Imp bounced across the room, kissed Geste, kissed Bredon, and then flung herself back in Aulden's arms, letting her white prison gown bunch up to her waist as she nestled onto his lap.

Bredon looked away, slightly embarrassed by Imp's lack of modesty.

Close beside him, Sheila draped herself on Geste and began to kiss him repeatedly, working her way downward. Startled, Bredon stepped back and again looked away.

Over by the food-bearing floaters and carts O, Brenner, and Khalid draped arms around one another.

To Bredon's shocked surprise these embraces led to other actions. Aulden raised his own gown and pushed Imp's higher as her hand fell between his thighs. Sheila pulled Geste's gown from his shoulders and worked his arms free, so that the garment dropped to the floor, followed by her own.

In short order the victory celebration turned into an orgy. Bredon stood to one side, watching.

He glanced around. Rawl was paying no attention to the others as he studied the walls of machinery, and Lady Sunlight was still standing quietly by the door, but the others were all enjoying each other, oblivious to their rather inappropriate surroundings.

Bredon stepped back against the banks of controls and closed his eyes. The thought came to him that at any moment, Rawl and Lady Sunlight would follow the example of their companions; he suppressed the thought, but kept his eyes shut. He did not want to see that.

Lady Sunlight watched the others uncertainly. She was still somewhat disoriented. Thaddeus had thrown her entire view of the universe into doubt; in her understanding of reality, no one kidnapped or tortured anyone.

That was over, though. She was free again.

There were still unanswered questions, however, such as just who this "Bredon" person was. He certainly didn't fit her image of the natives. He was not noticeably crude or unclean, and in fact he had proven very useful.

Perhaps it was time she reconsidered some of her long-held opinions.

Besides, there was a orgy going on, and she did not want to be left out. Rawl was never much fun, and could be so very irritating at times. O was hogging both Khalid and Brenner. That left Bredon.

She crossed the room slowly, wisp of doubt still lingering, and almost shyly put an arm around his waist.

Startled, he opened his eyes. He started to draw away, embarrassed, then stopped. This was something he had dreamed of, to have Lady Sunlight's arm around him, and he was not enough of a fool to throw it away.

"What's the matter?" she asked.

Bredon blushed and shrugged.

She remembered that, clean and intelligent as he was, he was still a native of Denner's Wreck, and guessed what was bothering him. The natives were fairly conservative, sexually—natural enough in a society with poor medical care and contraception. She looked at her companions and smiled. "Ah, yes," she said. "Not quite befitting the dignity of demigods, is it?"

"No," Bredon replied, still struggling with the realization that at long last Lady Sunlight was speaking to him, and that she even had her arm around him. He tried to get up the courage to put his arm around her, as well, but could not quite bring himself to do it.

"Well, we're human, really, as I suppose Geste and the others have told you, and we don't get this many of us together in one place very often, and we don't usually have such a good cause to celebrate. I suppose they just got carried away." She smiled again, this time directly at Bredon.

"I suppose so," Bredon agreed.

"You saved our lives, probably," Lady Sunlight said, suddenly serious. "Thaddeus was crazy. You must have done a lot of damage, to drive him down there undefended while Geste was still loose."

Bredon shrugged again. "Aulden made it easy," he said.

"Still, you did very well," Lady Sunlight insisted.

Bredon did not reply.

"How did you get involved with us, anyway?" she continued. "Just what were you and Geste doing together? Imp told me a little, while we were locked up, but she never said how you came to be with Geste in the first place."

Bredon blushed again and looked away, then looked back. "He played a joke on me," he said.

"Oh, he did? That's no surprise." Her voice was tinged with her habitual anger and disgust at Geste's pranks.

"Yes," Bredon said. "I . . . I got upset about it, and he promised me that he would do me a service as an apology."

Lady Sunlight nodded. "That was nice of him, I suppose. Was it a particularly nasty trick he played?"

"Well, no, not really. He made a horse talk, and wouldn't let me catch it." Bredon felt desperately stupid, trying to explain himself to her.

"You catch horses?" she asked, puzzled, her head cocked slightly to one side so that her hair tumbled in a golden stream over one shoulder. She had never given much thought to what the natives did with themselves.

"I'm a hunter," Bredon explained.

"Oh," Sunlight said, clearly neither understanding nor very interested. "So he played this trick on you, then promised you something to make up for it. What did you ask for?"

Bredon knew, in a flash of intuition, that this was his chance, the best opportunity he would ever have, perhaps the *only* opportunity. He turned and looked her in the eye.

"You," he said.

Taken aback, Lady Sunlight said, "Me?"

Bredon nodded.

Her anger at Geste grew. He had obviously thought that the whole thing was funny, this poor native lusting hopelessly after her. Bredon deserved better than that. Geste had even made a joke of his apology to the poor boy!

Sunlight looked at Bredon, eye to eye, and he realized that they were the same height. She glanced over at the bodies tangled on the floor, then back at Bredon. She spread her arms wide.

"Well," she said, "here I am."

Chapter Twenty-eight

". . . She appears rarely, but when she does, the people all fall to their knees and then prostrate themselves, all calling out, 'Glory to Starflower! Glory, glory!' For some this is sincere devotion to the Power that protects them, but for others the only motivation is fear, for they know that her anger can be terrible and her retribution swift if her followers dare to disobey . . ."

—FROM THE TALES OF ATHERON THE STORYTELLER

Sixteen wakes had passed since Geste put Thaddeus into the stasis field, and at long last all twenty-eight of the immortals resident on Denner's Wreck were gathered aboard the Skyland. Both of Thaddeus's unconscious bodies were safely tucked away in storage, the original still in stasis and the clone's needs being supplied by symbiotes and life-support machines. The other twenty-seven Powers were gathered in the Skyler's main lounge. Cheerful music played in the background.

Bredon, there at the insistence of Geste, Imp, and several of the former captives, made himself as inconspicuous as possible in a back corner.

"All right, Geste," Lady Haze demanded. "What are we doing here? What's so important we had to come in person?"

"I wanted you all here in person so that there won't be anyone refusing to abide by the majority decision," Geste replied.

"What majority decision?" Gold the Delver asked.

"One that we haven't made yet, but that I hope we will."

"All right," Lord Carlov said. "Get on with it; what decision do you want?"

"I have a bit of a speech I want to make first. Bear with me."

Several people shifted uncomfortably.

"Get on with it," Hsin of the River called.

"I will." Geste stepped up onto a floating table and began: "We came to Denner's Wreck on a holiday, came to get away from the problems of life in the mainstream of civilization. We came, and we settled down, and we've had a good time here, all in all—but we've been irresponsible as hell about it, and we've made a mess of the planet."

194

Several people stirred, but no one protested aloud.

"Not only that, we've done an incredible amount of harm to the people who were here before us. Thaddeus killed hundreds of them; I know Rawl has killed several, as well, in his self-appointed role as judge, jury, and executioner—"

"Only four, Geste," Rawl interrupted. "Four in four hundred years, and all four were murderers several times over."

"All right, four. And I'm sure some of the rest of you have killed people here, accidentally or otherwise—haven't you?"

Again, several people shifted uncomfortably, but no one spoke.

"You've *killed people*," Geste repeated. "Not animals, or plants, or machines, but *people*, as conscious and genetically human as any of us. We don't have any *right* to do that."

Several people did start to speak this time, Rawl among them, but Geste held up a hand and silenced them.

"I know all the arguments—they're just short-lifers, they're only losing a few years, they're so primitive that their lives aren't worth living, they deserve it. That's crap. They're *people*, and we have no business interfering with them."

"It's hard to avoid them, if we're going to live here at all," Brenner remarked.

"Not that hard," Geste replied. "The Skyler's avoided them all, and Shadowdark, and Arn and Hollingsworth don't see them very often, I'm sure."

"I don't, either," commented Lady Haze.

Lord Hollingsworth mumbled, "Never hurt any when I *did* see them, either."

"Furthermore," Geste went on, "even when we haven't killed them or messed up their lives directly, we've done it indirectly, just by being here and allowing ourselves to be seen."

"If you're talking about messing up lives, Geste—" Starflower began.

He held up a hand. "I know, I know, I've been guilty of plenty of interference myself—not up to *your* level, Starflower, but enough. No, too much. But let me finish. To these people, we're practically gods. They call us the Powers—you all know that. They credit Lady Sheila with controlling the weather and bringing the seasons; did you know *that*? Did you know that the Nymph is considered the goddess of erotic love? That Gold is lord of the underworld? That Sunlight is responsible for every flower that ever blooms? And Starflower here, who correctly admonishes me for my pranks, has been actively accepting their worship. We have completely screwed up the culture these people had when we arrived by allowing them to misinterpret us like this!''

"We didn't *ask* for this," Starflower retorted.

"It's none of our business," Lady Haze added.

"But it *is* our business, and at least one of us, Starflower, *did* ask for it—or do you claim that you never encouraged those ceremonies honoring you? We *are* responsible," Geste insisted. "When we came here, we took a vote on whether or not to introduce modern technology to these people, whether to make any of them immortal or establish interstellar commerce, and we voted not to do any of that. Why? Because we had no right to interfere in their culture—that was what we *said*. Do you remember that?''

He glared around at them all, then continued, "That was what we *said*, but what we meant was that it wasn't our problem, that is was more fun to play demigod and not worry about the poor savages. We interfered in their culture anyway. Hell, we didn't just interfere, we practically ruined it. We played God all over the place—and I was as bad as almost any of you, I admit it. We played at being gods while we preached noninterference. It's time to stop, now. It's gotten serious. One of us went berserk and killed hundreds of innocent people, and of all the rest of us, only three did anything—and even those three only got involved when Thaddeus threatened other immortals. He could have gone on killing people forever if he hadn't started interfering with *us*, couldn't he?''

He paused, and several people shifted uncomfortably. The Skyler's expression shifted from self-satisfaction, as she heard herself included in those who had helped, to uncertainty as she remembered how she had backed out toward the end.

"Well, it's time to stop the fun and games, people. Imp and Aulden and Sheila and I intend to take Mother and go back home, to get Thaddeus some psychological repair work—repairs that should have been done centuries ago, but which nobody wanted to get involved in. And when we get there, we're going to tell whatever authorities are concerned with this sort of thing that there's a planet here full of short-lifers who deserve better, and we're going to see that a proper development company is sent out here to Denner's Wreck to clean up our mess. Now, the rules of this little organization say that we need a majority vote to leave. We intend to get that majority vote right here and now, one way or the other.''

The Skyler asked, "Do you expect all of us to go back?''

Geste looked at her, surprised not by the question, but by the source.

"Not necessarily," he said. "You can stay if you like, but the terms will be a bit different. Mother won't be up there in orbit any more, to help out with long-range communications. And you had better not screw around with the locals anymore, because starting right now, you'll be held accountable when we get some proper authority out here. These people have rights, and we'll see that they're protected. Which brings up another thing—I think it's high time that we started providing these people with some of the benefits of our presence, as well as the inconveniences. It's time we started giving them a little basic technology, improving their agriculture, their medicine, and so forth. Anyone who stays should plan on doing what he or she can to assist the short-lifers in the area."

"That's fine with me," the Skyler said, "as long as I don't have to deal with them personally."

"I've been doing some of that already," Leila said.

"I'd also like to say," Geste went on, "if you don't care about altruism, that we haven't been doing ourselves any good staying here this long. It's too isolated, we have too much time to ourselves. Look at us! We've all gotten into ruts, become stereotypes. Listen to the music the Skyland is playing for us—pop-cult songs a thousand years old! Isn't it time we got ourselves out of this backwater and back into the mainstream?"

No one answered, and after a pause the Trickster concluded, "All right, then, that's my speech. Now the vote. Who says we take Mother and load Thaddeus aboard and go home immediately?" He raised his hand.

Imp's hand shot up, and Aulden's followed.

The Skyler raised her hand.

Lady Sunlight hesitated, then raised hers.

Sheila raised hers calmly and gracefully.

Madame O's hand rose, then Khalid's, then Arn's, Isabelle's, Lady Haze's, Leila's, and Nymph's.

"Oh, what the hell," Starflower said. "I was getting tired of it anyway." She thrust her hand up.

Rawl raised his hand, followed by Tagomi of the Seas, but by then it no longer mattered; the majority had spoken.

"Good!" Geste said, speaking loudly to cover the unhappy muttering of a few of the dissenters. "We leave twenty-eight hours from now—two planetary rotations. If you aren't aboard Mother by then, you're staying, whether you want to or not—and if you stay, remember that you'll be held accountable for your actions from now on." He stepped down from the table and turned away.

Bredon slipped out of his corner and made his way toward the Trickster. Lady Sunlight noticed him and followed.

He caught Geste at the door.

"Hello, Bredon," Geste said politely upon noticing him.

"Hello, Lord Geste," he answered.

" 'Geste' is fine," the Trickster said. "You don't need to give me any titles. And I was never a lord."

"All right. Geste, then."

"That's better. Now, you look like you're after something. What can I do for you?"

"When will you be taking me home?"

Geste looked at him, startled. "Home?"

"Back to my village."

"Oh! You know, Bredon, I hadn't realized that you *wanted* to go home; I had thought, somehow, that you'd be coming to Terra with us."

Bredon was speechless; his mouth opened, then closed, but nothing came out.

Behind him, Lady Sunlight said, "Oh, do come, Bredon; I think you'll be amazed. And back there we can get you a proper symbiote, adjust your body a little, extend your life span—we don't have the right equipment here yet."

"I can come?" Bredon managed at last. "Really?"

"Of course—if you're sure you want to."

"Want to?" The question seemed absurd. To travel above the sky, faster than light, to the homeworld of humanity—to live in the light of another sun—of *course* he wanted to go!

Then other images welled up, images of his parents, his siblings, Kittisha and Mardon and his other friends.

That all seemed unreal. He had learned so much since he had left his village. Could he ever really go back? Could he live the life of a hunter, using a grass rope and a spear, after what he had seen and done?

No, he knew he could not. He brushed the images of family and friends aside.

"Of course I want to come!" he said. "I'd like to go back to my village for a light or so, to tell them all what happened, though." *That*, he thought, would be quite a tale; he wondered what it would sound like by the time old Atheron had interpreted it into something the village could accept.

"But even if you can't spare the time, that's all right," he said. "Of *course* I want to come!"

"Good!" Lady Sunlight said, as she spun him around and kissed him.

Name of applicant: the-Hunter, Bredon

Honorific, patronymic, epithet, or other additional nomenclature: "son of Aredon the Hunter"

Citizenship number: None

Planet of origin: Denner's Wreck, catalog 2356-CS-6, 246-Aurigae III.

Place of origin: village, no recorded name, 28°16'30" N. 15°24'00" W.

Unaltered height: 1.71 meters

Education: None

State of health: Fair. No significant risk of contagion. No symbiotes.

Genetic pattern recorded: Yes, by sponsor

Neural pattern recorded: Yes, by sponsor

Sponsor: Sunlight, C.H., Lady, CN 0456-4530-5072

Clearance granted, 3-8-7154.

        —FROM THE RECORDS OF TERRAN IMMIGRATION